A Fistful of Death

Judy Spoon Ertel

WESTBOW
PRESS®
A DIVISION OF THOMAS NELSON
& ZONDERVAN

WestBow Press books may be ordered through booksellers or by contacting:

WestBow Press
A Division of Thomas Nelson & Zondervan
1663 Liberty Drive
Bloomington, IN 47403
www.westbowpress.com
844-714-3454

ISBN: 978-1-6642-9059-4 (sc)
ISBN: 978-1-6642-9061-7 (hc)
ISBN: 978-1-6642-9060-0 (e)

Library of Congress Control Number: 2023901581

Print information available on the last page.

WestBow Press rev. date: 04/14/2023

This book is dedicated to Jeanette, Louise, Linda, John S., Sharon, Karen, George, Earl…and especially to Kate and John L. with much love.

CHAPTER 1

"Hi, Travis T. Is anything wrong?"

"Mom, why do you always think that something is wrong whenever I call you?" asked my son.

"Possibly it's because you don't call me very often, Honey," I said. "I'm really looking forward to your visit," I added to be more positive. "You are still coming week after next?" A call from my son could be easy or difficult, depending on his mood and stress level. A visit by Travis to my home in Wanderwood was very rare.

"Yes, Mom," he reassured. "Paula wanted me to ask whether there is anything special that we should pack for the kids. I'm bringing a few of their favorite toys and, of course, their clothes for two weeks."

"Remember that I can do laundry, Travis. You shouldn't need more than a week's worth of clothes."

"Okay. That sounds good. I'll be sure to tell Paula. I'm looking forward to spending this time with you, Mom. I was lucky to get these two weeks off. It will probably be our only slow time at the company for the entire year."

My oldest child, Travis Taylor Girard, or Travis T as his college friends dubbed him, was a mid-level manager at High Plains Products in Lubbock. High Plains manufactured the popular *Grab 'Em* line of beef jerky snacks. With the competitiveness in the snack food industry, his busy job kept Travis tied to Lubbock most of the year.

"Travis, I'm especially looking forward to spending time with you. I'm planning some activities for us to do with Trent and Tricia. Do you have any idea of things Paula might like to do?" I queried.

"Paula's busy and can't come this time, so please keep it simple." Travis sounded tired and a little frustrated. "I just want to relax and spend time with you. Looks like my lunch order is ready. I'll call you later."

"I love you, Honey. Take care," I said.

"Love you, too, Mom. See you soon."

Lunchtime loomed, and I launched into food prep mode. I was shortly using my left foot to hold back Vanilla, my curious Siamese cat, as I eased out the back door and onto the patio. Since I was trying to balance a tray containing a bowl of salad (already dressed and tossed), a saucer piled with Fritos, a napkin, utensils, and a glass of ice-cold lemonade, this was no easy feat. The tray held my version of a vegetarian lunch. 'Corn is the main ingredient in Fritos,' I reasoned. 'The lettuce, ripe olives, radish, grated carrot, and pecans are definitely vegetable.'

The atmosphere in my back yard was soothing as I placed the tray on the picnic table and seated myself on the bench. 'Addie,' my conscience scolded, 'you know that grated parmesan cheese is not in any way, shape, or consistency a vegetable. And those croutons. Tsk! Tsk!' Sometimes I felt that my conscience could be too picky.

'I need the cheese for balance in my diet,' I mentally protested. 'Besides, wheat is vegetable.' I knew that warring with my conscience, even over a small matter like the contents of my lunch, was a losing battle. I carefully settled into consuming my salad and nudged my conscience into silence, at least for a while.

Lunching on my patio as I enjoyed my back yard was always a pleasant time for me. "George, I know that you must be appalled, but I put Abelia bushes along the back of the house in your precious natural yard. They look lovely with the sage bushes that I planted earlier in March. You know, George. It was before I started planning the kitchen remodeling project. I need to have that redo finished before Lindsey and I leave for the cruise in May."

Talking to my deceased husband probably seemed odd to some people, but my true friends understood. After thirty-four years of a very loving and intimate relationship, it was difficult to let go of George completely. He was so totally entrenched in my life and my mind. We truly were soul mates---even though he could be a little controlling at times. Like his attitude toward putting more plants in the yard. The *unnatural look* he called it.

Now George was discoursing on more important things with the angels in God Land. And I, Adelaide Bonner Girard, single widow, mother of four, and gardener extraordinaire, could plant anything I wanted any time I chose (within reason, weather, and budget). This month I chose sage bushes and Abelias.

Abelias were sweet little bushes that were supposed to grow well in our warm Central Texas climate. Cynthia Parkhal at the Grow 'Em Tall Nursery told me that Abelias should thrive, not take a lot of water, and not make a lot of mess or need a lot of tending. They fit my cardinal rule for gardening. *If it doesn't grow by itself, it doesn't belong in my yard.*

"Are you in the back yard, Addie?" Lottie Frisham called to me from the side yard by my house.

Lottie Frisham was one of my best friends and near neighbors in Wanderwood. We spent probably too much time together since I moved from Lubbock permanently to live in my former summer home at Wanderwood, Texas. I depended on Lottie to help me acclimate. What she didn't know about Wanderwood wasn't worth knowing.

"On the patio, Lottie. I'm finishing my lunch," I answered her.

Lottie was a picture in her usual colorful attire. Today her gray curls bounced above a mint green, mid-calf length, jumpsuit with embroidered, entwined daisies and roses down each side seam. I knew that my friend spent many hours on first sewing the jumpsuit and then on embroidering each flower and leaf. Her talents in needlework knew no bounds.

"The jumpsuit is finished! It's stunning, Lottie," I said, and I meant every word. Lottie finished her look with a pert yellow handkerchief tucked into one of the patch pockets and with yellow patent leather sandals on her bare feet. Her red polished toenails reflected the red of the roses. The effect was as stunning as I told her, and she deserved the accolade.

"Well, I finished the last of the embroidery yesterday morning," she said as she took a seat at the table. "Then I had to hurry to get the jumpsuit washed and ironed so that I could wear it today."

"All of that effort was definitely worth it," I complimented. "You have a boat load of talent and patience when you are working on your crafts. I would be too intimidated by the size and scope of such a project even to think of trying it."

"Why thank you for those kind words, Addie," she preened. "I wanted to have it finished before Travis T arrived with the family. I know that it won't be long now, and I'm looking forward to seeing Tricia and Trent again."

"Yes, I'm looking forward to their visit, too. In fact, I just spoke to Travis on the phone."

"Well, what did Travis have to say?" asked Lottie. For some reason, my neighbor and close friend started many of her sentences with the word *well*.

"Not much, as usual, except that Paula isn't coming with him," I said which started my brain to puzzling over why Paula wouldn't be on this visit.

"Paula's not coming? But I made plans for things to do with Tricia and Trent." Lottie was instantly well on her way to being distraught.

"No worry about that; Trent and Tricia will be here."

This information seemed to return Lottie to her happy place. "Well, how are you going to manage meals when your entire kitchen will be under construction?" asked Lottie. "Have you heard from Kilgore Pettigrew as to when he'll start tearing up your kitchen?"

"Kilgore said that the two weeks when Travis will be visiting is the only time he can begin my kitchen remodel," I explained. "Then he will have one more week to put the finishing touches on the kitchen. He has some other big renovation scheduled after that. Some whole-house remodel. A *major magilla*. His words, not mine."

"Well couldn't you postpone your kitchen until after the house *magilla*? Travis doesn't get to Wanderwood very often."

I knew that Lottie was trying to be helpful, but the situation was already a frustration for me. I had been trying not the think about it. Now the big issue was splat in front of us like the big, ugly, tangled mess that it was. "After the magilla house redo in Wanderwood, Kilgore has scheduled two jobs in Dripping Springs, kitchen and bathroom remodels. After those, he has another whole-house remodel in Woodcreek. And after Woodcreek---"

"I get the picture," she interrupted. "Basically, you're telling me that it's now or maybe next year."

"You are getting the picture," I sighed as I sipped the last of my lemonade. "Maybe it won't be so bad. I can pick up take-out from Lefty's Bar-B-Q. That will cover a couple of days each week. I'll get steaks for Travis to grill on the first Saturday after he arrives. You and Walter will come for that, won't you?"

"We wouldn't miss it!" Lottie enthused. "I'll bring something---maybe a macaroni salad. The kids will like that. And I can make the angel food cake with a glaze and sprinkles that Tricia likes so much."

"That would be a big help," I said. "And I may need to put a few things in your freezer while they're remodeling, if that would be okay. My refrigerator will be connected in the living room but no ice maker. I'll probably need to borrow ice."

"Well, Addie, if you need to, you can use my kitchen for some of your food prep and cooking. Since we're just around the corner, we could make some meals together. Things are likely to be a mess here with all that construction dust and debris."

"Lottie, that would be great!" I said and I leaned around the table to give her a Texas-sized hug.

"Also, Addie, I might be able to have Trent and Tricia over to our house for dinner. Thursday night could be good for you since you have your Library Friends meeting that night, don't you? And Travis could come with them to dinner, too."

"I do have a meeting of the Library Friends organization each Thursday night," I mused. "That would be a great relief, Lottie. Let's tentatively plan for Travis and the kids to eat at your house on Thursday unless Travis has other plans or unless that becomes inconvenient for you. I know you have a lot of activities during that time. "

"Well, do you have an update on when Travis will arrive?" asked Lottie. "Did he give you a definite timetable?"

"No. Only that they'll be here after lunch on the Saturday after next," I replied. My brain already was lost in the maze of Travis visiting, the kitchen remodel, and my commitment to help with work on the new library.

"Addie, will you still have time to go with me to the big Yard Sale in Hays County on Saturday?" Lottie questioned.

"Lottie, it seems that the next three weeks are some kind of vortex where too many things are going on at the same time in my life. However, I am definitely making time for the Yard Sale with you. I thought moving to Wanderwood might make my life simpler but, instead, my life gets busier and busier. I don't know how I can juggle it all and keep all of the balls in the air."

"Well, it looks to me like you're juggling bricks instead of balls," Lottie commented. "Balls would be easy. But you can work off some of that stress at the exercise class this afternoon. Karyne Layne will give us a fun workout."

"I don't know whether that will be enough. Let's go drown my sorrows in Dr. Pepper," I said as I picked up the tray and headed for the back door.

"Sounds like a winner," she agreed.

Lottie opened the door for me, and I entered the dim kitchen. I deposited the dishes in the old, stained and chipped, porcelain sink and set the tray on the worn and stained laminate countertop. The remodel of my aged kitchen was not happening soon enough. 'George and I should have updated years ago,' I thought.

"Weren't you talking to someone when I arrived?" Lottie asked.

"George," I said in explanation.

"What did he have to say?"

"You know George. He rarely answered me when he was here, and this time I'm glad that I got no reply. I never could bring myself to tell him some things when he was alive," I stated. "George could be so sensitive and would get huffy if I criticized what he did or didn't do. That must have been the manager in him. He seldom saw himself as we saw him. George didn't like his decisions to be challenged."

"What man does?" asked Lottie. "Men like to think their word is law."

Lottie's husband, Walter, was a great guy who had been a big help to me since my move from Lubbock to our summer house. Walter worked as the assistant manager for Kriender's Feed Store near Dripping Springs. If he was king of their castle, he let the queen run it any way she wanted.

"What'll it be?" I asked as I milked ice from the refrigerator door into glasses for Lottie and me. "I have tea, lemonade, or Dr. Pepper."

"Well, I guess a little lemonade couldn't hurt. It doesn't sound too exotic."

"There's nothing exotic about this lemonade," I said as I poured from the pitcher. "It isn't fresh squeezed. It's made from one of those powdered mixes."

"The way God intended," stated Lottie as we settled at the kitchen table. "Do you want the rest of that Pink Sashay yarn back? If not, I could use it for the elephant puppet that I'm knitting for Carolyne Gastbend's son, Harland."

"A pink elephant?" I queried and took a sip of my Dr. Pepper.

"Well, Marty Gastbend drinks a little more than he should. I wanted to see whether he could distinguish it from the other ones he's seeing."

"Honestly, Lottie, you can't be serious."

"No," she admitted. "I only wish that Marty would cut back on his drinking. I'm actually making the puppet gray with a pink shirt. The leftover Pink Sashay is about the right amount for that shirt."

"Use the pink yarn. The elephant does sound cute. How long will that take you to finish?"

"Well, Addie, I'm sure it will be done before your kitchen redo will get started. Have you made any changes in the plans since I talked to you Tuesday?"

"When I update this kitchen, I'm putting in a dishwasher," I said.

"When did you decide on the dishwasher? You haven't mentioned that before."

"The dishwasher was the last thing that I added to this project before I presented my plans to Kilgore," I replied as I put our empty glasses in the sink. Then I grabbed my Shapely Woman Spa Tote and headed for the front door. It's time that this kitchen came into at least the late Twentieth Century."

"Couldn't hurt," Lottie agreed following me out through the living room.

We slowly made our way out of the neighborhood through the winding streets in Lottie's gray van, finally turning from Heavenly Oak Drive onto Wanderwood Boulevard (RM 150A). Lottie headed the van for the center of town. Traffic was fairly light on what we laughingly called *The Boulevard*. We were the second car stopped in a line of three at the only signal light in the town. Lottie quickly made the left turn onto Brazos Street, turned right into the parking lot of our lone *shopping center*, or at least what passed for a shopping center in Wanderwood, and parked.

Twin Oaks Plaza was aptly named for a couple of huge, ancient live oak trees that sprawled like bookends, one at Brazos Street by one entrance and the other a short block away by the Trinity Street entrance. A block-long strip of shops surrounded the cracked-blacktop parking lot. The huddle of small stores consisted of Browder Brothers Handy Sack (grocery store), Ruger's On-Time Pharmacy, Shapely Woman Spa, Nelly's Gift Emporium, and Lefty's Bar-B-Q. The two smallest stores were currently without tenants.

Wanderwood State Bank perched like a moldering stone heap at the front of the parking lot adjacent to The Boulevard. Across The Boulevard, the Wanderwood Community Center, the *Evritt Gazette*, and LaDonna's Cut Yer Guff Hair Salon completed our little downtown area. Anything we needed that these shops didn't supply would have to be ordered or involve a trip to another, larger town.

Describing our town shopping center as small and rustic did not quite measure up to the true effect of folksy-ness. Lottie's gray van claimed a space among the clutch of cars near the spa. At least, it seemed like a parking space although the old blacktop was badly in need of repair and striping. Most locals just guessed at where the stripes used to be.

"Ladies, please form two lines." Karyne Layne was standing on a low platform at the front of the room, calling out and clapping her hands to no avail. The ladies were standing in small groups around the edge of the exercise area. Most were talking and adjusting their snug exercise garb instead of heeding her words.

Lottie and I soon tuned into the topic of the day. An editorial this week in the county newspaper, the *Evritt Gazette*, explored the pros and cons of setting up the new library in the old, red-brick, county school building. This building stood vacant and decaying on the corner of Brazos Street and Cypress Avenue, two blocks to the north of Twin Oaks Plaza.

The school district already approved the conversion of the school building into a county public library last month at a nominal rent. As usual, publication of the *Gazette* was somewhat behind the actual news event but Derald Markey, owner and editor of the *Evritt Gazette*, did not let that prevent him from using his editorial prerogative to create controversy. It seemed to me that controversy must sell newspapers and keep circulation numbers up.

Each participant's opinion on the editorial was still being bandied about as we ladies found our places for the class, forming two lines as instructed. Languid music seeped from Karyne's sound system, and we began our warm-up movements. This was followed by more lively tunes for a lot of foot stomping and jumping around on the well-worn carpet. Then a slow, soothing cool-down finished us off and prepped us for a half hour of stretching and additional suffering on the various machines. Over all, we gals had a fun, but strenuous, social hour where we could catch up on happenings in our little town.

As we donned our street clothes in the spa dressing area, I mentally groaned looking at the one-inch bulge around my waist. That bulge insisted on poking out over the top of the teal denim slacks that I had chosen to wear. At least my cleavage was an appropriate size for my five-foot-six height, though not as perky as I might wish. 'Addie, what can you expect at fifty-eight?" I chided myself.

Then, I noticed the hair---the slightly sweaty, straggly, auburn hair that stuck to the sides of the face looking back at me from the tall dressing mirror on the hot pink wall. I fished my brush from my tote and gave my hair a few fierce swipes and a few additional fluffs. 'Nope. You've got to make that appointment for a haircut at LaDonna's Cut Yer Guff Hair Salon before the cruise,' my exhausted brain sighed. 'Maybe a shorter cut like Lottie's would be good?'

I tugged on my pink pullover tee, snugging it down carefully over the offensive one-inch bulge. Giving a few more fluffing swipes at the hopelessly limp hair, I grabbed my clean socks and street tennies and strolled over to join the now fractious discussion of the possible or impossible town library.

The debate was taking place around the benches by the front desk. Lottie and Karyne were gesticulating with their arms to emphasize their points of difference as the discussion heated up. Who knew that a simple thing like a library could cause such a whoop-de-do? Karyne appeared to be pro-library while Lottie, for unknown reasons, seemed definitely against.

Since I was already working on the library project with the Library Friends organization, I opted to stay out of the foofaraw. Differences of opinion could get very heated in a small town. I seated myself on a bench in the corner. With interest, I listened to the combatants but did not join the fray. There was nothing to be served by making enemies.

CHAPTER 2

"Back up slowly! We don't want to crush it accidentally! I was directing Lottie Frisham as she carefully backed out of the space on a grass parking lot. What else could we do after, fumble fingers that I am, I dropped my brand new Chastique lipstick. The one in the new, limited-issue RasperBerrio shade. The errant lipstick bounced two feet and landed under the middle of Lottie's van.

"Adelaide Bonner Girard, I certainly know how to drive slowly in reverse," Lottie bristled. "I have been driving since I was fifteen." The tone in her voice warned me that I should close my mouth and wait to find the lipstick. Lottie stopped short, having backed only three feet.

Looking behind the van, I saw that another car was stopped in the driveway between the rows and was totally blocking Lottie's ability to back further. Worse still, the car was now starting to back up. I waved my arms and signaled that they should move on down the grassy lane since we were not vacating the space. This brought a scowl to the face of the previously hopeful driver. Perhaps he would prefer to be home in front of his television watching golf instead of ferrying a group of chatty passengers on this lovely Saturday morning in mid-March. No contest there.

Since I was wearing my new burgundy, brushed-denim shorts and the light pink blouse with the burgundy passion flowers backed by navy pin stripes, I didn't wish to be crawling on the dirt and grass on my bare knees. Nor did I wish to scruff up my navy skips or light pink socks which I thought completed my outfit so nicely. After all, it had taken me almost a week to find the pink socks tucked away in a storage bin under my bed.

I was accompanying Lottie Frisham to the Hays County Area-Wide Yard Sale. This event was being held on the grass landing strip at the City of Woodcreek by the Village of Wimberley, Texas. I finally broke the ancient wooden side chair from my living room. More than twenty years ago, George and I bought the chair at someone else's garage sale for eight dollars.

Actually, my retired next-door neighbor, Tom Hamilton, broke the chair by standing on it while trying to reach a silver serving tray that his wife, Marolly, needed to borrow. I located the tray on a high shelf in my hall closet, but Tom insisted on retrieving it for me. Unfortunately, Tom grabbed the rickety chair and stood on it before I could fetch my small kitchen ladder. Fortunately, Tom was unharmed; the same could not be said for the chair.

"Hop to it, Addie! We have to get there before the deadline!" Lottie fussed. I quickly retrieved the offending lipstick and watched Lottie park the van once more. I was totally surprised by her need to rush.

"What deadline, Lottie?" I had to run to stay with her rapid, long strides as we crossed the grassy field toward an entrance denoted by hay bales stacked to form a short fence on each side of a wide opening. In the distance behind the lanes of colorful booths, we could see a backdrop of privacy fences shielding the houses and trees of Woodcreek from the airport property.

"Well, everyone coming through the gate during the first half hour can drop entry slips into the drum for the big drawing. I collected entry slips from one hundred and forty-seven people in Wanderwood over the past two weeks---including yours."

"That was why you wanted the Yard Sale ad?"

"Yes, Addie. You obviously weren't interested enough in the drawing to pay attention to it." At five foot ten, Lottie had longer legs than I had and could set a mean pace when she was determined to cover some ground.

I dutifully trotted along toward the rows of booths as quickly as a fifty-eight-year-old woman could. "What is the prize that you are trying to win?" I wheezed, attempting to catch my breath while still scooting along behind my friend. I didn't dare to detain this woman on a mission.

"Well, there are lots of prizes. They are things donated by merchants from around Travis, Hays, and Evritt Counties. Things like *a dinner for two* at different restaurants, or *a free gift* when you visit a store, or *BOGO coupons.*"

"*BOGO coupons?*" I wondered what a BOGO was and why Lottie was willing to do the forty-yard dash for a chance to win one of them.

"You know. *Buy One Get One Free coupons.* BOGO."

We reached the entrance at last and joined the large group of patrons who were waiting to deposit their entry slips. Entering the drawing was not the only reason Lottie and I arose so early for the drive to Woodcreek. I thought that I needed that replacement chair for my living room since my son, Travis, was coming for that visit in a week. The Hays County Area-Wide Yard Sale seemed like a good place to find a chair at a reasonable price.

Lottie, however, was trolling for items which I was sure she did not need since her house, storage closets, and garage were as full as mine. You never knew what you would find at one of these area-wide sales. You could become excited about someone else's treasure or trash if you thought that you might find a use for the items they were selling. This was recycling at its best.

"We should keep an eye out for shelves or anything that might work for the new library---especially wooden kitchen chairs," I reminded Lottie as she dropped her last slip into the large wire drum which was filling rapidly with entries from a wide assortment of lookers and shoppers. "A number of people have already donated wooden table and chair sets, but some of those don't have all of the original chairs."

"Addie, the library won't look nice if it's furnished with a hodgepodge of mismatched tables and chairs," Lottie scolded, shaking the gray ringlets of her newest hairdo, courtesy of Lisa Quarles at LaDonna's Cut Yer Guff Salon. LaDonna's was the premiere and only hair salon in the small town of Wanderwood, Texas, where Lottie and I lived.

"Maxie Chalpers offered to sand and paint whatever furniture the Library Friends organization managed to collect," I explained, "Maxie's planning the project so that all of the furniture will blend, at least in color. The Friends talked about staining the furniture, but Maxie nixed that idea. She proposed the painting plan instead. We're going for the *eclectic* look."

"Well, Maxie does nice work," Lottie allowed. "She really has a talent for woodwork. Her carved wood figures are on sale at Nelly's Gift Emporium. In fact, her wooden birds are so popular, I wonder how she would have time to refinish any tables and chairs or bookshelves."

"I think that Maxie is very organized about her work," I defended the plan for furnishing the new library. "Of course, she claims that it's not *work* because she is doing what she likes to do. According to Maxie, she would be doing woodwork in her spare time if she wasn't able to earn a living doing it."

Lottie stopped in front of a booth featuring vintage glassware. The pieces were likely reproductions of classic styles in glassware and ceramics. They looked similar to pieces that I remembered seeing in my grandmother's curio. I could see that Lottie was more than a little interested.

"Lottie," I chided, "you can't need any more glassware. Your cupboards are as full as mine."

"Christmas shopping," she said as we wandered into the booth.

"You are Christmas shopping in March?" I questioned. "That seems like a stretch."

"Well, it's never too early to start shopping for Christmas," she replied.

"For vintage glassware?" I couldn't quite believe what she was saying.

"My niece, Clarissa, has this fascination for vintage things. I thought a small glass vase would be nice or one of those little glass shoes." Lottie looked carefully over a table of glass tchotchkes. "It would be cute in her room. I want to encourage her to appreciate nice things and practice keeping her things nice."

"Isn't Clarissa the niece who shares a room with *Ingrid the Incorrigible*? You're thinking that giving Clarissa something made of glass is a good idea?" I paused as my eye was caught by a cunning display of ceramic figurines. The delicate open-work and colors made the ceramic look like lace.

"Addie, Clarissa can keep it at my house until she has a room of her own. She has a box in my smaller spare bedroom for her things. She is ten years old now. She'll be a teenager in a couple of years."

"And this room of her own is going to happen when?" I picked up a ceramic figurine of a pretty young girl in a long, swirling dress. Giving myself a mind-shake, I put it carefully back on the shelf. 'Concentrate on chairs,' I mentally scolded myself.

"Well, Jeff and Terry are thinking of moving to a larger house," Lottie said. "They've outgrown that starter house they bought eleven years ago. I'm sure I've told you that they got the house when Terry was pregnant with Clarissa. Eleven years is more than long enough in a small house. The plan is to have separate rooms for Clarissa, Ingrid, and Dalton."

Lottie and Walter Frisham didn't have children of their own, but they spent a lot of time helping other people raise theirs. My children and grandchildren were included in Lottie's and Walter's huge extended family. They provided the love, and children of relatives and friends reaped the benefit.

We left the glassware space behind and moved on to another space which featured furniture. I didn't find an occasional chair for my living room, but I did purchase two oak, wheat-back, dining room chairs. The operator of the space tagged them with my name for pickup later and moved them to the back of his booth where other, earlier purchases, waited for the return of the buyers.

Lottie and I moved along one row of booths after another past numerous jewelry, clothing, and handicraft booths. The Yard Sale ad promised that there would be more than three hundred booths. It didn't lie. At lunch time we paused in our tramping from booth to booth to forage through the food offerings. I opted for a flavorful chopped barbecue sandwich and Fritos from the Kiwanis booth. Lottie got a cheeseburger and Cheetos from the Shriners.

I sank my teeth into the shredded beef, and the barbecue sauce tingled the roof of my mouth. 'No wonder our efforts at the Shapely Woman Spa aren't paying off in pounds lost. Even the long hike through these endless booths might not work off the calories from this lunch, but it really tastes good.' My thoughts and the scrumptious sandwich were permeating my entire being with a feeling of euphoria. 'Must be this excellent sauce,' I thought.

"Do you think that we can get through the rest of these booths in two hours or so?" asked Lottie. "I don't believe I can hike around longer than that."

"Probably," I answered, popping my last Frito into my mouth.

"Well, can you beat that!" Lottie exclaimed in a pseudo-whisper as she grabbed my arm.

"What?" my euphoric, food-induced bubble burst.

"Shh! Over there." She indicated an area of tables about thirty feet from us. "The table by the guy selling balloons. Can you believe that Anson Kerringer would show up at an event like this? With all of his money, you'd think it was beneath him. Uh-oh!"

"Who?" I was trying to focus on the tables in the direction that Lottie indicated. It was a struggle even to keep sight of the balloon guy in the crowd surrounding the food booths.

"Anson Kerringer, Addie," she hissed in a whisper as if anybody that we knew were close enough to hear us.

"Who is that?" I was sounding like an owl, but I didn't recognize any of the men at the tables by the balloon guy who had suddenly waved his clutch of balloons and caught my eye.

"Anson Kerringer. He's Mavis Corcoran's boss at that ticky-tacky new development on the north side of Wanderwood. You know, the developer of Champions Ramble."

"Oh," was all I said since I didn't know Mavis Corcoran well or know Anson Kerringer at all.

"Well, that isn't Anson's wife, Kissie, with him," Lottie added. "That's Viveca Laurin, Wanderwood's most popular realtor."

"She's a prominent realtor. He's a land developer. Sounds to me like a natural combination," I said trying pitifully to hold up my end of the conversation. At least I was honed in on the correct table finally. I recognized Viveca Laurin from her picture on her signs and from occasionally seeing her at Shapely Woman Spa. Viveca's flowing, glossy, raven hair, her sleek facial structure, and her flawless makeup were really eye-catching on her realty signs. However, today she had that lustrous hair pulled back and covered with a navy-blue kerchief. The makeup was toned down.

"And would you look at that outfit she's wearing," Lottie turned her hand palm up, indicating that she thought Viveca's faded jeans and Wanderwood Bobcats sweat shirt were unusual clothing for the realtor to be wearing. "I didn't think she wore anything but designer clothes."

"They look natural for this event. Anson Kerringer seems to be dressed in a similar fashion," I noted, observing his tan chinos and Dallas Cowboys sweat shirt. He had the prominent cheekbones and facial structure to suggest that he might have a Native American ancestor or two. His black hair was combed back nicely, giving him a definitely Hollywood, no-hair-out-of-place look. 'I wonder who cuts his hair,' I found myself thinking.

"Well, what are *they* doing here---together? She's still a married woman; he's a married man. She's separated but she never divorced her husband."

"Lottie, they're probably doing what we're doing," I reasoned. "Shopping the Yard Sale. It may be their day off. They probably are just good friends."

"Nonsense," scoffed Lottie. "Weekends are usually the busiest time of the week for realtors and people selling property---like a certain developer. Besides, Viveca has two children. Where are they?"

"With her husband?" I suggested.

"Hunh! Clark Laurin left Viveca cold about two years ago and took off for Brazil. No one's heard from him since. Not even his mother. At the time, the situation was a bit suspicious," Lottie explained. "He just locked the doors on his insurance agency one day, grabbed his bags, and left town. His office assistant, Shelby Draper, quit two weeks earlier to work at the Wanderwood Bank."

Lottie paused to dab at her mouth with her napkin. "There was some talk that Clark might have a girlfriend, Carla Mott, or maybe he possibly embezzled insurance agency funds. Viveca did the bookkeeping but claimed that she had nothing to do with the everyday workings of the agency. She also claimed that she wasn't aware of any relationship with Carla. It was very suspicious indeed."

"Anson and Viveca are leaving now," I commented. Lottie and I watched them weave their way through the tables around them, headed for the nearest lane of booths. They stopped briefly to deposit their trash in one of the yellow barrels scattered around the food area and stood pointing in different directions. Apparently, they were discussing which way they had been and which way to go next.

"Quick! We should follow them," said Lottie. "Let's see what they're really doing."

Kerringer and Laurin seemed to reach a decision and chose to turn down a different lane of booths.

"Why would we do that?" I asked. I gathered my lunch trash as well as Lottie's to deposit in the yellow barrels nearby. "I don't even know those people and couldn't care less what they're doing."

"Well, we haven't shopped that row yet," Lottie said. "At least, I think that we haven't shopped it yet."

Lottie was correct. She and I had covered numerous rows of booths but not the row where she dragged me to follow Laurin and Kerringer. The twosome was ahead of us in a booth selling Mexican serapes, dresses, and tchotchkes. I led Lottie into another nearby furniture booth. I shopped various wooden household goods. Lottie shopped the activities of Viveca and Anson. I emerged, having purchased three arrow-back kitchen chairs and a lovely oak captain's chair for my living room to be picked up later. Lottie emerged having more questions than answers about Anson and Viveca.

"Well, they aren't seriously shopping, Addie. They merely talk and walk. Neither one picked up anything from the tables or racks to examine. They aren't spending any time looking at individual pieces."

"Maybe they are looking for something specific," I suggested.

"In a commercial, Mexican souvenir booth? Get real!" scoffed Lottie. "They must have needed some place away from Wanderwood to meet. In this crowd, I guess they thought that they wouldn't run into anyone who knew them."

"Then they guessed wrong," I said.

"Well, not so much wrong," Lottie quipped. "I recognize them, but I don't actually know them. Anson and Viveca are part of that hoity-toity group who live in the Willem Club section of town. You know the place. McMansions on half acre lots. People foolishly thinking that they live the posh life. Bizarre! Can anyone possibly live the posh life in a town with no upscale restaurants, no fancy department stores, and no specialty stores full of designer merchandise?"

"Lottie, you're right about Wanderwood. Our town is not the place for upscale living," I agreed as I stopped to check out some cute crocheted hand puppets. The vendor caught my eye by standing in front of the booth with a red dog puppet on his hand and using the puppet to wave at passing shoppers. 'These puppets could be fun for Tricia and Trent (my soon to be visiting grandchildren).' I thought. Looking around, I noted that Anson and Viveca were now wandering through a double-sized booth full of Mexican pottery and dishes.

I purchased a red dog puppet and a brown dog puppet. Both puppets had long snouts with black noses at the end and goofy grins. The vendor assured me that these were popular characters my grandchildren would recognize and love. To be on the safe side, I also purchased a green dragon and a pink dragon puppet, as well as two super soft crocheted balls made from bright, multi-colored yarn. This vendor claimed that Tricia and Trent could not harm each other or anything in the house while throwing these *hausbols* around.

Lottie thought that the puppets were cute, and carefully examined them inside and out. "Look, Addie, the stuffing is totally enclosed by crochet. How do you keep the faces from peeling off? I've found that things don't always stick to yarn very well."

"We use a special epoxy glue," the vendor's wife explained. "This is the only glue that we have found which will glue felt to yarn securely. You can also mend broken dishes and pottery with it."

"Well, would you mind awfully telling me the name of the glue?" Lottie queried. "I really need something like that."

"I'll write it down for you.," The friendly woman grabbed a pad and pen from the back of a table loaded with merchandise.

CHAPTER 3

While Lottie was getting the glue information, I crossed the row to another booth to examine stacks of jigsaw puzzles. I was drawn to several stacks of illustration art puzzles. A colorful puzzle atop one of the piles featured a vintage, very humorous Norman Rockwell illustration.

"Addie Girard!" The vendor formerly arranging items in the back of the booth, was now turned toward me.

"Lacy Tindal! I haven't seen you since the high school band had their Concert After Dark!" I gave my good friend from Wanderwood a hug. "I see what you've been doing," I said as I lifted a puzzle box.

"I heard about the cruise that you are taking with your daughter, Lindsey. It sounds fantastic! Everyone's passing the info around---so much so that I don't know what to believe," Lacy bubbled. "Are you really going to the Far East?"

"No, merely to the Caribbean for a week or so," I demurred.

"We need to get together soon so you can give me the straight skinny," my good friend insisted.

"Lacy, you've been reading too many mystery books. *The straight skinny?*" I laid a couple of puzzles aside to buy. "How much for the puzzles?"

"Three dollars each," replied Lacy. "Bart and I worked them all, and we guarantee that all of the pieces are there."

My interest increased two-fold. "Sounds like a great deal," I said, setting aside two more boxes to my must-have stash.

At this point, Lottie joined us. "I have some shelves of mystery books in the back of the booth, Lottie," Lacy called. "I'm downsizing my collection."

"That's for me," Lottie said as she sailed past us toward some shelves in the rear of the space, "Hi, Lacy," she added with a wave.

"What's Bart up to these days?" I asked as I unfortunately found another two puzzles to buy. I might not work them until winter, but I knew the price was too good to pass up. Puzzles in the stores cost four or five times the price of these.

"Bart is getting us a quick lunch before all of the food stands start selling out of the good stuff." Lacy held a few puzzle boxes up for me while I sifted through the third stack. "This is actually Bart's new hobby---doing Market and Craft Sales. We want to remodel and update. He thinks that this will be a good way to declutter our house."

"How is that working?" I was thinking of the remodel that I planned to do on my seriously *dated* home. 'Should I declutter more?' I wondered.

"This is our first event," Lacy explained. "Bart's having a good time with it. Next event, we'll try clearing out some of Bart's stuff. Then we'll see how eager he is and whether this hobby will last." Lacy was continuously restacking the puzzle boxes as I went through them.

"Addie, things are slower at the dealership from April to August. There are so many end-of-school events in April and May. Then the blazing summer hits. No one wants to walk around on asphalt and concrete in all that heat and humidity. We thought that we could use a productive hobby."

Bart and Lacy Tindal owned Bart's Amazing Autos, located at the edge of Wanderwood on RM 150A. They were known as great supporters of town functions. This fact emboldened me to ask a favor. "Lacy, would you consider organizing a yard-sale fundraiser for the new library later this year? Maybe it could be after July Fourth or possibly in early Fall?"

"Are you in charge of that Wanderwood Library Friends group?" asked Lacy incredulously.

"No," Lottie answered for me, "but those who are in charge sure do know how to dump the grunt work on Addie and others."

"Lottie! I volunteered to help with cleaning and furnishing the building. Everyone in the Friends group is doing something."

"After Janet Makeshire turned the screws. Lacy, you know how Janet and her bunch are," Lottie persisted.

"Yes, I do know," Lacy agreed with Lottie. "They like to call themselves the *idea people*, and they are masters at *delegating* the grunt work to others. I wouldn't be so quick to volunteer with that bunch in charge, Addie. Besides, this library project seems like an expensive boondoggle---a lot of work for little return. Do you truly think that the people in Wanderwood will use this dinky library? How popular do you think it will be?"

I tallied up my purchases and pulled the necessary bills from my fanny pack. "Lacy, any town, even one as small as Wanderwood, should have a library. It's not only for the adults, but for the children as well."

"The children have a library at school to use," Lottie said.

"Now that library is *dinky*," I insisted. "By the time the school kids reach fifth grade, they have read most of the books in it. The kids need another reading option, especially in the summer. When the school is closed, the kids have too much time on their hands."

"I suppose that could be true," Lacy acknowledged. "Maybe I'll consider working on a fundraiser but only if you're in charge of it. Janet and the rest of her group are such dilletantes. At least you would make the effort to find other volunteers to help me with the event."

"I'm sure Janet's heart is in the right place," I offered weakly.

"Let's see whether her pocketbook is in the right place," Lottie put in. "Janet and her pushy friends are usually long on talk and nowhere around when it's time to pay up. Mark what I'm saying, Addie. You'll end up in charge of that library project and paying for it, too, while Janet Makeshire and her Willem Club bunch take all of the credit."

"Does it matter who gets the credit?" I asked. "So long as the citizens of Wanderwood get a library, our goal is achieved. A year from now, no one will remember who was in charge."

Lottie paid Lacy for her book selections which were numerous. "Don't let Janet tell you to pay for things yourself and you'll get reimbursed," Lottie warned. "You'll never see the money again. Ask Shelby Draper at the bank what happened on the *Build a Town Gazebo* project. Janet was in charge, and Shelby didn't get reimbursed for anything."

"There is no gazebo in Wanderwood," I stated.

"My point exactly. Janet and that Willem Club bunch were in charge," Lottie insisted. "Shelby wasn't the only one to lose money."

"She's right about that project, Addie," remarked Lacy. "We donated money for that gazebo. It never happened. When it came to actual physical labor, the Willem Club group, who took over the whole mess, always had activities that interfered with their participation."

"Thanks for the advice, both of you. I'll move forward more cautiously in the future, but I'm continuing with the project. I believe that Wanderwood needs a library, and I'm not the only one who thinks so. Good luck with your new hobby, Lacy. I hope that you and Bart succeed in your reno plans."

We moved on as Bart returned with plastic-wrap covered plates laden with barbecued turkey legs and French fries. Lacy headed for their cooler to get cold drinks. "See you later, girls," she called.

"Good luck with your booth, Bart," I called back.

"Thanks, Addie. Good bargain hunting," he added.

Lottie and I took a lane to the left seeking different booths to peruse. We tromped halfway down the row before we found something unusual. Before us was a booth filled with unique wall hangings, humorous and folksy wall plaques, and medium to large hill country scenes painted in acrylic. I was struck by a gray wood plaque that read: *Improve your home's view. Plant a hedge.* The sign by the opening said *Artistes Outré*.

Lottie grabbed my arm and dragged me into the shop. "Why is this booth so interesting to you?" I managed to gasp.

"Look in that booth across the way," Lottie said. "The one with the carved wooden bears in front."

I scanned through clusters of free-standing wooden figures and tables crowded with smaller carved figures. Toward the back, Anson Kerringer and Viveca Laurin were examining a large, interestingly carved wooden bowl. He tilted it up while she eyed the bottom, probably checking the price. Then they took the bowl to the vendor at the side of the booth. Lottie stood on tiptoe and craned her neck to the right.

"What are you doing?" I asked as I tugged on her arm to get her attention.

"I want to see who pays," she replied, shrugging me off and slapping at me ineffectively. "We should have brought binoculars."

"To a yard sale?"

"Well, that's interesting," she said smugly.

"What did you see?" All I could see was Laurin and Kerringer heading toward the booth entrance.

"I'll tell you later," Lottie said as she moved farther into the Artistes Outré booth. "Addie, you must have this." I turned to see Lottie staring at a large wooden wall painting. It appeared to be acrylic painted on a rectangle of weathered wood. The subject matter featured a small brick building surrounded by live oak and cedar trees. In the distance was an old-fashioned water tower. "Don't you recognize it?" she tittered. I shook my head. "It's the old, red brick school building at Wanderwood!" She was laughing now. "You could have the artist add a sign that says library on the front of the building."

I looked closer at the wooden rectangle. Sure enough, the water tower said *WANDERWO* on its curved surface. I glanced at the signature in the lower right corner. "R. Ratlief," I read out.

"Of course," Lottie said, no longer laughing. "Rebecca Ratlief. You met her at the Spa last week. She's the middle-aged brunette with the artsy blond streak through her hair. LaDonna told me that Rebecca moved to Wanderwood a few months ago and bought the Ottmers' place off Goliad Street."

"Yes, I do remember her," I said. "She told me to call her Becca."

"Were you looking for me?" We spun around and found ourselves facing the subject of our discussion. "Lottie Frisham. I thought I recognized that laugh."

"We were admiring this painting, Becca," I spoke up, hoping she didn't think that we were ridiculing her work. "You're very talented."

"Well, we were actually noticing that the subject is the old school building at Wanderwood," Lottie added. "I went to school in that building. Addie is one of those foolish people who think that the building needs to be a library."

"And Lottie is one of those people who are resistant to change," I laughed. "Have you chosen a side on the issue, Becca?"

"I'm one of those indecisive people who always straddle the fence," Becca Ratlief chuckled. "Some issues can become very heated in Wanderwood, so I hear. I can't afford to offend my small but loyal group of supporters."

"I didn't know that the art market would be affected by local politics," I said.

"Addie, the art market is affected by every issue-oriented wind that blows in a small town like Wanderwood. If I didn't take my work to other markets like this one, I wouldn't make a living. There is no art gallery in Wanderwood, and there's not enough traffic to support one. In Wanderwood, my only outlet is Nelly's Gift Emporium, and she can only handle very small vignette paintings and some of my wood carvings."

"You sound a bit frustrated," Lottie commiserated. "Couldn't you show your work in a big city gallery? More traffic there."

"I've tried Austin, Dallas, Houston, and San Antonio. No luck. There are so many artists in Texas, literally thousands. That means there is too much competition for the few really good venues," Becca explained.

I was disturbed to see Becca so distressed. "Perhaps I could talk to Janet Makeshire about displaying your paintings at the new library, if you were willing," I offered. "After all, we have to put something on the walls for décor. Your Hill Country paintings would look great! They would give the place some pizzazz. For now, I'd like to buy this painting of the old school building. Lottie said that I must have it, and I think she's right."

"Well, where would you hang it, Addie," protested Lottie. "You don't have a single wall that isn't *over*-decorated."

"It's the start of my re-do project. My inspiration piece."

"What inspiration piece?" asked Lottie.

"In the interior design books, I read that a person can choose some kind of inspiration piece and design a room around it," I explained. "I'd like that room to look as good as this painting." I laughed again as I handed Becca my credit card.

Becca took the credit card and removed the painting from its hanger. "I'll wrap this for you," she said over her shoulder as she headed for a table at the back of the booth.

"Lottie, I feel that I need to make changes in the house. I want to lighten and spruce it up. George and I owned that house for almost twenty years. While Travis T is here, it should be the right time to start. He can help me move things. It will give him something to do since Paula won't be with him."

"I still don't understand why Paula isn't coming." Lottie protested. "But you said that Travis was bringing Tricia and Trent. I made plans---things for the kids to do with Walter and me."

"Relax, Lottie," I reassured her. "Tricia and Trent will have plenty of time to spend with you and Walter during the two weeks that they are visiting. Paula simply wasn't able to come along on this trip."

"Well, why not?" demanded Lottie. My friend truly hated not knowing everything. She enjoyed the slow, usual pace of life in Wanderwood. Lottie hated change almost as much as my late husband George had.

"I don't know what the details are. Travis just said that Paula wouldn't be coming with them. I didn't press him for details. Oh, dear," I moaned, "I should have asked about Paula. I do care, but I don't like to pry. How do you find a good balance between caring and prying? I suppose that means that I'm a bad mother-in-law."

"Nothing of the kind," insisted Lottie. She carefully examined a pottery dish in the shape and color of a purple and yellow pansy. "I need to get this for---a friend."

I didn't ask her which friend. I was fairly certain that Tricia would go back to Lubbock with that dish in her suitcase. Lottie's fantasy life involving my children and grandchildren was harmless. Those dreams made her happy. I wasn't going to sprinkle unnecessary showers onto her parade.

Rebecca Ratlief returned to us with a credit card receipt to sign. "The painting is signed and dated on the back of the wood plank," Becca said. "Save the written receipt for provenance. It proves that you are the original purchaser because you bought the painting directly from the artist." Then she took Lottie's purchase and credit card and bustled back to her work table.

"Anson and Viveca are long gone," Lottie said.

"What did you see in that booth when you said that you'd tell me later?" I couldn't believe that I remembered to ask or that I even cared to know. Wading in the quagmire of Wanderwood gossip was something that I tried to avoid.

"Well, I saw Anson pull out his wallet, but Viveca put the bowl in her tote bag," Lottie replied.

"So?"

"Don't you see, Addie?" continued Lottie. "He bought the bowl for her. It was a personal gift. They weren't just on a business venture. They were here to spend some time together away from prying eyes. At this Yard Sale they were away from Wanderwood and away from Anson's wife, Kissie."

"I see that you've been reading romances as well as mysteries. That's what I see," I said shaking my head. "I suppose this is what we do in a small town. We watch our neighbors and wish we had as interesting a life as they seem to have."

"Well," Lottie went on, "since Viveca and Anson are gone, let's cover the last two rows of booths. Then we need to pick up those chairs that you bought. I don't know how we'll get all of those bulky things to the van."

"I saw a sign post by the entrance," I said. "While you were dropping off your entries for the drawing, I scoped out the area. The Civitans brought golf carts with trailers for picking up the big stuff."

"Where was their booth?" Lottie asked. "I didn't see it."

"Over near the entrance," I pointed. "No booth. It's only a table with a couple of Civitan members sitting behind it."

"Well, Addie, do you even remember where you bought those chairs?"

"Yes, Lottie, I wrote down the booth numbers on this pad," I said pulling a La Quinta note pad from my fanny pack. I double-checked the booth numbers as we hiked toward the Civitan table.

Once there, we learned to our dismay that we had to place ourselves on a wait list for the next available golf cart and trailer. Lottie and I were seventeenth on that list. We filled a little of the wait time by checking the list of prize winners which had been posted on a bulletin board near the drum for contest entries.

"Oh, my! Lottie exclaimed. "I won three great prizes!"

"What did you win?" I queried, thinking that the term *great prizes* could be relative to your expectations.

"Let's see." Lottie ran a finger down the long list once more. "I won a free checkup and cleaning service for my air conditioner. I need that for sure. It's from Farland's Heating and AC in Dripping Springs. They cover Wanderwood, you know." Her finger found another listing. "Here I won a free oil change from Lube-A-Lot. That's in Dripping Springs, too. Walter is going to like that," she crowed.

"And here I won a BOGO coupon. Wow! It's for buy two large pizzas and get two free at Izzy's Pizza in San Marcos. We can use that when the book club group hits the outlet mall early next month." Then her voice got louder. "Bingo! I can't believe it! You scored the best win of all!"

"Lottie, how could I score a win if I didn't enter the drawing?" Lottie's excited statement had me confused.

"The contest allowed only one prize per person, so I made out some of the entries with your name and address. My wins were under my name, Walter's name and Jeff's name." Lottie explained the details of her plan.

"So, what was this bonanza that I won?" I queried. "It would have to be top notch to beat your BOGO prize. That's a real score. Izzy's usually doesn't offer coupons."

"You won Dinner for Four at The Salt Lick!" she squealed.

"I've been hearing about that restaurant," I said. "Isn't The Salt Lick a barbecue place by Driftwood?"

"Not just *a barbecue place*, Addie," enthused Lottie. "The Salt Lick is the best barbecue place for five counties, and you know how close Driftwood is to Wanderwood. It's only a hop, skip, and a long leap."

"Then you and Walter can introduce me to the wonders of The Salt Lick as my guests, since I will be the possessor of a Dinner for Four prize. How do we pick up these prizes anyway?"

"Well, it says here that we go to the information booth which is over there to the right of the entrance by the food area," Lottie read from the prize listing on the board.

Surprisingly, Lottie was able to redeem all three of her prizes with no problem at the information booth. The tired-looking woman in the small structure seemed happy to be relieved of the prize certificates. She didn't quibble at all when Lottie asked for Walter's and Jeff's prizes. Small Texas towns. Aren't they great! So accepting.

Next, we found a table at the food court where we could both see and hear the ladies at the Civitan table when our name was called. We didn't want to miss our turn at the cart and trailer. With drinks from the Kiwanis booth, we sat down to wait. Watching the curiously dressed sale attendees was a bonus. To keep Lottie entertained, I stated, "Now that I've had time to think about it, you were right. This was an odd place for a developer and a realtor to meet."

"Addie, if this wasn't a romantic getaway for Anson and Viveca, what possibly could it be?" I'd gotten Lottie mentally back to speculating about the Anson-Viveca conundrum.

"I don't know that we have enough information to understand anything about it," I answered. "They were certainly talking a lot."

"Well, it might have something to do with Champions Ramble," Lottie stated. "Lots of people are talking about that lately."

"Champions Ramble? Oh, Kerringer's new development on the north side of Wanderwood," I acknowledged. "Isn't there a controversy brewing over that place causing a bunch of unhappiness---and talk?"

"Well, Anson Kerringer has no business doing what he's about to do," Lottie explained which didn't explain anything.

"Something's wrong with the housing development?" I asked.

"No. The housing development probably will help Wanderwood by the time it's finished," Lottie admitted reluctantly. "The problem is with the new road to Champions Ramble. Actually, the new bypass."

"The road to Champion's Ramble bypasses what?"

"Wanderwood, Addie! Don't you ever keep up with what's going on?" Lottie fussed. "When Kerringer's road is finished, that road will become the new RM150A. Where 150A now goes through Wanderwood, the road will be called RM150B. We'll be cut off, and all the traffic on 150A will go to his development. Anson Kerringer has a new area for commercial development planned along the new RM150A."

"That would cut traffic for all of the businesses along The Boulevard," I said. Now I definitely understood what made the road controversial. Those small business owners adjacent to The Boulevard depended on every dollar that came through the door to remain financially viable.

"You were away visiting your daughters, Madison and Lindsey, three weeks ago. That's when Anson Kerringer and the state road people held the hearing to explain the road plan. Those road experts were so pleased that a section of the winding highway will be straightened out. They thought that the residents of Wanderwood ought to be happy that it decreases the distance from Dripping Springs to Kyle by almost two miles, as if a mile here or there made a difference. The road guys assured us that the new road would not cost the taxpayers of Wanderwood a dime. It would just cost them their livelihood, we tried to explain. The people from the state didn't seem to care to hear it."

"Lottie, did a lot of people turn out for the meeting?"

"Well, no," she said with disgust. "Kerringer conveniently scheduled the meeting for Spring Break week. A lot of people were out of town traveling. Only a handful of residents attended the meeting. Now everyone's complaining, but it's probably too late. At the meeting, it sounded like a done deal. Folks are speculating that maybe money changed hands with some Representative or Senator. You know---a sizeable contribution to their campaign fund."

"Do you think that Anson Kerringer has friends who are that highly placed in state government, Lottie?"

"Well, Anson likely has more friends in Austin than in Wanderwood. You know that he and Kissie actually don't live in Wanderwood. Kissie and Anson have a condo at Champions Chase in Wanderwood, but their house is at Lakeway, northwest of Austin." Lottie checked her watch. "I hope that our turn to load comes soon."

"*Kissie* Kerringer? Is that her real name or a nickname or what?" I asked to distract Lottie from getting too antsy to leave. I would never hear the end of stories to our friends about how *Addie's library chairs* cost us so much time. However, expounding her extensive knowledge of everything to know about Wanderwood and everyone in it seemed to be Lottie's favorite pastime. I shamefully played on her weakness.

"Kissie actually is Kassondra," Lottie explained. "According to info from Lacy Tindal, Kissie's great-great-grandparents were royalty in an obscure duchy in the Alps during the early twentieth century, a Duke and Duchess or something like that. She and Anson sure do act like they think they're royalty. They seem to think that having a condo at Champions Chase over by Willem Club entitles them to special consideration."

"But why *Kissie*?" I persisted.

"Well, she was a cheerleader during high school at some Dallas suburb," Lottie said as if that explained the strange nickname.

"Addie Girard! Please come to the Civitan booth," blasted at the two of us over the loudspeaker, startling us. "Addie Girard. Please come to the Civitan booth. Your chariot awaits. Better rush or that chariot will be leaving without you and with someone else aboard."

'That announcer has a sense of humor---and a loud voice,' I thought.

For a twenty-dollar donation to Civitan, I was soon putting slowly around the yard-sale grounds in a gas-powered golf cart which was pulling a small trailer. At the same time, Lottie hiked to the parking lot to stow our bags of purchases and to bring the van up to an area near the entrance designated for loading large merchandise.

I hoped that Lottie found a place to park in the pick-up area, and that she wouldn't get too impatient to be going home. Possibly Lottie would speculate over Anson Kerringer and Viveca Laurin rather than thinking that her friend, Addie Girard, should be more considerate of her. My conscience was pricking me. I would have to do something very nice for Lottie to make up for this inconvenience.

CHAPTER 4

"What you have there, Addie, is *a fistful of death*."

"Tom!" I gasped. "Why do you say that?" I stared at the clump of weeds in my gloved hand. Kneeling on a mat at the school grounds clutching a noxious tangle of stems, leaves, roots, and soil was not how I expected to spend my Tuesday morning. When my next-door-neighbors, Tom and Marolly Hamilton pressed me to gather volunteers, how could I refuse?

"Deadly Night Shade," Tom Hamilton explained patiently. He scratched his salt and pepper gray hair with a garden-gloved finger. At around six feet, Tom was somewhat taller than my five foot six. His concerned, craggy face towered over me since he was standing and I was kneeling on the ground. "I thought that we rid the school yard of all that poisonous stuff a couple of years ago. Guess we missed a root or two, and now it has popped up again. Be very careful with it. You don't want to get the sap on you or come into contact with any crushed leaves. Those plants can be very deadly."

"Oh, my, yes," agreed Shelby Draper. "Hold on to that, and let me get you a plastic leaf bag. Just hold on to it until I get back. Do you have a trowel to dig out the roots?"

"Yes, I have a trowel." I answered, feeling rather squeamish at kneeling there holding what Tom Hamilton had called *a fistful of death*.

Tom and Marolly Hamilton were avid gardeners. That was why they volunteered to help me clean up the grounds around the old red brick school building. Shelby Draper from the bank was a fellow member of the Wanderwood Garden Club. She, along with Mavis Corcoran and LaDonna DeValle, made up the rest of the crew who were helping me to clear the weeds and tall grass from around the base of the ancient foundation. I was thankful that Maxie Chalpers came with her riding mower two days ago, and the rest of the grounds were freshly mowed and cleared of debris.

"Maxie used the last leaf bag from the box," said Shelby as she returned from her car, "but I have this empty plastic bag left over from my picnic last week. I think that it will do."

Shelby handed me a large, white plastic bag with the Lotta Lotta Fried Chicken logo on it. Carefully I tucked the plants into the bag, making sure not to contact the plant or drop any leaves. "Thanks, Shelby." Then I carefully dug out the roots, putting dirt and all into the bag.

"I found seven more of these Night Shade plants along this side of the building," said Marolly coming back from her inspection. "It would be best if you dug them out, Addie, since you already have handled the plants with your gloves."

'Lucky me,' I thought.

"I'm afraid you will need to be extra cautious taking off those gloves," Tom said. "Be sure to burn them when you get home, but not in your barbecue grill. Wear an allergy mask when you burn them, and don't inhale the smoke. Make sure that no animals are around. Luckily, I didn't find any Night Shade plants on the other sides of the building. They seem to be confined to this section of the foundation."

"You know that this is a part of Hattie Clumber's legacy, bless her sweet, confused soul," LaDonna said shaking her head. La Donna DeValle, owner/operator of LaDonna's Cut Yer Guff Hair Salon, wore her light brown hair clipped close on the sides and poufy on the top. It was her usual cut, but it looked newly trimmed. The cut went well with the casual clothes she normally sported. Today, her ensemble was navy deck shoes with white crew socks, navy denim capri pants, and a white ladies' tee topped by a navy and white flannel shirt with the sleeves rolled to her elbows.

"Hattie passed away about three years ago so you may not have known her, Addie." LaDonna continued. "When Hattie was the president of the garden club, one of the last things that she did officially was to get permission for the club to plant and maintain a garden area around this building. It was getting to be such an eyesore. She chose the plants and did most of the bed on this side of the building. *My pretty patch of heaven*, she called it."

"We found out some time later that the pretty purple-flowering plants were Night Shade," Marolly finished the narrative. Marolly was standing next to LaDonna and their outfits clashed a bit. The pumpkin-colored jumpsuit and brown cross trainers with her yellow, short-top socks peeping out did not blend with the navy and white of LaDonna's outfit. "The Night Shade plants all had to be carefully removed," she concluded. "I don't know how Hattie managed to plant them and not poison herself."

"Then this wasn't what caused her death?" I asked.

"Nope," said Shelby. "Brain aneurism. She passed very quickly. One week in the hospital and she was gone."

Everyone was trying to hide their teary eyes. It was truly a sad story about their dear friend. "I will take extra caution digging the plants out," I assured them. "And I will be careful disposing of these gloves, Tom." Burning the gloves was no big deal since they were probably more than five years old. Everyone stood over me and watched while I dug out the remaining plants. Then Shelby carried off the bag containing the noxious mess for, hopefully, safe disposal.

"Will you all be attending the Library Meeting on Thursday night?" asked Mavis Corcoran. She was a vague young woman, strangely dressed in black slacks and a matching off-the-shoulder blouse finished with black patent flats. At least the outfit seemed strange for the day's work of weeding at a school building. She had come with Shelby Draper, and I remembered Lottie telling me that she worked for Anson Kerringer.

"We will be there, Tom and I," said Marolly.

"Thursday is my late night at the shop," LaDonna apologized. "Sorry."

"I'll definitely be there," I stated. "There are some things that I need to go over with Janet Makeshire."

"If I don't get away from work too late," Shelby said, rejoining the group, "I think that I can make it. I plan to bring brownies for refreshments."

A discussion ensued about who might bring lemonade, tea, or other snacks. Then we all picked up our tools and left the grounds. This was the culmination of a three-day effort, and the school grounds looked neat under the shade of sprawling live oak and cedar trees.

'Those trees will need to be trimmed soon,' I thought as I tediously removed my gloves with the help of a plastic grocery bag from my stash in the back of my Jeep. Tying the top of the grocery bag containing gloves in a knot, I tossed it back into the Jeep and made a mental note to be sure to remove it later.

I pulled some hand sanitizer and a couple of stray napkins from the glove compartment to clean my hands and wrists. These napkins were stuffed into the grocery bag as well after I retrieved the bag and untied it. 'Hopefully that will temporarily remove any possible residue from the problem plants until I can get to Lefty's Bar-B-Q and wash my hands thoroughly,' I sighed. The restaurant was only two blocks away at Twin Oaks Plaza, but I was already five minutes late for a lunch date with Lacy Tindal.

I waved to Ramona 'Lefty' Aduddell who was tending the cash register. Then I looked around for Lacy Tindal's flaming red hair---at least this week it was red. She occupied a booth in the back corner away from the jukebox. Willie's lament for a certain southern state was currently playing. I stopped by the booth long enough to drop my backpack-styled handbag and excused myself to the ladies' room. After a good scrub of my hands and wrists, I was once more at the booth and slowly perusing the specials on Lefty's new menu.

Lacy adjusted her sage-green jacket worn over a pale yellow, silk ladies' tee and matching sage green slacks. The color looked marvelous with her red hair. "Bart tried the ribs with the bacon, rosemary, and jalapeno rub last week. He's been raving about them to all of our friends," said Lacy.

"Sounds good," I agreed with my face buried behind the tall menu.

"Ribs are messy though. Maybe I should have the brisket with that new dill and honey sauce and a little hot sauce to spice it up."

"Sounds tasty," I said with my gaze still on the menu.

"Or maybe I'll just have a dried-up corn fritter with some stale, leftover cod cake."

"Um-hmm. Sounds…" I lowered the menu as what she said penetrated my distracted brain. "Dried up corn fritter and leftover cod cake?"

"Stale, leftover cod cake," Lacy laughed.

"You have caught me," I chuckled, laying down the menu and holding up my hands in surrender.

"What has you so distracted?" my good friend queried.

"The library project," I confessed. "I heard something the other day that was very upsetting."

"What did you hear?" asked Lacy eagerly.

"I don't think that it's right to discuss it with anyone until I've discussed it with Janet Makeshire first." I tried to explain.

"So, Janet Makeshire is your new best friend?" Lacy huffed.

"This isn't like that," I insisted.

"Oh, it isn't like that? Not a friendship thing?" queried Lacy. "What kind of a *thing* is it? What's Janet Makeshire done now?"

"I'm sorry," I apologized. "However, you cannot tell anyone about this until after the meeting with Janet on Thursday night."

"Addie, it's okay. I won't tell a soul," Lacy reassured me.

We were interrupted by Brenda, Lefty's daughter, bringing our drinks. "If you need refills or anything else, just holler," she said. "It's very busy today, but I don't think that there will be any delay in your order. These regular plates that you ordered don't take extra time. It's the folks who want ten different substitutions who slow things down."

"You've had some difficult customers during the lunch hour, Brenda?" I asked, being nosy.

"Clariss Padget and Shaynie Millred came in slumming." Brenda made a face as she said the words. "They ordered today's special and then they each wanted a different sauce than the ones on the menu. Next, they insisted on substituting different sides. The whole point in having specials is to standardize what's on the plate so that we can make them quick and offer a discounted price."

"What they wanted was a custom order at an off-the-rack price," said Lacy indignantly. "We get that a lot at our business. Those people from Willem Club ask for everything under the sun. They demand that we give them the discounted price for in-stock vehicles, but they want a special-order vehicle that has all of the deluxe option packages. Last month Shaynie Millred stomped around our showroom wasting two hours of our time because we couldn't sell her a fifty-five-thousand-dollar car for the thirty-five-thousand-dollar price advertised on an in-stock, basic model. She left without buying anything."

"Mrs. Millred does like to raise her voice and complain," Brenda agreed. "Folks could probably hear her in the produce department at the Handy Sack when she was here today. If they have so much money, why do they complain so much about meals that are reasonably priced? The price on the special is only nine ninety-five. With the way Mrs. Millred carried on, you'd think we were asking a hundred dollars a plate."

"Brenda, you have other customers," Lefty called from the register.

"Sorry, Brenda," I said. "I hope we didn't get you into trouble with your mom. We shouldn't delay you, as busy as you are."

"Naw," Brenda answered. "Mom likes to keep me on track, but she wants me to take care of our really good customers, like you." She flashed us a smile and left to wait on a young couple towing a pair of preschoolers who had entered and seated themselves at a booth across the room.

"Do you and Bart get much business from the Willem Club area?" I had to ask as Brenda bustled away.

"An occasional tire to repair or the purchase of a new battery now and then if we advertise a special price," said Lacy. "They never buy cars from us. Now quit stalling and tell me what you think you don't want to tell me."

"I overheard something that was very disturbing when I was shopping at the Handy Sack yesterday. I was by the meat department, trying to decide whether to buy chuck steaks or round steaks for Travis to grill when he and his children are here visiting. They'll be here on Saturday," I explained to her.

"In the aisle behind me, Clariss Padget was talking to another woman that I didn't see. Clariss was boasting about Janet hosting a luncheon at LaDuc Bistro in Westlake last Friday and using money donated for the library to pay for it. I was appalled by what I heard. I wanted to speak to Clariss and her friend, but they left the store by the time I finished pricing the steaks. You know that I'll have to bring this up at the meeting on Thursday night, but first I want to talk with Janet Makeshire personally."

Brenda returned with our sandwiches and extra napkins at this point. We paused our conversation until she returned to her waitressing duties elsewhere.

"Addie, I guess that I shouldn't be surprised that Janet would do such a thing," Lacy said, having sampled her cottage fries. "However, it might explain where the money donated for the gazebo went. People who worked on the project were surprised that the money was exhausted so quickly with so little to show for it. We never got past drawing up the plans and clearing the property." She paused for a bite of sandwich and a sip of iced tea.

"Clearing the property, Addie, didn't cost anything because it was done by at least nineteen volunteers. Then, after our volunteers had worked so hard to clear the property, we were told that we were out of money. The property was sold to Anson Kerringer, supposedly to cover additional debts of the project. So far as I know, no one ever considered that anyone might have embezzled the money. I guess that makes us sound pretty gullible."

"People around Wanderwood do seem very trusting of their neighbors," I offered before taking another delicious bite of my brisket sandwich. "This is an amazing sandwich. The meat is so flavorful. Lefty must use something special in her rub. A secret ingredient or something."

The attempt to change the subject didn't deter Lacy. "You have to take charge of this library project and investigate what Janet has done with the money, Addie," she said, munching on another slice of fried potato. "And maybe while you're at it you can investigate what happened to the gazebo money."

"Lacy, I wouldn't know where to start. I only want to put an end to Janet *borrowing* the library money for her own purposes." The tea was ice cold and not too sweet the way I liked it. 'Maybe I could take a bottle of this tea home for later,' I thought.

"I'll help you investigate. You could be Holmes and I could be Watson," Lacy insisted.

"I think Holmes smoked a pipe," I stated.

"So?"

"I don't smoke---or take drugs," I added laughing. "I don't think that I qualify."

"Well, I'm not a doctor," she was also laughing, "but I think that we really do need to investigate this thing."

"This thing?" I questioned.

"You know, this misappropriation of funds by Janet Makeshire. A very simple case like this, even Nancy Drew could solve it."

"So now I'm Nancy Drew? Lacy, I truly wouldn't know where to start investigating." Another cottage fry found its way to my mouth.

"Addie, I know that you like to be in the know about things," Lacy said emphatically. "You're inquisitive."

"You mean that I'm nosy," I laughed.

"Also, I heard that you helped Lindsey discover who was taking things from her locker when she was in high school."

"Lacy, where did you hear about that?"

"Mandy Corcoran, Mavis's youngest sister, talks to Lindsey on the phone. It seems that Mandy and Lindsey have been phone buddies ever since you and George started vacationing here each summer."

"That locker thing was a have-to moment," I said after another sip of tea. "The missing items were turning up in embarrassing places, and they each had Lindsey's name on them. The library problem is a totally different situation."

Lacy set down her half-eaten sandwich. "On a different topic, Addie, I met this great guy at the Yard Sale. He could be someone to date."

I could tell that my friend was teasing by the smirk on her mouth as she sopped sauce off her chin with her napkin. I decided to play along. "You want to take a lover on the side? Does Bart know about this?"

"Get serious. Bart is my always guy. This new guy is for you." Lacy waved a cottage fry at me. "You need to get out more. You know. Have some fun."

"I'm getting out a lot these days," I explained, laughing once more. "Between the library group and preparing for Travis T's visit, I seem to be *out* more than I am *in*. Besides, I'm not looking for a dating relationship right now. I'm enjoying being just me alone. I need a less hectic time to search for my dream guy."

"Now I know that you're putting me on," Lacy said. "George was your grand passion, and every other man pales by comparison."

"Do you hear that, George?" I questioned. "Now our secret is out."

"Don't let her give you a hard time, George," Lacy joked. "Let her know what you think of that." Just then thunder boomed outside, sending us into a major laughing fit. We hadn't noticed the sky darkening as the clouds slowly covered the sky. After another crescendo of thunder, the rain started. "George, we get the message!" Lacy called in a low voice, and we were consumed with laughter again.

"George certainly did have a sense of humor," I stated when I managed to pull myself together, "but he sometimes took himself too seriously. Do you hear me, George? Lighten up!"

CHAPTER 5

The door of the Wanderwood Community Center surprisingly was unlocked when I arrived forty-five minutes early for the Wanderwood Library Friends meeting. The Community Center was located in a typical two-story, fieldstone-covered building with a high porch roof supported by rectangular, fieldstone columns. Formerly occupied by the realty company owned by Viveca Laurin, the building was sold to the village of Wanderwood when the realtor moved to a newer, more modern building closer to Willem Club on RM150A. The building's saving grace was that it was air conditioned.

I was glad that the Community Center was no farther than the center of town since I spent the day getting the house ready for the visit of my son, Travis, and my two grandchildren. It took me longer than I thought it would to vacuum and dust the bedrooms and then change the sheets to freshen the beds. The fact that I had to face Janet Makeshire over the misuse of library funds probably slowed me down even more than usual.

A relatively new Red Mercedes and a navy BMW convertible sitting by the front door in the Community Center parking lot suggested that Janet Makeshire and at least one other member of the Willem Club group were already inside. Her vanity tag, MAKEME, identified the Mercedes as Janet's vehicle. Who knew whatever else I might encounter inside the center? The building usually felt friendly enough, but now it seemed ominous.

I paused outside the door to try talking myself out of proceeding to what was sure to be an unpleasant confrontation. A loud noise caused me to start! I glanced across The Boulevard toward Twin Oaks Plaza. The source of the racket, an overly loud motorcycle, roared out of the shopping center and sped west on RM 150A. "You need to calm down" I told myself, summoning my weakening courage enough to open the door.

"That's all you can expect from these bumpkins!" Clariss Padget was at the front of the central meeting room talking to Janet Makeshire. "They don't come early to set things up, and everything falls on us."

Looking around, I saw that the long tables at the front and sides of the room were in their usual places and still bare. The chairs were laid out in four rows across the center of the room, as usual. 'What had Clariss and Janet set up themselves that they were complaining about?' I wondered.

I stepped tentatively out of the foyer. "Hello, Janet, Clariss," I called with more bravado than I truly felt. "I came extra early because I have something that I need to discuss with you."

"I'm sure that whatever you need can wait for the meeting," said Janet with a toss of her shoulder-length, golden blond hair. "You probably aren't familiar with meeting protocol. Library business should be discussed at the appropriate time during the meeting so that all of the participants can hear it."

My mischievous spirit reared its head, "If you really want us to discuss your party at LeDuc Bistro in front of the entire assembly, then I suppose it can wait until everyone is here."

"What are you nattering about now?" Clariss demanded.

"I'm talking about misappropriation of library funds for your own personal activities," my nervous brain allowed my unchecked mouth to blurt out. "Using donated library funds to treat your friends to an extravagant lunch at LeDuc Bistro is not a legal or acceptable expense for money which should be used to rehab the school building and set up the new library. I do intend to discuss this at the meeting, but I thought that I would give you a heads up so that you could prepare your defense."

"Defense!" Clariss shrieked. "Defense? We are in charge here. We don't need to defend our actions to anyone, particularly a nobody newcomer like you!"

"Clariss, calm down," Janet Makeshire said. "Adelaide is new here and simply doesn't understand how things operate around Wanderwood."

"Janet, I may be new to Wanderwood," I said more calmly than I felt, "but I am not new to the laws of Texas. The state Attorney General's Office is going to take a dim view of the way you and your friends operate. If you do not return every cent of the money that you spent at LeDuc Bistro as well as any other misappropriated funds, I'm pretty sure that Friends members will agree with the Attorney General. You don't want to be defending yourselves in state court for this illegal action."

"You don't know who you're dealing with, Adelaide Girard," hissed Clariss taking a step forward. "We have friends in state government who'll see to it that no one listens to a nobody like you."

"No matter whether they are friends of yours or not," I stated, stepping back in reaction to Clariss's threatening stance, "those elected officials will not want to be involved with charges of embezzlement."

"What embezzlement?" asked Janet, now starting to pay more attention.

"Misappropriating money for your own uses from a state of Texas authorized, non-profit corporation is considered embezzlement under state law." I hoped that what I was telling them was correct. I was no lawyer, but it sounded right.

Janet Makeshire stalked across the polished wooden floor until she stood no more than three feet from me, hands in fists against her slim hips. "You can explain to those deluded volunteers of yours how they're going to get along without the influence and status of people at Willem Club. They wouldn't have that non-profit corporation without our help and influence."

"Shelby Draper and Mavis Corcoran supplied, submitted, and processed the paperwork that secured non-profit status for the Wanderwood Library Friends organization. I have seen the correspondence from the state. I don't recall any of your names being on it." I was trying not to get too upset, but these arrogant women were stomping all over my equanimity of mind. Thanks to the stress of dealing with their egregious behavior, I was beyond upset!

"You want to be in charge," Clariss was almost growling, "but you'll see. You will fall flat on your face without Willem Club. The downfall of this whole project will be your fault."

"On behalf of all Willem Club members, we are withdrawing from this ungrateful organization. Just see how many friends you have when those volunteers find out that we at Willem Club are no longer backing them," Janet said through clenched teeth, "and that their failure is your fault! Clariss, we are out of here!"

"We'll expect that money you misused to be back in the library account by this coming Monday when the bank closes," I called after them as their designer stilettos clacked across the room and out the front door. The two upset women almost collided with Tom and Marolly Hamilton and Mavis Corcoran who were entering with boxes of supplies for the meeting.

"What was that about?" asked Marolly as she placed her box on one of the side tables.

Tom placed his box beside Marolly's and stepped back to take the box that Mavis was carrying. Tom's salt and pepper gray hair was styled in a classic businessman's cut, but it had gone a little long between appointments. He was definitely due for a trim. His salmon-colored polo shirt was buttoned to the top of the placket at the neck. A navy windbreaker completed his effort at a casual look. Brown, worn dress shoes in need of a polish below navy twill slacks made Tom seem like he could be out for an afternoon card game at the country club instead of setting up for a small group meeting.

"That was Janet and Clariss, speaking for the Friends members from Willem Club and submitting their resignation from the organization," I said with more than a little trepidation. I did not know how the group would react to this outcome or the money situation.

"Hallelujah!" said Tom. "How did you accomplish that?"

"Whatever you did," Marolly added, "I wish that I could have been here to see it. That should have happened weeks ago."

"You may have stirred up a hornet's nest," Mavis said with a frown on her usually smiling face. "What did you say to them?"

"I'll try to explain everything during the meeting." What Mavis said was causing me to worry. 'What will the rest of the Friends think and what will they say?' I wondered. My mind churned with visions of angry, shouting Friends members, but I said, "I don't believe that I want to explain it more than once."

'We should pull things together before more members arrive," said Mavis. She was ready for action in a no-nonsense outfit of blue denim work shirt topping burgundy boot-leg jeans. "Addie, I have the tablecloths in my box. We need to put those on the tables first. I went with some off-white tablecloths with an ivy print."

"That ought to look nice for a spring theme," approved Marolly. She was as easy-going as her husband Tom was conventional. Marolly seemed determined to enjoy her retirement in spite of Tom's cautious attitude. She was gaily dressed in a leopard print knit top over dark brown Jamaica shorts. From the top of her sensible oxfords, I saw brown and gold striped short-top socks poking up. Her hair, which was the color of straw, was held off her forehead by a gold hair band. "We brought a centerpiece of miniature pink and yellow roses for the main table, and one of red and pink tea roses for the refreshment table," she stated.

"With the tablecloths and centerpieces laid, Tom removed stacks of paper plates, napkins, and plastic utensils from a bin in his box and arranged them on the table that was set for refreshments. "I think we're close to ready," he said. "Do you have your book for recording the minutes, Mavis?"

"I need to fetch it from the car along with my plates of goodies," Mavis said. "Could you help me with that, Addie?"

"I'd be glad to, Mavis," I replied. "I need to get my plates from my car as well." I noticed that Tom and Marolly were already lifting a baking dish and a cloth-lined basket from their boxes.

In the parking lot, Mavis Corcoran grabbed my arm. "Tell me what is going on, Addie!" she demanded. "We can't afford to have Janet, Clariss, and the Willem Club bunch out of the project---at least I can't afford it."

"Why would the Willem Club group dropping out be a problem for you?" I asked, puzzled.

Mavis leaned into the back seat of her car to get her refreshment dishes, and I couldn't see her face to know how serious she was. "I work for Anson Kerringer," said Mavis. "Janet and Clariss will use their influence with him to make my life miserable. I may have to drop out of the Library Friends Organization. I can't afford to lose my job because you had some slight disagreement with them." She brought out her dishes, and I could see tears in her eyes.

"Mavis, I'm sorry that this is a problem for you, but it's more than some slight disagreement. I hope that you'll understand the importance when you hear what Janet and Clariss have been doing. We might as well disband the Library Friends and forget the project if we turn things back to them. I'll explain in the meeting."

Of course, explaining once was not enough for the twenty or so Friends members present to understand. Fortunately, no Willem Club members attended. 'Janet and Clariss probably called them all,' I thought. 'That group might be meeting somewhere else." This discussion would be horrendously difficult with them present. I hoped to avoid discussing all of the implications of the *misappropriation of funds*, but that question *Why?* raised its ugly head more than once.

"You should be able to see why I could not turn a blind eye to blatant theft of Friends' money," I detailed for the third time. "We cannot fund a library if some members drain off the funds that we raise and waste them on their own personal enjoyment. Janet and Clariss did not deny that they did exactly that."

"Why did Janet say that she did it?" asked Tom Hamilton, still dazed by the revelation of wrong doing.

"Janet said that *it's the way things work around here*," I stated simply, "and that we couldn't do anything about it."

"What did they mean by that?" asked Karyne Layne, owner and fitness guru at Shapely Woman Spa.

"I'll tell you what she meant," fussed Shelby Draper. "She meant that the Willem Club people could drain off all the money from this project like they have from every other project that we've proposed to improve Wanderwood. They think that we can't do anything about it if they blatantly take the money that's been donated and treat us like the chumps that we are. We've let them get by with it before so why shouldn't they think that? Remember the gazebo project?"

All of this confusion led eventually to a discussion of what to do about the resignation of the main officer positions. Mavis Corcoran, as the secretary of the Friends, and Shelby Draper, as the sergeant-at-arms, were the only officers remaining. The positions of president, vice-president, and treasurer were held by Janet Makeshire, Babs Vicenti, and Clariss Padget, all from Willem Club.

A discussion ensued over whether Mavis and Shelby should preside over tonight's meeting. At Mavis's and Shelby's urging the group decided to select a temporary interim president to serve until a new slate of officers could be properly chosen after notification of all members. After this matter was handled, we moved on to a discussion of how to gain access to the inside of the old school building for cleaning and painting. We also voted to paint the outside trim on the school building. Somehow, I was appointed to locate possible painters and also to locate area businesses to donate the paint.

A motion was made by new member, Lacy Tindal, seconded by Lisa Barncock, and passed by majority vote of the membership present that the names of the former Willem Club officers should be removed from the signature card at the bank. Shelby Draper agreed to do that. Two other members were chosen to do a review of the official minutes and documents to be certain that all other matters dealt with by Janet, Babs, or Clariss were legitimate. The best part of the meeting was the social hour which followed. All of the refreshments were great!

CHAPTER 6

"Trent! Put Vanilla down! Right now!" I insisted. "Come over here and give your Gammy a hug!" My seven-year-old grandson dropped the unhappy Siamese cat without managing to get bitten or scratched. Vanilla dashed in a mad climb to the top of the sofa and dropped into the middle of the narrow space behind it. Then Trent rushed into my arms as instructed and soon was talking to me in short, rapid sentences about the trip from Lubbock. The Saturday of their arrival was here at last!

"I saw a big bird in the sky, Gammy. The bird went around and around in circles. I saw goats and lots of horses." Trent held his arms as wide as he could. "A cow was standing in the water. Just one cow. He didn't stay with the other cows in the grass." For the age of seven, Trent was a bit chubby. He had Paula's thick, wavy hair and her sweet face. I thought that the rich brown hair color suited him.

"My, my," I said nodding. "That's a lot to see. You had a busy trip."

My son Travis stumbled in the front door pulling two over-stuffed, large suitcases. His shy, five-year-old daughter, Tricia, followed hesitantly dragging another small nylon suitcase on wheels. Travis was dressed in tan chino shorts and a Texas Tech Red Raiders t-shirt. He looked a little tired and frustrated. Tricia looked close to tears. I quickly gave Travis a hug and picked up Tricia, who, I found, seemed to have gained some weight since I last held her.

I sat down on one end of the sofa, gave Tricia a hug, and settled her on my lap. Tricia leaned her head against my shoulder and put her arms around my neck. "I wuv you, Gammy," Tricia said. She had a special place in my heart because she had that quirky auburn hair which made her resemble her dad when he was around kindergarten age and, also, me when I was very young.

'Tricia must have started another growing spurt,' I thought since she appeared to be at least two inches taller than the last time I saw her. If this continued, she would be taller than her older brother by the end of the year. Trent, unfortunately, did not seem to be participating in this new growth episode.

"I love you, too, Tricia," I assured her. "And I love Trent and your mommy and your daddy, too." I added. "I am very glad that you could visit me."

"That was a really long drive, Mom," Travis said as he settled himself on the other end of the sofa. "Will called me just as I was leaving. He wanted to know whether I had his guitar in my garage. Typical Will Girard thoughtlessness. I needed to get on the road quickly, and, as usual, Will was only thinking of himself."

"Your brother is younger than you, Travis."

"His call kept me from starting on time. We only stopped twice. We made a potty stop for gas and, of course, snacks and also a lunch break at Whataburger in Brownwood. I am beat, and I think that the kids seriously need a nap. Would you mind watching them take that nap while I look up an old friend?"

"You're beat, but you want to go out again to look up an old friend right away?" I was surprised by this announcement.

"You must know how it is," Travis explained. "Laddie may be available today but might not be around later in the week. I don't want to miss this chance to reconnect."

"Tricia does seem *nap-ready*, but I don't know about Trent," I mused out loud. "Okay, let me get them settled, and you can take off for a while." Teetering a bit, I somehow managed to get off the sofa with Tricia still in my arms and slowly lowered her to standing against my leg. "Trent, let me show you where you're going to sleep while you and Tricia are staying with Gammy." Tricia and I led him, now dragging his own suitcase, out of the room and up the stairs to the larger guest bedroom which featured twin beds.

This bedroom had belonged to my two daughters, Madison and Lindsey Anne, whenever we visited Wanderwood during the summers of their childhood. Now Travis and Paula's children would be occupying the room. I got Trent and Tricia settled on the twin beds under matching afgans (a gift from Lottie Frisham) that I kept at the foot of each bed.

I was looking for a book to read to them when I heard the car door slam and the engine start. 'Was that Travis leaving?' I wondered. A glance out the window showed that it was. 'Why didn't Travis wait until the children went to sleep?' My mind questioned idly. 'What is with that boy?'

I sat down on the edge of Trent's bed and opened the book that I chose to read to them, *Skiffles' Very Difficult Day*. This book was one of Travis's favorites when he was very young. 'Addie,' I chided myself, 'Travis is no longer a boy. He's a grown man with a wife and children.' I barely got to the part of the story where Skiffles turned his ankle before the children were sound asleep. Then I marked the place where I stopped reading, using a cute, tatted bookmark (another gift from Lottie) that I kept in the nightstand drawer.

Tiptoeing out of the room and carefully pulling the door almost closed behind me, I headed for the living room. I was expecting Kilgore Pettigrew, Wanderwood's guru for home repair and remodeling. Fortunately, I was able to snag Kilgore, a very busy man, to work on my kitchen remodel. Unfortunately, Kilgore was available only for the next three weeks to work on my project and then had other projects scheduled for the next eight months. He assured me that the work I wanted done could be accomplished in those three short weeks.

"Addie, I've worked out a list for you that shows the order and time that it will take for us to do each part of your kitchen redo," Kilgore explained, showing me the sheet and pointing out the various parts of the timetable. "We'll remove this old laminate countertop and the cabinet next to the sink on Monday. The new laminate countertop is on order and should be ready late next week. Are you sure that you want laminate? We could still change the order, but I'd have to know now."

Kilgore Pettigrew was a handsome man as his wife, Sara, often mentioned when she was working out at Shapely Woman Spa. He was tall, over six feet, and had a dark-skinned, angular face. Heading into the hot summer months, Kilgore cut his curly hair close to the scalp, but that didn't hide the wisps of gray that showed here and there. I was glad that Kilgore did not retire when he reached sixty-five, or there would be no one available in Wanderwood to do my remodel.

"I debated over what to use for the countertop," I explained. "I know that there are a lot of new trends, but they all seem to become dated rather quickly. Laminate is so practical, Kilgore, don't you think? If you drop a glass or plate on granite or quartz, it's broken for sure. With laminate you have the possibility that things won't break, and laminate is easy to keep clean. The real quandary was what pattern of laminate to choose. There are so many styles and colors."

"The pattern you picked, a simulation of granite, should look nice for a long time, Addie, and the darker color is a good accent," Kilgore wisely agreed. "That should go nicely with the lighter grayed-walnut stain that you've chosen for the cabinets, and both will go well with the Dinner Napkin White paint color that you selected."

"I don't know why they call the color Dinner Napkin White," I said. "It's obviously a pale beige, but it is light enough to make the cabinets and countertop stand out."

"Have you chosen the tile material for the back splash?" asked Kilgore, tapping his pencil point on the timetable where he had scheduled back splash installation.

"Next time I get to the Moore Décor Store in Dripping Springs, I will make a final choice," I promised. "I definitely have the tile narrowed down to five possibilities. Maybe when I see the actual stain on the cabinets that will help. Moore gets the tile from a distributor in Dallas. They assured me that it would not take much time to get so long as I choose something that is in stock in the distributor's warehouse."

Kilgore warned, "we'll start staining all of the cabinets as soon as the countertop is off and the cabinet sink is removed. I've scheduled Ernie Plott to do the plumbing for the dishwasher and install the new sink and faucet." His tapping pencil indicated another point on the timetable.

"Kilgore, is all of this demolition and construction in the kitchen going to cause a lot of mess in the house?" I interrupted him. I'd had all kinds of visions of problems that living in a construction zone might cause.

"Of course, Addie, there will be a lot of dust, but we will install sheets of plastic over the two inside doorways to minimize the impact of that dust on the rest of the house. There also will be some noise from time to time. You might want to consider activities away from the house during the day when work is happening."

"It's a relief that the dust will be somewhat contained," I said.

"You remember that I told you when we were first planning this remodel," Kilgore continued in his detailing of the work to come, "the stove, refrigerator, and kitchen table will have to be out of the kitchen for the entire three weeks. My crew will put them back in place after the walls are painted and the tile flooring is installed. Of course, like I mentioned when we were discussing your plans previously, we don't have room in this timetable for problems or delays."

"Problems or delays?" I questioned.

"Don't worry, Addie," Kilgore tried to reassure me with a smile on that handsome face. "I can't see that we'll have any delays so long as you get that back splash chosen by next week."

"I'll see that you have it on time, Kilgore."

'How am I going to get everything done?' I worried as I stood on my front porch and watched Kilgore Pettigrew's truck go down Serenity Lane and turn right at the intersection with Peaceful Way.

"Addie, was that Kilgore Pettigrew I saw leaving?"

I turned to find Lottie Frisham walking up the driveway wearing her fuchsia jogging shorts and hot pink tee that said *I'm One In A Million!* on the back. 'She is so right about that,' I thought. 'She is one friend in a million.'

"Kilgore was here to show me the timetable for my kitchen remodel," I told her. "With all that I have going on this week, I don't know how I will handle the remodel and everything else. When Travis scheduled this visit, I couldn't foresee the problems with the Friends Organization or that this remodel would have to start now."

"Well, I told you that I would help you take care of Trent and Tricia," Lottie stated emphatically. "When do you think Travis will get here?"

"He's already here and gone," I told her with some consternation. "Travis arrived with the children about half an hour ago. Then he took off almost before I could get Trent and Tricia settled for a nap. "

"Tricia and Trent are here---now?" Lottie questioned.

"They are taking a nap in Madison and Lindsey's room," I answered her. "And Travis took off like a shot. He said that he wanted to *reconnect* with some friend named *Laddie* that he knew years ago."

"Laddie?" said Lottie. "You don't mean Amanda Ladd, do you?"

"Amanda Ladd?"

"Well, she's the only person around here that I know anything about who calls herself Laddie," Lottie remarked. "Amanda Ladd is probably around the same age as Travis. You may not have met Amanda. She moved into her parents' summer home in Willem Club a couple of months ago. The Ladds live in The Woodlands north of Houston."

"How do you keep up with all of these people, Lottie?" I asked, feeling a bit disturbed by her information. 'Why was Travis *reconnecting* with Amanda Ladd?' I wondered. 'What is my son thinking?'

"Well, I didn't really know Harold and Ellen Ladd. They didn't live in this area of town and were here only during the Summer. Their children, Little Hal, Bobby, and Amanda, would turn up often at various church and local activities. I remember that Harold and Ellen liked activities where they could drop their kids off and pick them up later. They expected someone from the church or the community to take responsibility for their children---like free babysitting services. Maybe that's how Travis met Amanda. He attended a lot of those same activities."

"You'd think that I would have met her, Lottie. I took my kids to a lot of community activities during those summers," I said.

"Remember that you let me take the kids to activities as well, especially ones that my church sponsored," Lottie suggested. "You were awfully nice that way. I always liked that about you, Addie."

"You gave me regular breaks, Lottie, and I appreciated that about you. Like tomorrow. What time will you be picking up Trent and Tricia for the Welcome Back to Spring Party? I was hoping to rest a bit this weekend. Kilgore is bringing his crew early Monday morning to tear up my kitchen."

"Then I'll be here around six. The party starts at seven-thirty, but I want to show Tricia and Trent a few things that have changed around Wanderwood since they were here last Fall. I especially want to show them the old school building, now that you've been elected President of the Friends organization. Then, too, I need to get to the church early to help set things up for the party."

"That's Interim President; I have the office until the next regular election. I'm glad that Marolly and Shelby agreed to be Interim Vice-President and Treasurer. They are really avid workers. Selma Haythorne agreed to replace Shelby as Sergeant-At-Arms---temporarily."

"Well, Shelby is good with numbers, and everyone likes Marolly," stated Lottie. "With the new group of officers in charge now, I almost could consider supporting the Friends---almost."

"I wish you would join us, Lottie," I sighed. "I have too much to do this week for the Friends. First, I have to obtain permission from the school board to have access to the inside of the building so that we can clean up and paint. Then I need to find some businesses that will donate the paint or money to buy the paint. Marolly is going to help me with that. She thinks she knows a couple of painters who will help out. Also, I need to set up a committee to plan fundraisers for the Summer and Fall." The enormity of my list made me pause momentarily to shift mental gears.

"Kilgore says that I absolutely must pick out material for the cabinet backsplash in the next few days, so that it can be ordered. And, of course, I want to spend time with Travis, Tricia, and Trent while they are here. That's why it's helpful that you wanted to take them to the party this evening. I thought that, if I could get some of these things out of the way by phone or in person by Wednesday, then I could concentrate on having fun with Trent and Tricia. Maybe Travis and I could take the children to BoompaLand on Thursday or Friday."

"Well, Addie, I like BoompaLand but Walter doesn't care for it. You know that he isn't into amusement parks."

"Then you should come with us, Lottie, if you have the time. We'll have a lot of fun, but I'll have to let you know the details later. Timing may depend on how things go next week."

"I'll look forward to it," Lottie said. "I came by to ask if you wanted to take a walk down to the pond and back because I thought that Travis wasn't here yet. Maybe I'll take a shorter walk since you are on babysitting duty right now." She started down the driveway toward Serenity Lane at a good clip, a pace that I expected would probably decrease once she rounded the corner.

"See you later," I called after her.

CHAPTER 7

"Trent! Tricia! Stop running up and down those stairs! Stop right now! Not next week!" I knew that my grandchildren were merely excited about going to the Wildlife Safari near New Braunfels with Lottie and Walter Frisham, but their boundless energy was making me frazzled. I could hear Lottie's voice in my head saying, "Addie, chill out a little. Children will get excited once in a while." And then, of course, Lottie would be preening because it was a day trip with her that had them so excited.

"Why don't the two of you sit on the living room floor and play pass the ball until Aunt Lottie and Uncle Walter get here?" I suggested. This led to shrieks of *Pass the ball! Pass the Ball!* from the overactive twosome, and a mad dash for the plastic bin that had become a makeshift toy box in the corner of the living room. That, in turn, caused a number of toys to find their way out of the box while Trent and Tricia dug out the purple, black, and white soccer ball which I purchased at the Handy Sack for them last week.

No sooner were Trent and Tricia settled on the floor than the doorbell rang. 'Addie Girard,' I fussed to myself, 'whatever it is that they're selling, you're not buying!' I knew that Lottie was not at the front door. She usually came in the back door after cutting across the Hamiltons' back yard and only occasionally knocked. Besides, she and Walter weren't due to pick up Trent and Tricia for another half hour.

"That's the door bell, Addie. Aren't you going to answer it?" Marty Gastbend said as he appeared in the doorway to the kitchen, holding back the plastic sheeting while wiping his face with a dark blue kerchief. He tended to take frequent breaks from his work on the kitchen cabinets. Marty arrived much too early on this Wednesday morning.

I could have told him that I heard the doorbell myself, but I merely said, "Thank you, Marty." He returned to my devastated kitchen. I headed for the front door, stiffening my mental backbone to deflect even the most avidly persistent salesperson quickly.

When I opened the door, I was totally shocked to find Viveca Laurin standing on my porch. Viveca was obviously in *Number One Realtor* mode as reflected by the mauve power suit that she was wearing, complete with a lovely floral scarf that looked like exquisite silk. I couldn't recognize the designer of her sleek, high-heeled sandals. However, I was certain that they were expensive.

"Adelaide Girard?" she inquired.

"Yes, I'm Addie Girard. And you are Viveca Laurin, one of our local realtors," I answered her. I was somewhat nonplussed that she would know my name or where I lived---or that I even existed.

"I apologize for dropping by without an appointment, Addie, but Kilgore didn't think that you would mind. I needed to discuss with you a matter that is really urgent. I hope you have some time now."

I stepped back so that she could enter my small foyer and led her into my now toy-strewn living room. "Please have a seat, Viveca." I indicated the sofa which seemed to be the only clear seating in the room. Travis left a pair of beat-up tennis shoes and a sad-looking golf hat on George's old recliner before my errant son scooted out the door mumbling some excuse for leaving without more explanation.

Backpacks for Trent's and Tricia's trip to the Wildlife Safari occupied the wooden captain's chair which I purchased at the yard sale. The loveseat contained bags of Friends pending paperwork that I needed to review. Mavis told me that Janet and Clariss seemed to have no time to pick them up or deal with them. I wasn't sure when I would have time to deal with them either.

I picked up a few of the toys from the walkway in the middle of the room with my curiosity turning cartwheels at this unusual twist of events. "May I offer you something to drink?" I suggested, trying to settle that overactive curiosity of mine. "Perhaps a cold glass of lemonade?"

"Why, thank you, Addie." Viveca smiled her best *make the sale* smile.

I restrained an overwhelming desire to pick up more toys and made my way past my hulking refrigerator into the dining room. Taking two glasses from a covered tray by the microwave on the sideboard, I poured lemonade from a lidded pitcher that I was keeping on the tray by the glasses. The ice clinked the sides of the glasses, and I had to be careful not to splash the sticky lemonade. I almost forgot to snag two napkins from the sideboard as I headed back to join Viveca on the living room sofa.

"Thank you so much," Viveca enthused as she took a sip of the ice-cold lemonade. "This is very refreshing on a warm day like today."

I got right to the big question that was hanging in the air between us. "What can I do for you, Viveca?"

"Please, call me Viv," she verbally sidestepped the question. "All my friends do."

I tried it out. "Viv, is there something in particular that you need from me?" My curiosity was now convinced that this was a very important subject.

"Actually, Addie, the issue is probably so trivial that you're likely to wonder why I came in person instead of merely calling. I wanted you to understand how very essential this matter is to me." She paused and apparently was waiting for a response from me.

I was perplexed as to what she meant. My impatient curiosity was screaming in my brain, *'Just answer the question, Viv!'* But I said, "What could this issue possibly be?"

"Your little kitchen remodel," she finally stated. "Addie, I'm more than a little embarrassed to ask it, but would you mind awfully postponing your project? I suppose it might be a small inconvenience for you, but Kilgore mentioned that you had your grandchildren visiting. Naturally, I thought *what a splendid way to give you more time to spend with them.*" Viveca paused to take another sip of lemonade and then plunged ahead.

"As you may know, my full house remodel has been scheduled for some time," Viv continued. "Now I find that it needs to be moved up several weeks. You see, I have the opportunity to make my house the model home for Champions Ramble. Anson Kerringer offered to pay for the installation of many upgraded finishes which will be featured in Champions Ramble homes. I'm sure that you can understand how this puts more emphasis on completing the project earlier than originally planned."

"What a fortunate happenstance for you," I threw in to hold up my end of this off-the-wall conversation. "I'm sure that you have put in many hours of planning for your remodel."

Viv cleared her throat, sipped, and continued, "I'll be having all of the walls repainted to a more *au courant* color. Then, of course, all of the countertops and plumbing fixtures must be redone. And, yes, the lighting fixtures have to change. The floors will have new surfaces. Everything has to look new and match with plans for the homes in Champions Ramble. My house will be upgraded in every room." Finishing this spiel confidently, she paused for more lemonade.

I was totally at a loss what to say to that long statement, so I sipped some lemonade as well. Then Trent broke the tension when he hit Viv in the knee with the soccer ball. "Oh, Viv, I'm terribly sorry. Trent, please be more careful!" I scolded half-heartedly. "I think that you should pick up these toys now before Aunt Lottie and Uncle Walter get here. Let's see who can put the most toys in the toy box," I suggested.

'Bless her sweet, obedient heart,' I thought as Tricia quickly got up from the floor and began gathering toys and placing them in the bin one at a time. Trent followed her lead less enthusiastically. 'This interruption will give me a moment or two to think of a reply for Viveca,' I thought. And the doorbell rang again.

'What now?' my brain muttered, but to Viveca I said politely, "won't you excuse me a moment, Viv?" Then I somewhat ungracefully scooted for the front door, but Lottie was already entering followed hesitantly by Walter.

"Addie, we're here to pick up Tricia and Trent for the trip to the Wildlife Safari," Lottie announced unnecessarily. All toy gathering ceased instantly and was replaced by shrieks and squeals of delight. Lottie glanced at Viveca Laurin.

"We see that you have company, so we'll get out of your way," added Walter.

I made quick introductions as I checked once more to be sure that Tricia and Trent had hats, sunscreen, and bottles of water in their backpacks. Lottie and Walter assured me that the kids were going to have fun and that they wouldn't be back late.

Then, Walter preceding her, Lottie gave me a questioning look as she herded my now giggling and squirming grandchildren out the door.

I shrugged my shoulders, said, "I'll call you later this afternoon," and closed the door. Then I returned to an expectant Viveca Laurin She was still seated on my living room sofa sipping lemonade.

Marty Gastbend appeared again at the kitchen door, "Addie, it seems that the stain didn't make it into my truck this morning. I have to go back to the shop to get it. I'll need it today when I finish sanding the cabinets."

"That's okay, Marty, but I hope that this delay won't slow things up," I cautioned. "Kilgore set a really tight schedule for getting this kitchen remodel completed on time."

"Not a problem," Marty replied. "I'll see you shortly with the stain." Then he headed to the kitchen door and was gone.

I turned back to Viveca. She smiled, once more, expectant. "Viv, could you come into the kitchen for a moment?" I asked. I walked away from her past the plastic sheeting into the kitchen to check Marty's progress.

Viveca quickly joined me in the disaster area that used to be my aged but well-organized kitchen. The appliances were gone. The sink was gone. The countertop was gone. There was a gaping hole where the new dishwasher would go when it arrived. Tools were scattered about the room. Dust from the sander covered the vinyl tile floor and every remaining surface. "As you can see, Viv," I apologized, "postponement is not a viable option."

"Addie, honey, you are so right," Viv said, laying a comforting hand on my arm. "Seeing this, I am somewhat dreading the beginning of my project."

We returned to the living room and continued our discussion of Viv's whole-house remodel. Then we segued into a discussion of the difficulties with the converting of the old school building into a library. Viveca was in agreement with me that the town was growing and needed a library.

"Addie, having a library in Wanderwood will really enhance the quality of life. My clients regularly ask what amenities our community offers. Now I'll be able to tell them that we'll have a library soon, and I want to help that along. I want to join the Friends and help you make that happen."

"Viv, that's great! We need all the volunteers we can get. This is a large effort---"

We were interrupted by a trill from Viv's phone which she instantly whipped out. "Addie, I'm afraid I have to go," she said as she read the text message. "An out-of-town client has arrived a day early and wants to view properties in Champions Ramble. I have the exclusive contract as the only realtor who can market the development."

"It's been my pleasure getting to know you, Viv," I said as we quickly headed for the door. "I'll see you at the Friends meeting on Thursday."

She, in return, punched buttons on her phone. Viv gave me a slight wave of her fingers as she dashed for her sleek, silver Grand Cherokee.

CHAPTER 8

"You have to do it, Addie," said Lacy Tindal as she nibbled on a crunchy, golden onion ring. Just after one o'clock on Wednesday, Lacy and I were once more meeting at Lefty's Bar-B-Q for a late lunch. "Checking things out won't take you that much time. You're so...inquisitive...that you're a natural to find where the gazebo money went. I know that you can find the answers."

"Lacy," I said with a sigh, "I know that you aren't aware of what's been happening around my house. Tricia and Trent totally wore me out trying to keep them occupied on Saturday since Travis left and didn't come back until after ten in the evening. Luckily, Lottie Frisham took Tricia and Trent to a Welcome Back to Spring Party at her church for a couple of hours that evening. A reasonably peaceful Sunday morning worship service followed by lunch at Lotta Lotta Chicken in Dripping Springs led to naps by all of us on Sunday afternoon. I really needed the rest."

"But that's over and done," Lacy protested as she slowly dipped an onion ring into Lefty's special barbecue sauce which she had plopped in a puddle on one side of her plate.

"Sunday evening, I cooked what may be the last meal that I will cook for at least three weeks. I wanted to talk with Travis about activities we could do together with Tricia and Trent. He insisted on going to the Handy Sack to get some snacks for him and the children---for three hours. The children and I were in bed and asleep when he came back."

"You'll have more time later today to talk with him, Addie," Lacy tried to console me while she cut her barbecued chicken breast. "Next time we come here, I want to sample Lefty's Chef Specialty."

"I haven't heard about that dish. Is it new?" I asked. My bowl of Mama's Chili Stew (small portion) was so down-home delicious that I couldn't think the Chef Specialty would be better.

"I think that it features an ostrich burger," Lacy explained, "and some kind of spinach-bacon hush puppies. Then you can choose another side. We can try it when we get together later this week. You can tell me about your success in the big meeting."

"I don't know how I even have time for this meeting with family visiting and my kitchen torn up. Kilgore arrived with his crew as he promised at seven-thirty Monday morning. As soon as the kitchen stove was moved to the garage and the heavy refrigerator was relocated and connected in my living room, Travis ducked out with an excuse about making a lunch date with Laddie *to talk over old times*."

"You were by yourself with Trent and Tricia again?" she commiserated. "How did that go?"

"We took the socker ball to the back yard. Tricia and Trent chased that ball and each other for over an hour. They have an unfathomable amount of energy. We drove to Handy Sack and they helped me with grocery shopping. They napped while I worked on Library Friends paperwork. I'm trying to figure out what Janet Makeshire actually did while she was President of the Friends. Yesterday, I took Trent to Donovan Park pond to fish and chase the squirrels while Lottie took Tricia on a mysterious shopping trip to which, fortunately, Trent and I were not invited."

"I thought that Travis came to spend time with you," remarked Lacy as she sliced more chicken breast.

"So did I, Lacy." I considered ordering another small bowl of chili stew but gave myself a mental slap for that thought. "Tuesday afternoon, I taught Tricia and Trent how to play this new game, Tallywack, which I purchased particularly for their visit. I could have kissed Lottie when she begged me to let her and Walter take Tricia and Trent to the Wildlife Safari near New Braunfels today."

"So that's why Lottie missed the garden club meeting," said Lacy.

"Yes. Lacy, I truly needed her help because, wedged into all of this activity, I had updating discussions with Kilgore Pettigrew about details on the kitchen remodel. Kilgore insisted on double checking the color of the stain for the cabinets and the material chosen for the countertop."

"The kitchen redo sounds like it's become a larger project than you first envisioned." Lacy dipped another onion ring. "Lately, it seems like every group that I'm a member of is having some kind of event in honor of Spring. At the dealership, we've been a little busier than we expected for this time of year, but your week is much more hectic."

"For the library, I had to squeeze in a rushed meeting late this morning with the Superintendent of the school district. That netted me the keys to the old brick school building and permission for the Friends to do the cleaning and painting. Even when Tricia and Trent weren't with me, I was busier than an underdog candidate on the day before the election."

"Sounds like it," Lacy said as Loretta came up on the jukebox to brag about her parentage.

"While the children are at the wildlife safari with Lottie and Walter this morning, I was looking forward to devoting some time to Travis T. I wanted to catch up and find out what Paula is doing while she's staying at home. But Travis made some feeble excuse early this morning about buying some new shoes. He couldn't seem to get out of the house fast enough. Also this week, would you believe, Viveca Laurin dropped by unannounced."

"The realtor?" asked Lacy. "What did she want?"

"She wanted to ask me to postpone *my little kitchen remodel*. Lacy, can you picture me doing that after the kitchen is already so torn up? When I left for the meeting with the Superintendent, Travis had not returned."

'What was going on with my son and Amanda Ladd?' my curious mind wondered. 'Don't be such a Nosy Josie!' I scolded that meddling mind. 'He's probably bored and looking for something different to do during his time off. But what?' This question hung there in the cortex of my over-active brain with no answer forthcoming.

"That's why we can now enjoy the quintessential food of Central Texas--- barbecue," Lacy stated vehemently.

Lefty's Bar-B-Q was very busy for a noontime in Wanderwood. Willie replaced Loretta on the jukebox, belting out a tune about his life on the road and how much he and his friends enjoyed it. Lefty Aduddell was dividing her time between the cash register and helping her daughter, Brenda, serve and bus tables. While Lacy verbally tutored me in my duties as chief navigator for the Friends group, she unashamedly licked Lefty's excellent sauce from her fingers.

"Lacy, I don't see how I can waltz into Anson Kerringer's office at Champions Ramble and ask him to donate the paint for the library project," I protested. "He lives at Willem Club. Those people have made it plain that they are no longer supporting the Library Friends."

"His business isn't in Willem Club," Lacy insisted. "You need to remind Anson that he could use some good public relations with the residents of Wanderwood who are very upset over that road he's proposing to build. Put the pressure on him. I'm sure that you can get him to cough up a few measly gallons of paint."

"Thirty-two gallons of paint," I emphasized, "is more than a few measly gallons."

"That much, huh?" she asked, starting on her last onion ring.

"Maybe more," I answered. I had tamed my craving for fries or onion rings and was feeling very virtuous as I finished off my side of coleslaw. "Maxie Chalpers' rough estimate is thirty-two gallons. If we could get that much donated, I think that we could buy another gallon or two. We might find that we are short before the painting is finished."

"Do you really need that much paint?" queried Lacy doubtfully.

"That old school building is larger on the inside than it looks like on the outside, and we'd like to put on two coats to help cover the flaws. We're thinking that we may be able to open a wall between two of the classrooms to create a meeting room. That room could be rented occasionally to community groups to raise extra funds for supporting the library. Our plan is to hire a librarian and use Friends volunteers to help out with operations."

"Sounds like you are making good plans, but, Addie, you need to work on developing some gumption when it comes to requesting donations. Tell yourself that you have to learn to talk to people with your hand out. It's important to the success of the library. Before you go into Anson Kerringer's office, remember to tell yourself the worst that can happen is that he'll say *No*."

"The worst that could happen, Lacy, is that he'll jump up from his chair, grab me by the arm, and personally escort me out of the building in front of everyone who's sitting in his office waiting room." I shuddered as I visualized that all-too-probable possibility.

"There is no way that could happen as you describe," Lacy insisted as she stabbed a fork into the last chunk of her dill pickle spear.

"Why do you say that?" I queried, dabbing with my extra napkin where I could feel the chili stew broth dripping down my chin.

"First, Anson doesn't have a waiting room at Champions Ramble. The offices are in a portable metal building---kind of like a mobile home. The only waiting area is inside the front door where Mavis Corcoran works. She's the receptionist and general office flunky. You know the type of position. Mavis greets people, does the filing, keeps track of appointments, puts together mailings, types letters, makes the coffee, empties the trash, and who knows what else."

"I met Mavis recently," I said. "She's been a great help with the work of the Library Friends because her days off are during the week. I didn't know that she was responsible for so much. However, her job sounds more like a secretary position than a receptionist."

"If he called her a secretary, Anson would have to pay her more," Lacy scoffed. "Anson is known for taking advantage of his employees. He has a difficult time keeping office and sales staff because of that."

I shook my head and tsked a couple of tsks.

"Jack Cartoff was at our car lot last week looking at this sweet, low-mileage, navy Volkswagen van that we are featuring in our pre-owned vehicle ads. Jack's on the sales staff at Champions Ramble, and he said that the down payment on the car might be a stretch for him. When I suggested that maybe he could ask Anson for an advance or a raise, he got upset. Jack told me that he and Benny Olesford were the only salespersons who haven't quit. Jack also said he knew that they would be let go if he or Benny were foolish enough to ask for a raise."

"That's cold," I said. "Now I'm sure that I wouldn't dare to ask Anson Kerringer to donate the paint!"

"Addie, all you have to do is go in the front door and tell Mavis why you're there. She'll get you in to see Anson. You explain to him about the library needing conscientious supporters from the business community. Tell him how you're going to recognize the substantial donors. Remind him that donating is great for public relations. Bart and I get this kind of request all the time."

"When you describe it, Lacy, it seems so simple," I sighed.

"Addie, it is that simple. You can do this," my friend assured me. "When are you going to go to Champions Ramble?"

"If I'm going to get it done before the library meeting, I have to go to Champions Ramble this afternoon. Tricia and Trent are on the wildlife safari with the Frishams this morning and will be doing crafts with Lottie all afternoon. She's even making supper for them."

"Sounds like your schedule is pretty tight," said Lacy.

"Tomorrow night is the Friends meeting, and I'm wanting to have at least some of the paint donated by then. During the day, I plan for Travis, the children, and I to make a trip to BoompaLand. Then, on Saturday, I'm planning to have Travis grill some steaks that I'm buying at the Handy Sack. I knew that by then the kitchen would be unusable," I explained. "Oh, dear, I'd better have Brenda add some gallon bottles of fruit punch and tea to my bill to take home. And maybe I'll get some potato salad for Travis and a large container of Lefty's Polka Dotted Mac and Cheese for Tricia and Trent. And some of this chili stew, too."

"What's Polka Dotted Mac and Cheese?" asked Lacy.

"It's Lefty's recipe that she added to the menu last month---a way to get kids to eat vegetables," I told my friend. "She adds finely diced carrots, extra-finely-diced celery, and green peas to regular mac and cheese. I've tried it for supper, and you hardly notice the vegetables. If Tricia and Trent like it, I can nuke the leftovers for their supper on Saturday. I'm searching for things that I can heat in the microwave while my kitchen stove is in the garage."

Lacy gave my arm a pat. "Refrigerator in the living room. Stove in the garage. Where do you have the microwave?"

"It's in the dining room," I said, "on top of my grandmother's sideboard. Lacy, I'd better get the potato salad and the Polka Dotted Mac and Cheese ordered before I forget it." I managed to get Brenda's attention and signaled for her to come to our table.

"Maybe I'll get some of that Polka Dotted Mac and Cheese, too," Lacy said. "I have trouble getting Bart to eat vegetables. When he's home, he likes to sprawl in front of the TV and eat what he likes to call *comfort food*. Apparently, Bart doesn't find vegetables very comforting, unless we're talking about potato chips or tomato sauce on spaghetti and pizza."

CHAPTER 9

"Addie Girard, get on with it now!" I scolded myself out loud. I had been sitting in my car in front of the metal mobile office building at Champions Ramble for almost five minutes. I was working on summoning up enough false courage to go into the building. "How difficult could it be to talk to Anson Kerringer? He's just an ordinary person like you," I chided myself.

"Just an ordinary person with at least two expensive homes and lots of bucks in the bank," I answered myself. "Just an ordinary person who makes a habit of bullying his employees," I added. "Yes, George, I know that this is not productive thought." I answered George's nagging voice in my head that also was telling me to get out of the car and do the work that I had come to do. "You think that I took on responsibilities for the Friends organization that I shouldn't have tried to do," I huffed.

"I'll have you know, George Girard, that I am a very resourceful person. I have good friends here in Wanderwood who are backing me and depending on me to get that paint for the new library. I am not going to let them down now. I am going to find some way to be Addie Girard, fundraiser extraordinaire! We are going to have that library, or my name isn't Adelaide Bonner Girard!"

I grabbed my purse and shoved open the door of my Jeep before I might lose that new-found bravado. "All you have to do is talk to Mavis Corcoran after you go in that door," I told myself. "Mavis is one of my new library helpers. That part should be easy. Lacy said that Mavis can get me into the office to see Anson Kerringer, and Anson Kerringer I will see---if he's here."

I looked around as I mounted the steps. The grounds around the metal office building seemed deserted so far as I could see with all of the wooded area surrounding it. No cars were in the parking lot except my green Jeep. 'Maybe there's a staff parking lot in the back,' I thought. 'Anson Kerringer might want to reserve this front lot for prospective homebuyers. A wealthy businessman like Anson might not want his customer parking lot cluttered by Mavis Corcoran's beat-up Volkswagen Bug with the lime green *KIDS IN RESIDENCE* sticker on the back.'

I hastily pulled my mind back from these thoughts to an actual thought of opening the front door. "All you have to do is talk to Mavis Corcoran after you go in that front door," I told myself once more as I reached for the knob. I truly believed I had convinced myself that the process would be that simple.

Once inside the front door, I was in a small anteroom office where I was prepared to speak to receptionist Mavis Corcoran. I faced, instead, an empty desk. A burgundy desk chair, neatly drawn up to the small receptionist's computer table-desk, did not appear as if someone had left the room and would soon return. The desk looked as if the receptionist had left for the day with everything neatly put away. I listened carefully to the silence in the vacant room. I could hear no voices from any adjoining offices.

'Where is Mavis? Where are the salespeople?' I wondered. 'Maybe the salespeople are out showing houses to prospective customers,' I answered my wondering mind. "Mavis, are you here?" I called hesitantly. There was no answering voice. No *Sorry, I had to step into the other room*. Only an eerie silence. "Mr. Kerringer?" I called out once more tentatively as I looked around the room for access to other spaces. 'The front door was unlocked. Therefore, someone must be here' I mentally encouraged myself.

A short hallway to the left, flanked on each side by two small schefflera plants in burgundy ceramic pots, seemed like it might lead to offices. "Mr. Kerringer?" I called again as I headed into the hallway. Two small offices with doors standing open were off this hallway.

Each of these offices had a desk, desk chair, two upholstered (burgundy) occasional chairs, one window flanked by sheer curtains, a large plat map of the Champions Ramble development on the wall, and a small schefflera plant (same burgundy ceramic pot) in the corner. The walls of the front office, the hallway, and these two offices were typical mobile home wood paneling which was painted light gray. What these offices didn't have were occupants.

I started to feel really annoyed with myself. "Maybe you should have made an appointment," I berated myself. I checked the one door in the hallway that was closed and found that it led into a unisex bathroom. This room, also, thankfully, had no occupant. I retraced my way down the short hallway to the receptionist's office. Still no Mavis. The room was as I left it moments before.

I headed for another short hallway to the right of the front door. A third time I called, "Mavis? Mr. Kerringer?" Down this hallway were what looked like two more offices. However, the first room turned out instead to be a room with a round table in the center surrounded by six of the burgundy occasional chairs. The light gray paneled walls of this room featured the same plat map of the development and numerous color pictures of various styles of houses. No one was home.

The other office contained a nicer desk than the sales offices and a larger, more imposing desk chair. It still featured the same pair of burgundy occasional chairs and schefflera plant in a burgundy pot, but it had two windows and, above the desk, a large painting of golfers on a difficult-looking green. The painting had an ornate gold frame. The office didn't have Anson Kerringer seated behind the desk, before it, or anywhere else in the room.

Off this hallway, there was also a closed door. 'Does this place need two bathrooms, or is this a supply closet?' I wondered as I slowly opened the door. "Mr.

Kerringer?" I called for the benefit of anyone inside what appeared to be a staff breakroom in the back corner of the building. A small dinette, a few kitchen cabinets, and a sink were in this room. And Anson Kerringer was in this room---crumpled in a heap on the floor! His once interesting facial structure which had suggested Native American ancestors was now frozen in a contortion of pain. He was obviously very dead.

"What the---" I stared at the stricken figure on the floor of this room which reeked of stale vomit and another noxious odor, an awful smell which was somewhat reminiscent of a soiled diaper. I backed from the room, being careful not to touch anything, and scooted directly for the front door. I didn't want to be in the building if I, too, threw up. I pulled a tissue from my handbag and quickly opened the door, sucking fresh air in big gulps as I cleared the porch at a run.

"Get hold of yourself, Addie Girard," I scolded as my shaking fingers tried to dial 911 on my cell phone. On the third attempt, I was finally successful. "I need the Evritt County Sheriff's Department," I told the calm and professional sounding operator who answered the call. "I'm Adelaide Girard and I'm in the town of Wanderwood in North Evritt County. I'm at the sales office of the Champions Ramble development. I just now found Anson Kerringer dead on the floor. Could you please send deputies to see about this?" The words tumbled from my mouth in a rush.

The operator was asking me something, but I wasn't taking in her words. I grabbed for the door handle on the passenger side of my Jeep and yanked. It was locked! I desperately rummaged for my keys in my handbag and was relieved to hear all of the locks click open as I punched the button twice from habit.

I still had the cell phone to my ear, and I realized that the 911 operator was politely but repeatedly asking me something. "I'm afraid that I'm feeling a little dizzy. Could you say that again please?" I requested. She repeated the question. "No, I don't think that I'm in danger," I answered sliding into the seat, closing the door, and hitting the lock button---twice.

"There doesn't seem to be anyone here but me…and…and the deceased person," I stammered. I belatedly looked around the area but did not see another single person. The wooded area surrounding the office and my Jeep seemed to close in on me. Every tree looked like it might be hiding someone lurking and watching.

Over the phone, I heard the operator reassure me that a sheriff's deputy should be arriving soon to assist me and that I shouldn't leave the area. She asked me to remain on the phone and then proceeded to disconnect me. I broke the connection as well and dropped the phone into my handbag. "George, how could this happen to me?" I asked as I leaned my head against the window and awaited an answer. As usual, George was not listening to me and said not a word.

I waited faithfully in my car for at least fifteen minutes before curiosity and boredom overcame my fright. I unlocked the car and slipped out cautiously. By this time, I was wondering about the possible employee parking lot. The driveway continued around one end of the building, and that was the way that I decided to go.

Today, I was dressed purposefully in a trim, slate-colored suit. I chose the one with the waist-length jacket sporting decorative red buttons to match the red and gold crest on the breast pocket. 'Dressing for success is the order of the day,' I had thought. As I rounded the end of the building, there it was. A second parking lot behind the building and a shiny black Jeep Wagoneer. This was probably Anson's car. No other vehicle was on the lot. I returned to my car, hoping that the deputies would arrive soon.

I passed a little more time by thinking forward to next month and the cruise that I would soon take with my younger daughter, Lindsey Anne. Remembering that Lottie had once commented about Lindsey Anne being smarter than Madison, I mentally pictured my two daughters side by side. 'Madison is such a social butterfly that it's difficult to know how smart she really is,' I thought. 'Her social flitting may hide a very bright person. People may not see the *smarts* behind all of the activity. Of course, both of my daughters were very clever and beautiful to me.'

By the watch on my arm, almost an hour passed before the deputy at last pulled into the parking lot at Champions Ramble. This deputy, wearing a faded and somewhat wrinkled uniform, appeared to be about eighty years old as he dragged himself out of an unmarked car. He waddled over to me, shifting his utility belt around his ample girth as he walked.

"Ms. Gerhardt?" he questioned as he neared the Jeep.

"Girard," I corrected. "Adelaide Girard, Deputy."

"The dispatcher wasn't too clear about what you wanted, Ms. Girard. Could you tell me the nature of your problem?" He took a small flip notebook and a pen from his shirt pocket. "Of course, I'll need you to give me your full name and address first." He clicked his pen and poised it over a blank page in his notebook."

"My name is---" I started.

"Hold on a moment. I have to get the date, time, and location down first," the deputy interrupted me. He pulled a clip-on case for eyeglasses from his other shirt pocket, extracted a pair of wire-framed glasses, and put them on. After he replaced the case in his pocket, I waited while he checked the watch on his thick, hairy wrist for date and time, I supposed. The hair on his arms was as gray as the hair on his head. That hair was still thick and stuck out in numerous directions. Seeing him face to face, I dialed back my age estimate by about twenty years. This man was, after all, a working officer. He had to be under retirement age.

"Next, I need to introduce myself," he stated carefully. "I am Evritt County Sheriff's Deputy Augie Dawge, and I'm here in answer to your 911 call that you made..." Deputy Dawge checked his watch again.

"About an hour ago," I finished for him. "I believe that the time on my cell phone was three-forty-three p.m."

"Okey-dokey," he noted my answer. "I can double check that fact later, but right now I need to get your full name, address, and telephone number." His pen was poised once more over the notebook.

"My name is Adelaide Bonner Girard and I live at 135---"

"One moment, Ms. Girard," he interrupted again. "You'll need to spell that name for me. My report needs to be accurate."

I complied and went on to spell Serenity, merely for the sake of accuracy he said. After I gave my phone number and repeated it twice to help the accuracy of his report, he asked me, once more, to explain my problem.

"Deputy Dawge," I started, trying to control my emotions, "my problem is that an hour ago, approximately, I found Anson Kerringer on the floor in the staff breakroom, and he was deceased."

"You should have told me that right off, Ms. Girard," he fussed.

"Deputy, you wouldn't let me tell you *right off*," I fussed back in my defense. "You told me that I had to wait until you wrote down my name and address."

"Sorry, Ms. Girard," the deputy apologized. "This has been a very long day because we're shorthanded at headquarters. A number of our staff is in Corpus Christi for a special law enforcement training seminar. I'm usually manning a desk at the station in Handlen. But, as my supervisor said, we remaining officers must take up the slack. At least that's what he said right before he left for Corpus."

"Your apology is accepted, Deputy Dawge," I reassured him.

"Thanks, Ms. Girard. Now what do we do next?" He seemed to be asking himself, but I answered for him.

"You call for the coroner and the crime scene investigation team. At least, that's what the police do on TV."

"Why do you think that this is a crime scene?" he demanded.

"I think you're supposed to investigate all suspicious deaths like it's a crime scene, aren't you?" I asked.

"Oh, yeah, that's right," Deputy Dawge agreed, "but maybe I should see this scene first. Do you think that you could show me where you found Mr. Kerringer? While we've been jawing out here, he may have recovered."

"Don't I wish," I said, "but Anson Kerringer is definitely deceased."

"Have you seen a dead body or two, Ms. Girard?" The deputy looked at me somewhat skeptically.

"My husband is deceased," I said, shuddering at the thought of Anson Kerringer's dead body, "but you'll know that Mr. Kerringer is deceased when you see him. I probably shouldn't go back in there since it's a crime scene."

"You're right again," he slapped his forehead. "What was I thinking? We have to preserve the integrity of the crime scene. Did you touch anything?"

"I'm sure that I didn't touch much," I said, "the front door knob, the door knob on the bathroom, and the doorknob on the breakroom."

"You used the bathroom?" Deputy Dawge asked incredulously.

"No," I reassured him, "I only opened the door when I was trying to find a staff member or Mr. Kerringer. The door was closed and not labeled. I didn't go into the room." Deputy Dawge was scribbling furiously in his little notebook so I continued with my description of my activities. "As I said, I also touched the doorknob of the breakroom. It was closed and not labeled. I thought Mr. Kerringer might be in there and he was---at least his body was."

Deputy Dawge paused in his scribbling. "I'm not sure whether I can go in there without touching anything," he again seemed to be talking to himself.

"Perhaps you could view the scene through the breakroom window," I suggested, trying to be helpful and move the process along. "I believe that there was a window in that room. It would be at the back corner on the right end of the building." I pointed in that direction.

"You'd better show me, Ms. Girard."

"I'll try, and possibly you could call me Addie," I said. "And your name is Augie?"

"Yes, Ma'am. Addie," said Augie Dawge as we headed around the end of the metal office building by Anson Kerringer's office. When we rounded the corner, I pointed out the window that I thought would be the scene of the crime. The bulky deputy tromped officiously up to the window and peered closely at the scene inside.

"I'll be whipped with a horsetail!" Augie exclaimed as his eyes took in the contents of the room and settled on the body of Kerringer. "Did he look like that when you saw him, Addie? Come here and look."

"Augie, I'd rather not see that again," I said giving another shudder. "He was all scrunched up and holding his stomach. His face looked like he died in a whole lot of pain. Is that what you're seeing?"

"I'm afraid so, Addie, but if you don't check the scene, how will we know if he's moved since you saw him?"

"Augie, I'm sure that Anson Kerringer hasn't moved since I saw him last. Dead people can't get up and walk away. No one has been in that place to move him since I left and closed the door. I've been sitting out front most of the time since I called 911." I was starting to tremble again, but I tried to focus on my explanation. "Maybe you should call for the coroner and the crime scene team now, Augie. This is probably as sure as you're going to get that he is deceased."

Deputy Augie Dawge took one last look through the window and sighed. "This really stinks. Whoever gets the call gets stuck with the case," he said as we strode back to the parking lot. "And I was hired to be a file clerk. For twenty-two years I've been a file clerk. Now, thanks to some poorly-timed seminar in Corpus, I have an actual case. And it's maybe a murder! That's the worst case of all to have." He shook his head woefully.

"Augie, the sheriff's department might reassign the case to a more experienced investigator," I offered to encourage him.

"Like who, Addie? All of the real investigators are in Corpus and won't be back until next week." Deputy Dawge surveyed the woods surrounding the mobile office and impatiently made a few more scratchy notes in his notebook.

I was afraid that he might cry any minute and totally embarrass himself. "Make the call and see what happens," I proposed. "I was told that Anson Kerringer had friends in state government. Maybe the department will call in a state investigator."

"Oh, that really makes my day! Now you say the victim had friends in state government! That's all I need. People in state government sticking their noses into my first case! This case gets worse and worse, Addie! I'm a doomed man."

"Not as doomed as Anson Kerringer," I said.

CHAPTER 10

Clang! Clang! The noise was coming from somewhere in my house! I looked at the clock. Seven-forty! 'Why is there clanging in my house at seven-forty on a Thursday morning?' I asked my sleepy, befuddled brain, but it had no answer for me. 'The Grandchildren are here!' my sleepy, befuddled, and panicky brain suddenly shouted.

I slipped out of the bed, grabbed my light-weight robe from the chair where I had tossed it the night before, and rushed for the hallway. I tugged on the robe and tied the sash as I ran to the bedroom that had been Lindsey's and Madison's room when they were younger. Mercifully, Trent and Tricia were still sleeping. Carefully, I pulled the door shut as quietly as I could. Then I headed for the stairs.

Another noise, metal scraping on metal this time, led me to the disastrous deconstruction zone that was now my kitchen. Travis sat straddling a wooden dining room chair in the middle of the room. He was munching what looked like toast and jelly. A pair of legs were sprawled on the floor, projecting from the cabinet where my old sink used to be.

"Morning, Mom. Plumber's here," Travis informed me.

"Hi, Addie," said Ernie Plott as his head and torso emerged from the cabinet with a pipe wrench in his hand. "Kilgore sent me to change up the pipe fittings for the new sink and dishwasher," he explained. "I'll put in the actual pipe work after the new countertop is installed. Then I'll put in the new sink and garbage disposal. That should happen in about a week or so. After the countertop is set, I'll also be installing the new dishwasher."

"Thank you, Ernie. I saw that you were on Kilgore's remodel schedule for today, but, somehow, I didn't expect you to start so early," I stated, trying to calm my startled brain.

"I was sure I told Travis that I would be here at seven-thirty when I called to confirm my plans yesterday afternoon," Ernie seemed bemused.

I looked at Travis who was looking anywhere except at me. "Mom, I meant to tell you, but you got home so late yesterday. Lottie already was here to drop off the kids, and she wondered where you were."

"Some unexpected things happened yesterday afternoon, Travis. I was unavoidably detained." My explanation seemed lame even to me. "I'll call Lottie later to thank her for her patience and try to explain if she doesn't show up here in the next half hour."

"Does Lottie have something planned for Trent and Tricia today, too?" he questioned.

"Travis, I'm sure that Lottie will be curious about why I wasn't home when she got here yesterday," I offered as explanation. I waited a beat or two for Travis to ask why I was late the previous day, but that didn't happen.

"Actually, I was hoping that today you and I could take Trent and Tricia to BoompaLand. Lottie wanted to go along. And she wanted you and the kids to come for supper with her and Walter tonight because I have a Library Friends meeting to attend."

"I don't know, Mom," Travis's voice took on that whiny tone that he could get when he wanted to get his way. For some reason, he was starting to blush. "I sort of promised Laddie that I would help with a problem at her house, and then we were going to grab some lunch."

"Amanda Ladd is certainly monopolizing your time," I said. "You and I have scarcely had any time together since you got here five days ago."

Travis was now beet red from the neck up. "I-I didn't think that you knew Laddie," he stammered. "She told me that she didn't know you."

"No, I don't know Amanda Ladd," I stated, emphasizing the word, *Amanda*. "Of course, you must know that Lottie knows, or knows about, almost everything and everyone in Wanderwood."

Ernie Plott was cleaning up his trash, picking up his tools, and returning the tools to his toolbox neatly. "Addie, I wanted to get this done early because Marty Gastbend is scheduled to be here to finish the sanding and staining on the cabinets. He's taken on Jasper Moody to help him finish up quicker," said Ernie as he closed the toolbox and crossed to the door.

"Jasper Moody?" asked Travis. "I remember him. He was kind of a goofy kid, always joking around and getting himself into trouble. He is probably grown up by now and more responsible."

"Not much," said Ernie. "I like the guy okay, but Jasper's not always reliable. He's still kind of goofy, but he tries hard. Sanding cabinets shouldn't be too much of a stretch for Jasper. See you at the Friends meeting, Addie." He left through the kitchen doorway. We soon heard his truck starting and backing out of my driveway onto Serenity Lane.

Travis was finished with his toast and started for the sink with his plate before he remembered that we no longer had a sink. He paused and seemed unsure what to do with the plate.

"Where did you leave the jelly knife?" I questioned.

"In the downstairs bathroom lavatory," he answered and turned toward the living room.

"There are paper plates, napkins, and plastic utensils under the towel on the sideboard next to the microwave in the dining room, Travis," I noted. "I meant to tell you before now, but I didn't recall it the few times that I have seen you. Please return that chair to the dining room table. It might get stain on it in the kitchen. Kilgore wanted to keep the room clear *for construction purposes*." I took the dirty plate from him and held the plastic sheeting away from the doorway so that Travis could bring the chair through to the dining room.

"And while I have you here, I should tell you that I'd like you to grill some steaks Saturday for lunch. I thought that we could eat on the patio. I got some potato salad and cole slaw from Lefty's Bar-B-Q yesterday. There are bottles of Lefty's tea and fruit punch in the refrigerator next to the gallon bottle of lemonade that I stirred up."

"Sure, I can do that, Mom," Travis said in an offhand manner. "Grilled steaks sound good, but I really need to go now if Laddie and I are going to get her work done before lunch."

"I surely would like to have some time to talk with you, Travis T. There are things about my day yesterday that you should know."

"Yeah. We'll have time to talk later, maybe this evening, but I do have to go now, Mom." Travis reversed directions, gave me a quick hug, and was out the kitchen door before I had two seconds to protest further.

"That wasn't too productive, Addie Girard," I scolded myself. The knock on the back door startled me. With the plate still in my hand, I opened the door.

"Morning, Addie," Marty Gastbend greeted me as he strode into the kitchen followed by, no doubt, his new helper. "Jasper and me'll have these cabinets stained before the day is out. Ain't that right, Jasper."

"You ain't just wolfin' no one, Marty," Jasper Moody agreed as he slouched across the room and leaned against the wall opposite the door. Jasper was wearing stained, faded tan overalls on top of a purple and yellow plaid flannel shirt with the sleeves cut off. His high-top, green tennis shoes were laced only halfway up and the tongues on the shoes hung out at odd angles.

'He is obviously a person who goes his own way fashion-wise,' I thought.

We were interrupted by Lottie breezing through the doorway right behind the odd twosome. "Addie, we have to talk," she insisted. "Hi, Marty, Jasper," she added in the pair's direction.

"Mornin' to you Lottie," said Marty.

"Hey, Miz Frisham. Terrible morning for the race, huh?" Jasper said with a smirk.

"What race is that, Jasper?" I asked.

"The human race," he snorted and guffawed. "Old 'un but a goodie," he choked out as he slapped his leg.

"Jasper Moody, grow up!" Lottie fussed at him, apparently to no effect. "Why don't we go upstairs, Addie." Lottie grabbed my arm and pulled me toward the living room. "Are Tricia and Trent ready to go to BoompaLand?"

"They may be waking up with so many people banging in and out the kitchen door," I said. "After I rinse this plate, let's check on them." I quickly disposed of the plate and jelly knife and then started up the stairs with Lottie close behind me.

When we were halfway up, Lottie grabbed my arm again. "It's all over the Channel Seven News about you finding Anson Kerringer dead in his office," she hissed. "The Sheriff's Office is calling it a suspicious death. What was suspicious about it?"

"Lottie," I suggested, "possibly this discussion could wait until we have Trent and Tricia on a ride at BoompaLand?"

"BoompaLand!" shrieked Tricia as she appeared at the top of the stairs in her pajamas. "We're going to BoompaLand!"

A sleepy-eyed Trent came out of the bathroom also in his pajamas. "Did you wash your hands, Trent?" I questioned. With an audible sigh, he turned around and went back into the bathroom, presumably to wash his hands. I listened for the sound of running water.

After getting my ecstatic grandchildren dressed and feeding them their breakfast in the dining room (some toaster tarts and chocolate milk, I'm embarrassed to admit), we assured Marty Gastbend that we would return before he was finished for the day. Then we headed for BoompaLand. Lottie turned her gray van left instead of right when we reached Wanderwood Drive, and we headed away from the center of town on RM 150A toward Austin.

I was glad that Lottie was driving since that left me free to keep an eye on Trent and Tricia in the back seat. I got Trent and Tricia to sing their favorite traveling song, *Who's Going Down The Road Today?* I knew that it would take them a while to sing all twelve verses, and that they might be distracted enough to allow us to talk…quietly.

"Why is the *Thing* with Anson suspicious?" Lottie went straight for one of the top questions as she negotiated through one of the meandering, curvy stretches of RM 150A.

"The *Thing* with Anson is suspicious because it's an unexpected *Thing* and also because the authorities don't know what caused the *Thing*." My explanation didn't seem to clear up any *thing*.

"Addie, on the News, Betsy Rauss said that Anson was alone when the *Thing* happened. Where were Mavis and the rest of the staff? Surely Mavis and at least one of the two sales people should be in the Champions Ramble office on a Wednesday afternoon."

"Mavis wasn't there. The whole building was empty when I got there except for Anson Kerringer, of course." I described the scene, explaining how I had been looking throughout the building for Anson to ask for a donation of paint for the library project. "Anson was on the floor in the staff break room, all doubled up."

"…Anson came over the hills and up the lane," came two sweet singing voices from the back seat.

"Lottie, perhaps we should postpone this discussion until we reach BoompaLand,"

I cautioned. She nodded her head as she skillfully manipulated the van through a sharp s-curve on the Hill Country road that was RM 150A east of Wanderwood. I could see why the state highway department might want to straighten this section of 150A. Farmers used this road as an access to the nearest market town or to Austin. The city of Austin was not only the state capital of Texas but also the biggest market town in this part of the state.

About four miles from the eastern town limits of Wanderwood stretched a bucolic piece of commercial/residential property known around the area as BoompaLand. Tourists had been known to make a detour off Interstate-35 and drive the twenty-five or more miles of treacherous, winding country roads in search of this eccentric mini amusement park. The fact that they returned to their homes and related to their neighbors that they made this pilgrimage accounted for the large numbers of tourists each year who did locate and enjoy BoompaLand.

As Lottie explained the history of BoompaLand to me some time ago, a young couple named Stevie and Tallia Prookes were impressed by the movie *Overboard*. Stevie Prookes especially liked the part about designing and building their own folksy miniature golf course as their way to live happily ever after. Unfortunately, the Prookes ran out of money by the time they nearly finished the fifth hole. Staring at impending bankruptcy, they came to their senses and were able to sell the property to Carl and Della Bumper.

The Bumpers were a couple who retired from traveling and working the carnival circuit around the Midwest United States. Their idea of *happily ever after* was to have their own small carnival that did not move. Using the five-hole miniature golf course as a beginning, Carl added a medium-sized carousel (much used) with only seven of the stationary horses and two benches remaining aboard. Through sagacious purchasing on the internet, Della helped Carl add a number of metal cars from various kiddie rides as well as a wooden lion and tiger. Three more benches of various styles completed the carousel ride. An old stable building contained some carnival-type games.

Carl and Della lived on the property in a large, reasonably new, double-wide manufactured home. The aging couple operated the mini park from the months of March through October. Two years ago, to deal with water-drainage issues, the Bumpers added a duck pond with ducks to feed and a small petting zoo. This year the petting zoo featured two spotted lambs, a young goat, an alpaca, two middle-aged Black Labrador dogs, and three elderly Maine Coon cats. I learned last year that Tricia and Trent totally adored the carousel, the petting zoo, and even the mini-golf, attended by Carl, Della, and Della's two sisters who loved kids.

I was surprised to see as many as seven cars already in the small parking area as Lottie pulled her van into an end parking slot not too far from the admission gate. Trent and Tricia popped their seat belts before I could exit the front door. Lottie came around the van to take them in tow as soon as I could open the sliding door by the middle seat.

My two happy grandchildren were hopping up and down and shrieking excitedly to Aunt Lottie about what they wanted to do first and later. I felt a slight pang of jealousy as Lottie, Trent, and Tricia preceded me through the front gate. I stopped at the booth by the entrance and paid the reasonable entrance fee of seven dollars per person.

Lottie could scarcely wait until we had Trent and Tricia strapped on the Lion and the Tiger (their favorites). We were headed for a nearby bench under a live oak tree before she let loose. "Adelaide Bonner Girard, spill it all! Why didn't you call me last night to tell me what happened? I know that you couldn't talk about it in front of Trent, Tricia, and Travis last night, but you could have called."

"Lottie, it was horrifying! Anson Kerringer had thrown up on the floor. He looked so awful, scrunched up the way he was, lying there and clutching his stomach! And the expression of horrible pain on his face! I tell you it was horrifying!" I stopped talking and realized that I was shaking and nearly in tears. Speaking more quietly, I said, "I think that he was poisoned."

"Poisoned? Addie, are you sure?" Lottie asked, amazed by what I was telling her.

"I guess that wasn't on the Channel Seven News, huh?"

"Well, no, or I wouldn't be asking you about it," Lottie stated flatly. "Did Kevin Dorting treat you nicely? If he gives you a hard time, you let me know. I know his mother, and she'll straighten him out."

"Who is Kevin Dorting?" I totally was not getting the meaning of her statement.

"The main investigator of Evritt County. You must have talked with him yesterday," insisted Lottie.

"No. I talked with a deputy named Augie Dawge," I informed her.

"Augie Dawge! That man is a file clerk!" spluttered Lottie. "He has never been a regular deputy like Kevin Dorting or Bobby Opperson. Sheriff Bishop Post would never send Augie to investigate a death, even a natural one."

"Maybe Kevin Dorting and Bobby Opperson are in Corpus Christi with the group that went to a big law enforcement conference," I suggested. "Augie Dawge said that most of the staff were in Corpus, including the Sheriff."

"Addie, Evritt County is in real trouble if they have to rely on Augie Dawge to investigate anything." With that statement, Lottie got up and went to help Tricia and Trent off the carousel. We bought them each a small swirl of cotton candy on a paper cone, and we moved on to the stables to try the carnival games.

"What are you going to tell the people at your library meeting about what happened at Champions Ramble?" asked Lottie while Trent and Tricia tried to toss rings over the necks of soft drink bottles. We had stepped away a short distance to talk out of the hearing range of the excited, squealing and shrieking, twosome and their flinging rings.

"I was hoping that maybe the topic wouldn't come up. It was bad enough being interviewed by Channel Seven and at least three other remote on-camera interviewers. We have so many other pressing topics to cover at the Friends meeting. Everyone might be too involved in those items to worry about Anson Kerringer."

"Wake up and smell the hot mocha! Of course, they're going to want to discuss what happened at Champions Ramble," Lottie protested. "These are Wanderwood people. You can't get an infected splinter in your finger without everyone for twenty miles asking you about it."

"Yes, Lottie. I know what you're saying is the truth, and I'm glad you brought it up. I guess I was trying to avoid facing the issue."

"Well, what are you going to tell the Friends?" she nudged. "After all, you were representing the Friends group when you went to Champions Ramble. Weren't you going to ask for a donation?"

I thought for a minute or two, but my tired brain was having difficulty presenting me with possibilities. "Maybe I'll postpone the Anson discussion until after the meeting?"

"Yes, well, that might work, but it only delays the inevitable questions and your need to answer them," Lottie allowed.

"I think Tricia and Trent have tossed their last ring," I said. Amazingly, Tricia and Trent, with some help from Della Bumpers, had won two bottles of Dr. Pepper.

"I won it for you, Gammy," said Tricia, her grin lighting up her entire face.

"Cause you like Dr. Pepper," Trent added, not to be upstaged by his sister.

"Thank you so much!" I tucked the bottles into my tote and gave each of them a hug. "You are the sweetest grandchildren ever."

Our next stop was the petting zoo where we found that three young emus had been added during the previous week. Food, of course, needed to be purchased to welcome these new arrivals. Della's sister, Nelda Cremper, was at the petting pens to supervise the feeding of the animals in the petting zoo. She cheerfully explained to the children what each animal liked to eat.

"Well, I heard you tell the Channel Seven interviewer that no one was at the sales office when you got there," said Lottie. "Where was Mavis Corcoran? Where was the sales staff?"

"Not present. I have no idea where they were. It was so strange, Lottie. The sales office was unlocked but deserted. I went through the whole place calling out for Mavis and Anson Kerringer and found no one. Until, like I told you, I found Mr. Kerringer lying dead on the breakroom floor." I shuddered involuntarily at the remembrance of that macabre scene.

"You probably should prepare yourself for some of the Friends members wanting to hear every grisly detail."

"That's a distressing thought, and---oh, dear! Mavis Corcoran will probably be at the meeting if something hasn't happened to her, too. Perhaps I should have checked on her."

"Well, if Mavis is at the meeting, that could actually be a positive," Lottie commented.

"I don't see how," I moaned.

"Mavis will deflect some of the attention away from you," crowed Lottie. "She worked for Anson Kerringer!"

CHAPTER 11

"Travis, you should not be fussing at me," I insisted. "I certainly would have told you about finding Anson Kerringer if you had been here for me to tell you." My wandering son was finally at my house that afternoon and sitting on the living room sofa with a sour expression on his face. Trent and Tricia were taking a long nap after their trip to BoompaLand and a stop at Lotta Lotta Fried Chicken for lunch.

"I absolutely had a right to know that my usually sensible mother is out running around Wanderwood discovering dead bodies," he grumped. "Then you had to appear on the TV news bragging about it."

"Stop! I did not want to talk to the TV interviewers. And you would know about what happened if you bothered to stay here long enough for me to tell you." I was not about to allow my oldest child to think that he was free to boss me around. "You have no one to blame but yourself, Travis. I told you this morning that I had problems yesterday, but all you could think about were your plans with Amanda Ladd."

"Thanks to your activities, I won't have to worry about seeing Laddie again soon," he continued to fume. "First, you deliberately antagonize the people at Willem Club, and now you finding this body is being flashed all over the TV News."

"Travis, what does either of those situations have to do with Amanda Ladd?" I was having difficulty following the logic in what he was saying, if there were any.

"Laddie lives at Willem Club in her parents' house, Mom." Travis must have thought that this explained his entire peevish attitude because he stopped speaking and turned on the television.

I reached over and picked up the remote from the coffee table where he had dropped it and turned off the TV. "I don't believe that I understand what you are trying to say, Travis. Why should the Friends' difficulties with a few people at Willem Club have anything to do with you or Amanda Ladd? Amanda is not a member of the library group. If she were, I'm sure that I would know."

"Why are you involved with that crackpot library group? This town is too small to support a library," Travis groused.

"Wanderwood is growing. More people are moving in every month, Travis. I happen to believe that this library could be a really positive thing for Wanderwood--something that all of the people here and in Evritt County can use."

"The residents of Willem Club won't be likely to use it. You made sure of that." He held out his hand for the remote.

I placed the remote across the room by the television. "If it were up to some residents at Willem Club, no one in Wanderwood would get a chance to have a library. Some of those people were misappropriating the library funds that others donated."

"So you say. It seems to be your word against theirs," Travis stated emphatically. "Laddie told me about it."

"How does Amanda Ladd know the truth about what happened?" I asked. "She isn't a member of the Friends. She wasn't there."

"Laddie belongs to the Country Club and knows Janet Makeshire and Clariss Padget very well. They told her how you took over the Library Friends organization and accused them falsely of taking money. Why did you do something like that?"

"Travis Taylor Girard! You need to listen to me, *your mother*. Do I lie to you?" I paused, waiting for an answer, but I didn't get one so I continued. "Janet and Clariss admitted taking the money to throw a lavish party at a fancy restaurant in Austin. They told me that I could not do anything about it because *that's the way things work around here*. Their words, not mine. They were mistaken. I did do something about it." I took a deep breath and forged on with my explanation.

"I brought it before the Friends group at the regular meeting. The group itself decided to remove Janet, Babs, and Clariss as officers after Janet and Clariss resigned from the club and stomped out right before the meeting. That was not my decision. Luckily, Janet and Clariss returned the money after the members insisted that they do so. It was a very large sum of money. Amanda Ladd might want to check into the real facts before she finds herself spreading lies."

"Laddie wouldn't lie to me," Travis insisted.

"She might if she were repeating lies that other people told to her," I said. "Amanda Ladd was not present that night at the meeting. She is only repeating second hand information from very biased sources. The residents at Willem Club have chosen of their own free will to withdraw from the Friends organization. I'm fairly certain that having people in town know that some of them took library money and used it illegally is rather embarrassing. And, Travis, I never wanted to be Interim President of the organization nor did I ask to be."

I was interrupted by a knock on the front door. Opening it, I was faced with Lottie Frisham comforting a very upset Mavis Corcoran. The young receptionist for Champion's Ramble and Library Friends member had obviously been crying. Lottie eased Mavis forward into the foyer.

"Addie, we need to talk with you," said Lottie. "Privately," she added when she saw Travis. "Mavis is very distraught."

"Please, come in," I said stepping back to allow them to enter the living room. I retrieved the remote from the television and handed it to Travis. "We need to finish this discussion later, Travis," I said as I followed Lottie and Mavis into the dining room. They seated themselves at my dining room table, and I heard the sound from the TV. "Can I get you something to drink? I have water, soft drinks, iced tea, lemonade, and fruit punch."

"Why don't I get that, Addie, while you talk to Mavis," said Lottie as she popped up from her chair. "I see that you have paper cups on the sideboard, and the Fridge is in the living room. What would you like, Mavis?"

"A soft drink, maybe? Do you have Dr. Pepper?" Mavis hesitantly requested.

"A Dr. Pepper, definitely. Maybe I'll make that three Dr. Peppers. I'll be right back," Lottie said, grabbing three paper cups from the stack on the sideboard and scooting out of the room.

I took napkins from the sideboard and placed them on the table. "I'm truly sorry about your loss, Mavis. Were you and Mr. Kerringer close?"

"No. We weren't close at all. Addie, he was a terrible boss, but I needed that job." Mavis paused to dab at her eyes and blow her nose with one of the napkins I had provided. "And then, yesterday morning...well, almost noon really...Anson Kerringer fired me." Mavis stopped speaking to try smoothing her short, straight brown hair. I wondered whether her lavender peasant blouse had been hastily donned. The fact that she was wearing a pair of bright orange slacks and black patent leather sandals encouraged this notion.

"Oh, my," was all that I could think to say.

A thump and then a bump came from the kitchen followed by a shout from Marty Gastbend, "Jasper! How did you do that?"

"Excuse me a moment, Mavis." I jumped up and dashed to the kitchen and almost collided with Lottie, followed by Travis, entering from the living room. Marty was kneeling on the floor with the can of wood stain dangling by its wire handle in his hand. The can was dripping, spilled stain was oozing across the floor, and Jasper was standing across the room with his hands in the air.

"Honestly, Marty, I don't know how it happened," Jasper whined.

"I'll clean this up, Addie. Don't worry about it. You're replacing the flooring, right?"

"Yes, I'm putting in vinyl plank," I answered. Quickly, I crossed to the cabinet where the sink used to be and grabbed what was left of the roll of paper towels hanging there. I tossed the roll to Marty and searched for something good to say. "I like the new color for the cabinets," was all that I could dredge up. What a disaster!

"Jasper," said Marty, "could you go out to my truck and find me a big blue can that says stain remover on the front?"

"No problemo," said Jasper as he sauntered out the kitchen door.

"That should get him out of my hair for a while," said Marty as he sopped up the stain with paper towels. He stuffed the gooey towels into a plastic bag from Handy Sack that I retrieved from my sack of recyclables. "I surely am sorry, Addie. Hiring Jasper was a mistake. I should know better."

"Why did you hire him, Marty, if you know he's not a good worker?" asked Travis.

"His parents are my neighbors," Marty said, still apologizing. "He broke one of my hand sanders earlier. And now he spilled the stain on the floor. I'll tell him that I won't need him for the rest of the project and pay him off today."

"I hope his parents won't be upset," I said.

"I'm sure they're used to it," Marty replied.

We left Marty to clean up his mess. Travis went back to the sofa and what appeared to be a golf match that he was watching on TV. I headed back to the dining room, and Lottie returned to her drink preparation. Mavis, amazingly, was still sitting where I had left her at my dining table.

"I apologize, Mavis," I said as I sat down opposite her once more. "I'm having my kitchen remodeled."

"I hope you got Kilgore Pettigrew to do the project," she said and blew her nose into another napkin from the stack on the table.

"Yes, Kilgore is overseeing the remodel," I assured her, "although I haven't seen much of him so far. He stops by to check the progress and then is gone."

"Don't worry, Addie. Even when you don't see him, Kilgore rules with an iron hand. He's the best in this area. He regularly worked for Mr. Kerringer's companies as a subcontractor." Mavis's expression reflected something startling that had apparently just occurred to her. "Oh, dear, what am I going to do? I don't have a job anymore!"

I was struck by this statement. "You did say that he fired you yesterday morning. Why are you so surprised that you don't have a job today?"

"Because Anson fired me regularly," Mavis explained with a sniff, "but he always rehired me after a few days. The company couldn't manage without me for longer than that."

"Why is that?" I asked her without considering the implication concerning her skills or even a hint of an apology for being nosy.

"I was the glue that held the company together," she stated flatly. "Jack Cartoff and Benny Olesford are terrific salespeople, but neither is very organized. And Anson is---was even worse. He continually forgot appointments, mislaid papers, and was moody and hyper. Probably because he drank so much coffee."

"Speaking of drinking, here's your Dr. Pepper, Mavis," Lottie said as she set the cup in front of the distressed woman.

"Is there still ice in the dispenser, Lottie?" I asked. "The icemaker isn't connected."

"There is still plenty of ice. If you don't have enough ice trays, I'll lend you some," offered Lottie. She set a paper cup in front of me and seated herself at the head of the table between Mavis and me. "Do we need coasters, Addie? This is a wood table."

"That's okay, Lottie," I replied. "I spread a plastic tablecloth under this cloth one because Trent and Tricia are here."

"Wise move," Lottie commented.

"While you were in the other room, Mavis was telling me that Anson Kerringer fired her yesterday morning. It's no wonder that she's upset over that fact...and his death, of course."

"Oh, Mavis, I'm so sorry," Lottie soothed. "How could he do a thing like that to someone as important to his business as you were?" Her comments suggested that Lottie heard some of our conversation before she returned with the drinks. "You were the person who kept that company organized."

"Like I said to Addie, Anson always rehired me in the past. Now I realize that won't happen. I'm totally out of a job this time." The tears started flowing again as Mavis grabbed for another napkin.

"Well, Mavis," said Lottie, reasonably, "His family has to get someone to deal with the business. It is still an operating business with houses being built and obligations to clients. Maybe they will hire you back, at least temporarily, to straighten things out."

"Do you really think so?" Mavis asked hopefully.

"Mavis, I probably shouldn't ask, but why did Mr. Kerringer fire you this time?" Containing my curiosity was never easy for me.

"That was strange," Mavis said. "He came out of his office in a rage and accused me of stealing money from his office. I tried to tell him that I didn't steal money from him, but he wouldn't listen! He told me to pack up my things and get out, so that's what I did. I didn't even take time to make a fresh pot of coffee."

"Coffee?" Lottie and I both said at once.

"I usually made a fresh pot right before noon so that the staff and customers could have fresh coffee if they wanted it," Mavis explained. "I was drying the coffee pot when Anson had his fit. I left the pot on the counter, grabbed my purse and extra shoes, and left. I don't keep much at the office because it's so open to everyone."

"Well, did Anson say why he thought that you would do such a thing?" asked Lottie. "Did he tell you why he thought that you took this money that he was missing?"

"He was babbling about a special fund, a special project called Sendero Gardens, and he wasn't making much sense," Mavis sniffed. "He was always talking about big projects that he was going to do, but he never said anything about this Sendero Gardens. I didn't know what money he was yelling about. I never handled any money for Sendero Gardens. I think sometimes he yelled at me when he was actually angry with someone else. Someone he couldn't afford to offend."

Lottie spoke up, "Mavis, tell Addie why we're here. Tell her what you told me."

"Oh, yeah," Mavis said and blew her nose again. "I need your help awful bad, Addie, because I think that deputy is going to blame me for Anson Kerringer's death. I didn't kill him but Augie Dawge is saying that I did!" Mavis dissolved into all-out crying now with tears falling almost faster than she could mop them up.

I grabbed more napkins from the sideboard. "Mavis, calm down. I don't see how Augie could accuse you when you weren't even there when he died. Wasn't Mr. Kerringer alive when you left?"

"The deputy didn't believe me when I told him that," wailed Mavis. "He...he said that I had to prove when I left and where I went after. And I can't!"

"Mavis, calm down," Lottie said. "We can hardly understand what you're saying, dear." We waited a minute or two while Mavis Corcoran tried to regain control of her emotions.

"What time did you leave the office after Anson Kerringer fired you?" I asked. "Let's try to carefully establish the facts. I feel certain that if we work on the facts, things will look better for you. Maybe recounting what you did after you left Champions Ramble yesterday will jog your memory." These words rolled out of my brain and through my lips though I had no real idea of the truth in them. How was I supposed to help Mavis Corcoran establish an alibi?

"Do you really think so?" sniffed Mavis straightening up in her chair.

"Let's give it a try, dear," said Lottie. "Like I told you, Addie is good at figuring things out. What time did you leave the office, Mavis?" she repeated my question.

As I said, I was starting to make a fresh pot of coffee for the lunch hour and the early afternoon. I do that right after eleven if I can because people tend to come in during the lunch hour. I don't usually go to lunch until one-thirty. Mr. Kerringer liked it that way. It didn't take me long to get my purse and shoes. I checked my watch when I got in the car and it was eleven thirty-seven."

"Why did you check your watch?" I asked.

"The deputy asked that, too," said Mavis. "After thinking about it for a minute, I realized that I always check my watch when I leave work. That helps me keep my schedule straight, you know, because I have two children with their own schedules. I had some time before they got out of school, so I went to Dripping Springs to just shop around. With two kids, I don't get much spare time to browse the gift shops and clothing stores by myself."

"A little alone time," Lottie encouraged.

"Yes, that's it," Mavis agreed and blew her nose which now seemed a bit congested. "Actually, I was still trying to figure out what money Anson was missing. I couldn't understand why he thought I would take anything after working for him several years. And I wondered what kind of project Sendero Gardens might be since I'd never heard Anson mention it before then."

She paused for breath, and I jumped into the void. "Mavis, what stores did you visit in Dripping Springs? That would be the place to start tracking your movements."

"Addie, I tried to remember when I was talking to Deputy Dawge. When I was shopping, I was wandering around not paying much attention to which shop was which. That deputy got me so nervous that I couldn't think. I couldn't remember the name of a single store."

"If you can't remember the names of the stores, let's try something else. Why don't you think about the merchandise that you saw, Mavis," I suggested. "Try to picture something that you saw and really liked."

"There was this cute denim outfit with eyelet lace ruffles and a vest to match. I thought my daughter Shelley would love it, but when I looked at the price tag, I knew that I wouldn't be able to afford it."

I pounced on that statement. "You looked at the price tag?"

"Yes," said Mavis.

"Whose price tag was it? Picture the tag and the price," I instructed. "What was the price, and whose tag was it---the shop."

"I see it!" Mavis yelped. "Forty-seven dollars! Lace and Spurs! They have a rose made from lace pictured on their tags. Their merchandise for kids is really cute but a little too pricey for me."

"Well, now we're getting somewhere," Lottie crowed.

"Did you browse through either of the stores next to Lace and Spurs?" I questioned.

"I did!" Mavis scrunched her face and thought for a few seconds. "The one on the left," she added as she vaguely waved her left hand in the air.

We heard a phone in the living room with a nineties rock song for a ring tone. "That's for Travis T," I assured them. "What we need to do now is drive to Dripping Springs. We'll see whether the shop keepers can remember you shopping there yesterday."

"Now?" asked Mavis. "Will we get back before my girls are out of school? I have to be there when the classes dismiss. Salley and Shelley are very active. I don't want them to get in trouble at the school."

"Well, no doubt we will be back long before your girls are out. And I'm sure they could behave for a few minutes if we're not," Lottie said with a straight face. "We need to jump on this possible answer for your problem of *no alibi* after Anson fired you."

"We would need to go now while Travis T is here to watch Trent and Tricia," I explained. At that moment we heard the front door close and, before we could get up from the table and cross to the living room, we heard Travis T's car leaving. "I guess I should revise that plan. My son, who is supposed to be here to visit me, has run off and left me hanging again."

"Addie, maybe you should have a talk with him…a serious talk," said Lottie.

I scanned the living room, crowded now with the large white box of a refrigerator sitting where the replacement wooden occasional chair used to sit. The wooden captain's chair from the Area-Wide Yard Sale was wedged into a corner between the sofa and loveseat. The room did not contain my errant son. "We were having that talk when you arrived."

"Oh," was all Lottie said in reply.

"However, we don't want to wait another day to check with those shops," I stated. We'll take Tricia and Trent with us. I'll see whether they've waked up. It shouldn't take me much more than ten minutes to get them ready to go."

"Maybe we should wait until after school so I can pick up my girls," insisted Mavis. "The kids could entertain each other, and we could get them a snack at Shermy's Drive-In after."

"No, Mavis," I countered. "You came to get your alibi problem solved, and we have to get on with that. I have other plans for this afternoon, and I'm sure that Lottie has plans as well."

Forty-five minutes later we were pulling into a parking space three doors down from Lace and Spurs. This shop was a very touristy collection of denim and gingham clothing for women and girls. Much of the garments were adorned with bows and ruffles. A string of bells attached to the door jangled as we entered. The shop was not spacious, but cutesy accessories abounded. The owners made use of every available inch of space to display as much merchandise as possible while still being artsy in their presentation.

Mavis was showing us the denim outfit which attracted her attention when a woman wearing a blue bib apron came through a doorway in the back of the shop. She looked around the shop and headed toward us. "Did you bring your daughter and your friends back to see that skirt and vest you were eyeing yesterday? She would look just precious in that outfit with one of these ruffled blouses." The woman was fingering a yellow blouse with ruffled eyelet lace down the front and eyeing Tricia.

Lottie hovered over Trent and Tricia who were giggling about some hair ornaments made with bows and feathers. I chatted up the shop keeper to verify the time that Mavis was shopping on Thursday. The woman was friendly and determined to be helpful. We had equal success in the shop next door.

Then we celebrated with cherry nut bars at Shermy's Drive-In. In spite of our protests, Mavis insisted on paying for the snacks. She proclaimed us her heroes for saving her life and reputation. The effort had not taken us more than forty-five minutes.

Next, I enforced a stop for my purposes at Moore's Décor Store. I had to get the backsplash on order. With assurances that the tile was available and would be delivered early the next week, I hopped back into Lottie's van, and we concluded what we thought was a successful trip to Dripping Springs.

CHAPTER 12

The trip to Dripping Springs was successful, but what I found at home somewhat deflated my state of euphoria. Marty Gastbend was packed and gone for the day. Only three-fourths of the cabinets were stained. Marty obviously hadn't started applying the layers of acrylic over the stained cabinet surfaces. A large brown splotch showed on the kitchen floor where Jasper spilled the can of stain. A very unhappy Kilgore Pettigrew stood in the middle of the room surveying the lack of enough progress.

"We will have to do a little night work on the staining to make up the time, Addie, but we have to get the project finished on schedule. I start on that complete redo of a four-thousand-square-foot house near Willem Club immediately after your project concludes. Viveca Laurin is not a lady with a lot of patience. I have to start on time. She wants a complete update covering the entire house."

"I appreciate that there isn't a lot of extra time for my kitchen redo, Kilgore," I agreed.

"We'll pick up the flooring for your kitchen tomorrow evening, and my delivery person will bring it to your house Saturday morning," he continued, once more checking his clipboard. "You'll need a place set aside for stacking the boxes of flooring. It will be a lot of boxes."

"Yes, I have ample space set aside in the garage, Kilgore. The vinyl plank will be okay there, won't it?"

"The weather isn't too hot yet. The inside of your garage should be fine," the contractor assured me.

"Viv told me that she's having the decorative surfaces of her entire house redone," I commented, unconsciously using the diminutive form of her name.

"Oh, she told you? Viveca Laurin will make some serious money when she sells that house, especially after the redo." Kilgore strode across the floor to check the finish on the newly stained cabinets more closely.

"When I talked with *Viv* recently, she did mention that she was making a lot of changes to the house and that the project would start after mine." I said, speaking the truth. I never spoke to Viveca Laurin when I saw her at the Shapely Woman Spa. Her visit and discussion of the redo had been a complete surprise. "She didn't tell me then that she was moving. I wonder where she will drop her hat next?"

"I think she said that it would be Grand Cayman where all she will have to worry about is an occasional hurricane," Kilgore said absently. "This color on the stain is coming out even better than I had hoped. Marty does good work, but he shouldn't have hired Jasper Moody to help him. I understand why he did it, but that young man is always more trouble than help."

"Marty meant well hiring Jasper, I'm sure, and the old vinyl tile will be covered by the vinyl plank," I said while thinking, 'The excuses that you will make for a friend in a small town.'

"You're very understanding, Addie, and I appreciate your kind words. I believe that Marty appreciates it, too. As I just said, my delivery person, Chuck Frengill, will pick up your flooring materials tomorrow late and deliver it here Saturday morning early. Have you chosen the tile for the backsplash yet?"

"I ordered the tile this afternoon at Moore's Décor Store. They had your specifications. Wanda said that the tile would be in the first of next week," I announced. I was proud that I had managed to accomplish something positive for the project.

"Having the flooring and tile in-house will help to get us back on track. I'll double check that backsplash material with Wanda at Moore's. The countertop is due to be set by Monday of next week, so the staining has to be done by then. Saturday morning, Marty will be working in here to apply the layers of acrylic over the stain."

"I was planning for Travis to grill some steaks Saturday morning. Lottie and Walter Frisham are going to be here for lunch," I explained. "I was hoping not to have workers underfoot then or the odor of fresh chemicals permeating the house since I am serving food to guests."

'Can't be helped, Addie," Kilgore insisted. "Chuck Frengill is available with his truck only tomorrow morning to deliver your flooring. The stain and acrylic coating must be done by Saturday afternoon before the countertop is set on Monday. We have to keep this project on timetable, and that timetable is very tight. There is no room in the schedule for problems. I'm sure that I explained this to you when we started the project."

"Yes, you did, Kilgore," I acquiesced. "We'll work around these issues somehow." I did understand that Kilgore used part-time workers, like Chuck Frengill, who worked at other jobs during the week. That was life in Wanderwood. Many of the residents worked more than one job. That made getting volunteers for the library effort more difficult for me, the new Interim President.

That evening, Ms. Interim President was having more than a little difficulty convincing noisy members to settle down so that we could discuss library business at the first meeting since Anson Kerringer's death. Watching the news, I saw that Channel Seven reporters were still badgering the Evritt County Sheriff's Department for new details concerning the murder investigation. The developer was a Lakeway resident, and the TV station thought that people in Austin would want to know all of the details of his death. Since Wanderwood was in the Channel Seven viewing area, I could understand Friends members wanting more information.

After a promise that we would definitely have a Kerringer question and answer session during the refreshment period afterward, the Friends meeting finally was able to proceed in a proper fashion. Under the category of old business, Marolly Hamilton reported that members of the Wanderwood Garden Club collected paint brushes, paint trays, and drop cloths and donated them to the Friends. I reported that Marolly and I were still working on getting the paint donated and asked the members to suggest possible donors.

Under the heading of New Business, a committee of Maxie Chalpers, Tom Hamilton, and Velma Plott were appointed to start working on a timetable for getting the painting done. Maxie Chalpers offered to figure an estimate of cost for removing all or part of a classroom wall to form the meeting room as well as getting the school board's permission to remove that wall. I thought she was really sweet to offer so much useful assistance to the project.

The meeting proceeded in a neat and orderly fashion until we got to the refreshments. Viveca Laurin, one of our newest members, for some reason thought that I would know when the Champions Ramble offices would reopen. This topic brought a huge uproar since some of the Friends members worked on Champion Ramble housing crews or for subcontractors. Explaining to the group that the possible reopening would be up to Kassondra Kerringer restarted the uproar.

Worse still was their insisted-upon recounting of my grisly discovery of Anson Kerringer's body. Members wanted to know details of progress on the investigation (Didn't know) and why they weren't being informed through the area TV news (Couldn't guess). I didn't want to tell them that there probably wasn't much progress. They were appalled that a substantial part of the Sheriff's staff, all six of them, were in Corpus Christi instead of working on this important murder case.

Members were sympathetic over my trauma in finding the body. They were comforting as I described the destruction in my kitchen (a timely diversion from the murder). This destruction, I explained, caused a great deal of difficulty in trying to cook for my visitors. The saddest thing for Friends members during the social hour was my refreshment offering of store-bought cookies on a paper plate!

I awoke with a feeling of foreboding on Friday morning but tried to shake it off. The Friends meeting had caused a restless night of poor sleep. I had yet to get my Saturday lunch get-together completely organized, and I knew that I still had a few things to discuss with Travis.

However, the Travis discussion was postponed due to the fact that he was MIA. A note fastened to the refrigerator door in the living room informed me that Travis went to San Antonio to find some *things that he needed*. There was no information about what those *things* entailed or when he would return.

In the kitchen, Marty Gastbend appeared to be finishing up the staining process so that he could start applying the waterproof acrylic finish on Saturday. I opted for a matte finish so that the cabinets would not have too much shine. My thought was that a high gloss finish would be more difficult to maintain and could show fingerprints and smudges more easily.

My plan for this Friday was for Travis, Trent, and Tricia to accompany me to south Austin to visit the Wildlife Center and the Lady Bird Johnson Wildflower Preserve. That had been my plan. Travis T obviously was pursuing his own agenda. I took my grandchildren to San Marcos instead to view the ducks, landscaping and architecture at Texas State University. Tricia and Trent really enjoyed the ducks and flowers. The buildings not so much, except for the bridges around the theater building and except for Old Main, it's gothic, pointed roof towering over the campus.

Lunch at Izzy's Pizza Parlour perked the twosome right up. The Novelty Fun Room full of arcade games was a hit. Birthdays were being celebrated at three different tables, so the kids got to watch Izzy's staff deliver a cupcake with a lighted candle and sing happy birthday to each celebrant.

Travis had not returned yet from San Antonio by the time Trent, Tricia, and I dragged our shopping bags into the house at one-thirty. I soon had the children playing with the hand puppets and the hausbols from the Area-Wide Yard Sale. Trent grabbed the red and brown dogs and managed to learn how to separate his fingers into the head and arm holes. Tricia struggled more with the dragon puppets although she did finally manage with her fingers only inside the heads.

When they tired of the puppets, the hyper children moved on to throwing the hausbols at different targets but mostly at each other. As they inevitably became too aggressive with the soft balls, I knew that I needed to get them more settled before their naps. With some instruction, I had Trent and Tricia building houses with playing cards in the living room. I didn't want to start their naptime until after Kilgore Pettigrew arrived for an update meeting. He insisted that we must talk. My imagination inflated this *talk* to some ominous showdown.

Kilgore showed up five minutes early and started an inspection of Marty Gastbend's work in the kitchen. However, my conference with Kilgore was delayed by two frantic calls from Shelby Draper and Marolly Hamilton concerning the progress I'd made on the paint acquisition (none) which led to a discussion of Anson Kerringer's death (tragic) and the possibility of any other paint donors (none known).

"I'm sorry, Kilgore. Library Friends business," I apologized. "Now you have my complete attention."

"Addie, this issue is not the fault of Moore's Décor. There was merely a glitch on the computer at the distributor."

"Moore's---the backsplash tile? What kind of glitch?" I queried, fearing that I might have to start over on selection for some horrible reason.

Then Kilgore said the very words that I dreaded. "That pattern of tile was discontinued in all of the colors. The computer at the Dallas distributor showed that they had tile in stock, but that tile was already promised to a housing developer in Tyler. If you could shift your order to one of your other possibilities, it likely wouldn't cause another delay. Moore has promised to get rush shipping. They feel very disappointed about the problem."

"I would like to cooperate with your suggestion, Kilgore," I apologized, "but all of my final selections were from that same pattern. They were just different shades of the same tile. I'll try to get together with Moore Décor on Monday to find another tile for the backsplash---something that is in stock and available."

"I'm sure that will work out fine, Addie, since we can't do the backsplash until the countertop is set anyway, and the staining has to be finished before that can happen." I could hear the undertone of frustration in Kilgore's voice. This project was definitely causing trouble in Kilgore World.

No sooner did Kilgore leave by the back door, than I heard someone come in the front door. I was hoping that it was Travis.

"Addie?" Lottie called from the living room.

"Aunt Lottie!" shrieked two card-house builders.

I joined them and sat down on the loveseat while I picked up the playing cards surrounding it. "I'm glad you came over, Lottie," I said with a slight sigh.

"I saw Kilgore's truck backing out of your driveway as I came across the lawn from my morning walk," she mentioned, removing the TV schedule that Travis left on the side cushion of the sofa. She seated herself in its place. I thought that Lottie's teal Bermuda shorts and crisp top in a teal, yellow, and white plaid set off her fluffy gray curls nicely.

"Yes, he was letting me know that my kitchen project is not up to his usual standards. Marty didn't finish staining all of the cabinets yesterday so he'll have to be here Saturday working while we're having the steaks," I said in exasperation. "I didn't plan to have someone extra under foot while we're trying to relax."

"Well, I really didn't mean to do it," she huffed.

"What are you talking about, Lottie?" I questioned. "What did you do that you didn't mean to do?"

"I invited Mavis and her children to the barbecue lunch tomorrow," Lottie stated. "It was one of those situations when I had to do something to help her feel better. She did lose her job, you know."

"Oh, dear," I said with another sigh, "I'll have to rethink my plans. Maybe I have some hamburger patties in the freezer that I can thaw for the children. I'm sure that they don't need steaks, really, but I don't have buns. I've been clearing things out of the fridge and freezer to get ready for this kitchen project."

"I have hot dog buns," Lottie offered, "If you think that the kids might prefer hot dogs. I have wieners. With hot dogs, you'd only need mustard and possibly chili."

"I may have a can of chili in the box of things from the kitchen pantry," I said. "If not, I can run to the Handy Sack. How much chili do you suppose we'll need?"

"Well, Walter will put chili on his steak," said Lottie. "I'm just warning you ahead of time. He does love chili."

"Then we must have chili," I laughed. "I bought plenty of potato salad and cole slaw from Lefty's Bar-B-Q. I have sweet tea, lemonade, soft drinks, and water. Travis and the kids finished off the fruit punch."

"Addie, maybe I should bring a green salad, too, as a supplement to the potato salad. You know how Travis likes potato salad," she suggested. "You could run short on the potato salad or cole slaw with six adults eating."

"Six adults?" I asked. "How do you get six? I was sure that I was now only planning for five adults." With the help of my two pint-sized assistants, I managed to pick up both decks of cards. "I have only a few steaks."

"Well, you probably didn't count Marty," said Lottie. "We will have to offer for him to join us, you know."

"Thank you, Lottie. I didn't think about Marty maybe expecting to eat," I said as I put the cards into their boxes. "I planned to cut the steak for the children in half. I suppose that I can cut them all in half."

"Well, while Travis is grilling steaks and wieners, he could also grill those hamburger patties, if you have them."

"Lottie! What a great idea," I congratulated her. "Whatever is left over, I can use for a lunch or supper on Monday. Kilgore says that they'll be setting the new kitchen countertop on Monday. It's going to be great to see the new kitchen start to come together and, especially, to know that the whole room will be finished in another two weeks. I am ready for life to get back to normal. Having a working sink with running water and a dishwasher besides will be a great start to things being normal."

"Is life ever normal here these days, Addie, since you---?" She paused. "Oh, now I remember why I came over to see you," Lottie interrupted herself. "I wanted to take Tricia and Trent to a hayride and marshmallow roast at the Cartoff's ranch this evening. Hannah Cartoff called to invite them out of the blue. I was so surprised."

"Marshmallows!" squealed two rambunctious children who proceeded to jump up and down and dance around the room chanting, "Marshmallows! Marshmallows!" as they started tossing the hausbols around once more.

"Why did she call you to invite Tricia and Trent?" I asked, a little wary of the sudden invitation. "Do you think it's possible that she thought they were *your* grandchildren?"

"She said that she didn't have your phone number. A friend had seen us together yesterday in Dripping Springs. You're invited, too, of course. I felt sure that you would want to go."

I was puzzled by this statement. "Why would I want to participate in this hayride?"

"Addie, Jack Cartoff works in sales at Champions Ramble."

The light was dawning over the mottled landscape of my weary brain cells. "Are you sure that Hannah Cartoff called you, or did you call her?"

"Addie!" Lottie seemed a bit offended, but, at this point, I wasn't sure that the emotion wasn't feigned. "I don't have the Cartoff's phone number. But, if I had that number and if I knew about this hayride, you can be sure that I would have called. The Cartoffs either have information or want information. We need to help Mavis."

My brain cells were starting to jog lazily across that mottled landscape of confusion in my head. "How is going to this hayride likely to help Mavis?"

"Well, don't you wonder why Jack Cartoff's wife Hannah would call me, a person who doesn't know her, and invite me, you, and your grandchildren to a hayride? I wonder how long this hayride has been planned or if it was a spur of the moment idea? Don't you wonder about that?"

"Of course, I wonder," I laughed. "Are you going to explain this to me or do I have to come over there and slap you cockeyed? After my conference with Kilgore, my patience is teetering on annihilation."

"The hayride is just a ruse, don't you see? Jack and Hannah want to talk with you," Lottie explained patiently. "This hayride event has to have something to do with Anson Kerringer's death."

"But why me?" I wondered out loud. "Why would these people that I don't know want to talk with me?"

"Because you found the body, ninny!" laughed Lottie.

CHAPTER 13

I left a note for Travis T since he had not returned by the time we left for the hayride. I usually associated the cooler fall weather with hayrides and marshmallow roasts. Apparently, some people in Wanderwood did not hold with that tradition, so here we were on a warm early-April night driving down an asphalt paved driveway to the *Cartoff Ranch*. A small storage building painted red and shaped like a barn in the back yard was the only thing that suggested *ranch* on the Cartoff property. Houses in this developed area on the east edge of Wanderwood, like the Cartoffs' place, were on half acre lots.

Lottie parked her van on an expanded parking pad of stone pavers next to the driveway, easing around a small trailer. This trailer was stacked with half a dozen bales of hay and was hitched behind a green, medium-sized lawn tractor. The makeshift hay wagon was sitting, facing the street, on the driveway before an ill-kept Texas-style home.

Paint was peeling from the dormers that protruded out of the rusting metal roof of the well-aged house. If the exterior had not been covered in fieldstone, I would have expected its paint to be peeling as well. Weeds overgrew the landscape beds in front of the porch, and the gray mulch obviously was past needing to be replaced.

Lottie and I followed the sounds of shouting, squealing children to the back yard. There a man in blue jeans, a red plaid flannel shirt, and a straw hat was working on building a fire in a piled-up ring of rocks that might possibly pass for a fire pit if the observer had a vivid imagination. Six or seven children were already chasing each other around the large back yard. We hadn't seen any cars other than one ancient, beat up Chevy in the carport. I surmised that the children belonged to the Cartoffs and possibly some of their near neighbors.

"You must be Lottie Frisham and Addie Girard," said a woman in her late twenties or early thirties who was unloading cookout supplies on a well-worn picnic table atop a fieldstone patio. This patio was obviously a do-it-yourself project made from native limestone rocks and cement. The woman was dressed in black denim shorts, white tennies, and a red cotton t-shirt sporting a logo touting Pikes Peak and Colorado Springs. "I'm Hannah Cartoff. That's Jack working on the fire for the marshmallow roast."

At Hannah's mention of marshmallow roast, Tricia and Trent shouted, "Marshmallows!" and started jumping around again. The rest of the children in the yard stopped what they were doing to eye Tricia and Trent.

"Nadia," Hannah Cartoff called to one of the girls nearby, "this is Trent and Tricia. Why don't you introduce them to your friends while I talk with Lottie and Addie?"

Nadia shyly but obediently came forward. She looked to be seven or eight years old. "We're playing Chase the Jack Rabbit. Do you know how to play that game?" Tricia and Trent both slowly shook their heads in reply. "Come on. We'll show you." Nadia motioned for them to follow her over to the group of kids who were now obviously wanting to get back to their game. Amazingly, Tricia and Trent tagged after Nadia and were soon learning the intricacies of Chase the Jack Rabbit.

"No doubt both of you are wondering why I called and invited you here," Hannah Cartoff said.

"Well, you want to talk about Anson Kerringer's death, don't you?" blurted out Lottie.

"Actually, yes," said Hannah, seeming a bit embarrassed. "We heard from Deputy Dawge that you found Anson's body, Addie. We, Jack and I, were wondering what you were doing at Champion's Ramble."

"And I was wondering why Jack wasn't at Champions Ramble when I was there," I spoke up. "Apparently we all seem to have a need for information about that day."

"Well, let's sit down and talk about it, why don't we?" suggested Lottie, indicating some metal folding chairs and mismatched lawn chairs. They were set up in a rough semicircle cluster on one side of the small patio.

"I went to Champions Ramble to hit Anson Kerringer up for a donation of paint for the new library project," I stated when we were settled. "Why wasn't Jack, or Benny Olesford, in the Champions Ramble office when I was there on Wednesday afternoon? I expected them to be there working on selling houses. Of course, I expected Mavis Corcoran to be there as well."

"That screaming fit that Anson pitched," answered Hannah bluntly. "Jack told me that Anson was almost apoplectic over some missing money. Benny and Jack knew better than to hang around when Anson was in one of his horrible moods."

"Truthfully," interrupted Jack Cartoff, straw hat pushed to the back of his head, "Anson ordered us to get our unprofitable carcasses out the door and go troll for some clients before he fired us, too."

"Well!" said Lottie. "Did he usually talk to you like that?"

"That was mild language for Anson," said Jack. "We heard him ranting at Mavis about stealing some money from his office. The money supposedly was scheduled for a new project. I thought that Anson wanted us out of the office so that he could work on that project. Benny thought that Anson might be expecting an important client, and that was why he wanted us out of there. We didn't mind leaving as opposed to being fired---again."

"Anson fired you before?" I asked incredulously.

"Anson Kerringer lived for power trips where he could lord it over his staff. He fired each person on the staff at least every other week," Jack said in a matter-of-fact tone. "But he always rehired us. No one else was foolish enough to work for him for very long. He never could keep other salespeople for more than a few weeks."

"Why did you keep working for him?" I asked, my curiosity jumping up and reporting for duty.

"Money and the job," Jack said simply. "We need the money, and jobs in Wanderwood aren't easy to find. At least, you don't find jobs that pay better than minimum wage. Benny and I live at Wanderwood. Our kids are in school here."

"I work in Austin for a better paying job," explained Hannah. "And Joy Olesford is a Human Resources Manager in Austin. I'm a registered Nurse."

"Someone has to be here in Wanderwood to see about our kids," Jack said. "You know. They might get sick or have to be picked up at school for some reason. The job at Champions Ramble doesn't pay enough…didn't pay enough…but it let us be here for our kids. Now we don't have that income, and we really need it."

"Did Anson fire you, too?" Lottie asked.

"No, but he might as well have fired us," Jack said.

"The office is closed until Deputy Dawge figures things out. As if that's ever going to happen," Hannah said in a discouraged tone.

"Jack, can you get another job?" asked Lottie.

"I'm looking for other work, but my prospects don't look good," said Jack. "What I need is for the office to reopen. You know the deputy, Mrs. Girard. We thought that you might talk to him or to Kissie Kerringer about reopening."

"I'm truly sorry that you and the Olesfords have this problem," I apologized. "I have barely met Augie Dawge, and I have never met Kassondra Kerringer."

"Well, I've known Augie Dawge for many years," commiserated Lottie. "I know that he is out of his element when it comes to investigating a murder."

"Murder?" questioned Hannah. "Why would you even think that Anson Kerringer was murdered? Everyone is saying that it was food poisoning or some weird virus."

"Addie thinks that Anson Kerringer was poisoned," Lottie stated with more matter-of-factness that I thought was warranted.

"Actually, that's just a guess," I insisted. "I saw Anson Kerringer sometime after it happened. He died very suddenly and painfully. If he were suffering from food poisoning, you would think that it would involve more time to take effect. Jack, you should have noticed symptoms earlier when you were in the office. Did he seem ill earlier?"

"Anson didn't seem ill at all when we were there around noon," replied Jack, "only extremely angry. Hannah, I'd better get the kids onto the hay wagon now. They're getting tired of Chase the Jack Rabbit." He strode off to round up the children. Shortly, we heard the lawn tractor start noisily and chug off down the country road.

"Addie, couldn't you at least try to talk with Deputy Dawge or Kissie Kerringer?" pleaded Hannah. "Jack has to get back to work soon. We don't want to lose our house."

"I would really like to help you, Hannah, and I'm sure Lottie feels the same way as I do. We want to help Mavis Corcoran, too. Has Jack ever mentioned a project called Sendero Gardens? It seems that's what Anson Kerringer was shouting about when he fired Mavis."

"Jack mentioned that name to me, too, but he said that he didn't know what Anson was raving about." Hannah set a tray of paper plates, napkins, and utensils on the picnic table, reminding me that I might need to restock the tray on my sideboard. "Jack insisted that he'd never heard of Sendero Gardens."

"Well, something that Jack didn't say was where he went after he left the office that day," mentioned Lottie.

"Oh, that," Hannah chuckled. "Benny and Jack went where they always go whenever they're fired. They went to a late lunch at Lefty's and then sat around talking with whoever showed up to eat. Lefty finally asked them to leave so that she could mop up before the after-school group showed."

"Life in Wanderwood," commented Lottie.

"They went to Lefty's. Mavis went to Dripping Springs to shop. How do you suppose a perfectly healthy Anson Kerringer ended up dead within the next two hours?" My curiosity was suppositioning out loud, but I just let it ramble.

"Well, maybe Benny Olesford was right," replied Lottie. "Maybe Anson was expecting someone. An important client or someone else who was important to him. Why else would he not want the staff in the office?"

"Addie, please talk with Deputy Dawge for us or even Kissie Kerringer," pleaded Hannah once more.

"Hannah, I can't imagine either of them wanting to talk with me," I said.

The hayride didn't last too much longer. The children played several more games, while Lottie and I played twenty questions with Jack and Hannah. We didn't manage to winnow any additional information from Hannah or Jack Cartoff. The marshmallow roast, however, was a lot of fun for the kids and a nice break for Lottie and me.

CHAPTER 14

Travis still was not home when I managed to escort my two happy and excited grandchildren up the stairs for their baths and bedtime. Tricia and Trent made new friends. Lottie and I made two new acquaintances. Who knew what Travis was making---possibly trouble for himself and his family?

I was determined that Travis and I would sit down on the sofa when he returned and finish that *serious talk* that we started earlier. I heard his car and the front door as I was reading *Skiffles Finds A Lucky Penny* to a couple of almost snoozing grandchildren. Their new friends had worn them out. Now I needed to ask Travis about his friend, Amanda Ladd.

Tiptoeing down the stairs, I looked in the living room but saw no six-foot tall form on the sofa. I found him in the dining room eating a peanut butter and jelly sandwich from a paper plate. Another plate held the plastic knives for the peanut butter and the jelly. "Travis, we need to talk," I started as I screwed on the lids to the two open jars and closed the wrapper on the loaf of bread.

"Mom, I'm really beat. I've just spent two long hours trying to explain to Laddie how it wasn't your fault that you happened to find Anson Kerringer dead in his office."

"Travis, I am beat, too, but we have to have this conversation now." His words hit my tired brain cells like a brick. "As far as I can see, you wasted two hours trying to explain something that doesn't need explaining. I don't think that you would be having that conversation with Paula who knows the kind of person that I am."

"You're right, Mom," Travis fumed, running his hands through straggly blond hair that was already mussed. "I wouldn't have that conversation with Paula because she wouldn't be around to hear it. She'd be at one of her college classes or at her part-time job at the plumbing company."

"Paula is taking college classes at night?" I questioned.

"No, the classes are in the morning, but she's gone Monday, Wednesday, and Friday for these classes," Travis continued to complain between bites of sandwich. "Then on Tuesday and Thursday mornings she does part-time office work for a plumbing company."

"You mean that she's only away from home while the children are in school and you are at work?"

"That's what I said, isn't it?" He was in a major grump.

I fetched a glass of milk to go with his sandwich and got one for myself, as well.

"I don't see what your problem is with Paula wanting to finish her college degree or make a little extra money to pay for the extra expense."

"Mom, it doesn't look good." Travis adopted that patronizing attitude which I found particularly annoying. Apparently, he hadn't outgrown that habit.

"Look good to whom?" I was clearly at sea where his problems were concerned.

"To our friends. To my business associates." He spoke as if to a backward child. "What she's doing makes it look like we need the money, and we don't. And college. How am I supposed to explain that? She's thirty-two years old, Mom."

"Yes, Paula is thirty-two and she's the mother of two children. And she is your wife, Travis." I spoke slowly, mimicking his slow manner of speech. "That does not mean that Paula is no longer a person with ambitions of her own. Why shouldn't she finish college if she wants to do so? She put her college career on hold to work and get *you through college.* Now it's her turn to resume working on her degree."

"But, Mom, she's thirty-two!"

"There is no age limit on college. I can totally understand Paula wanting to do those things," I continued to try explaining Travis's wife to him. "Think about it from Paula's point of view. Tricia and Trent are in school for maybe seven hours of the day. I went to work part-time at the furniture store when Lindsey started school."

"Mom, that was different. Dad had his own business. It was natural for you to help out."

"Travis Taylor Girard." It was my turn to fuss. "Your father and I owned that store together. I was an equal partner. And, listening to you now suggests that you are the one with the problem, an attitude problem. You're not thinking of Paula as an equal partner in your marriage. You're relegating Paula to merely an extension of yourself and your life and your ambitions. Paula obviously has ambitions of her own."

My speech was ramping up in speed, and I tried to slow it down. "Your words suggest that you don't think of her as a mature, intelligent woman who can make decisions on her own. Your words suggest that you believe she shouldn't have a thought that isn't directed by you. My marriage to your father wasn't like that."

"Mom, my friends at work and my friends in the neighborhood are all laughing at me and telling me that I shouldn't let her do these things. Laddie agrees with them."

"Since when are your friends at work and your neighbors and Amanda Ladd in charge of your marriage?" I asked. "Did you ever once stop to think that maybe the person you should be talking with and listening to about your marriage is Paula, your wife, your partner?"

Suddenly a pounding on the front door stopped us cold. "What now?" I asked, looking heavenward. "Why can't we ever finish this conversation without someone knocking on the door?" I got up and headed to the front door with Travis close behind me.

On the doorstep, in full uniform, stood Deputy Augie Dawge. "Adelaide Bonner Girard?" he asked.

"Deputy Dawge, you know that I'm Adelaide Girard." I smiled at him, my upsetting conversation with Travis T slipping into a pending file in the back of my mind. "Won't you come in?"

He stepped through the doorway. "Adelaide Bonner Girard, I am placing you under arrest for the murder of Anson Kerringer," the deputy stated in what seemed to be his best official tone.

In spite of my shock, I managed to say, "You are doing no such thing." Then I added in a reasoning tone, "Augie, you don't want to embarrass yourself by making a premature arrest. Also, you wouldn't want the department to be sued for false arrest, would you?"

"Well, of course not!" he spluttered. "But the Sheriff is all over my case about not getting your formal statement and about not arresting you on the spot Wednesday afternoon, Addie."

"Sheriff Post is back from Corpus Christi?" I questioned.

"No," Augie Dawge said. "He and the other deputies are still in Corpus at the Special Law Enforcement Conference."

"Come into the dining room so that we can talk about this reasonably," I urged.

"No," Augie insisted. "The Sheriff said that I had to bring you in, his exact words. 'Bring her in, Augie' is what he said to me on the phone."

"Augie," I chided. "*Bring her in* doesn't usually mean the same as *arrest her.*"

"It doesn't?" Augie took off his deputy hat and scratched his head.

"I'm sure that the Sheriff meant for you to bring me in for some official questions and to get my official statement."

"I don't know," Augie whined slowly.

"Mom's right," joined in Travis, being suddenly the supportive son that I was missing. "Well-trained investigative teams complete their investigation before they consider making an arrest. Formal arrests need to be based on solid facts and evidence so that you don't get the department sued, like Mom said."

"Well, we have the facts," insisted Deputy Dawge. "Everyone else has an alibi and Addie doesn't have one, so she's the one."

"Augie," I scolded, "you can't really know who *everyone else* is under the circumstances. A lot of other people could have come through that office between the time that the staff left and the time that I arrived. The door was unlocked." My brain cells were on a roll, inventing possible scenarios for other people coming into that office, a whole parade of other people. "Do you have a witness who can establish exactly who came into the office during that period?"

"Of course not!" said Augie. "Anson Kerringer was alone after the staff left."

"You don't truly know that to be fact, Augie," I insisted. "I heard that Benny Olesford thought Anson pitched a fit and told the staff to leave because Anson was expecting an important client. He didn't want anyone around when the client arrived.

My point is that during the two-hour span of time that Anson supposedly was alone, he could have met with one or more clients."

"I don't know," Augie protested.

"That's a big hole in your *Anson Was Alone* theory," I continued. "What we need to do is find out who that important client or clients might be. It's probably someone associated with that Sendero Gardens project that Anson Kerringer was raging about. Did you find information about Sendero Gardens in his files or on his computer?"

"No, Mom," Travis interrupted. "What you need to do is give the deputy your official statement and let the Sheriff's Department handle the investigating."

"Augie, Travis is right. We should go down to the Sheriff's Office so that I can give you my official statement," I acquiesced quickly. "My grandchildren are asleep upstairs, but Travis is here with them. I can go with you now."

"Mom, maybe you could do the statement tomorrow?" Travis suggested.

"We're grilling steaks tomorrow, Travis," I stated. Amid all of the chaos permeating my life, I was determined that this one sane event was going to happen. "Walter and Lottie Frisham are coming for lunch. Marty Gastbend will be here to finish staining the cabinets. And you specifically told me that you would be here to grill the steaks."

"I told Laddie that I would call her later. I need you here." Travis had that little boy whine in his voice again.

"Nonsense, Travis," I said. "Deputy Dawge's time is important. He needs official facts so that he can get on with his investigation. I wouldn't want Sheriff Post to be unhappy with Augie because of me."

"Mom, I believe that we were talking, and you were the one who wanted to talk," reminded Travis. "Don't you still want to finish our discussion?"

"But you were going to interrupt it with Laddie's call," I countered. "We won't be long." Then a fractious thought popped into my scattered brain. "Oh, Travis, when she calls, you should invite Amanda Ladd to the cookout tomorrow. I think it's time that we met. Come on, Augie. Let's get this done." I grabbed my purse, opened the front door, and walked out, followed more slowly by Deputy Dawge. Travis had no chance to make excuses before Augie Dawge and I were gone.

After a brief discussion on whether I should sit in the front or the back of the patrol car, we were on our way with me properly ensconced in the front passenger seat. I was glad that Augie had the good sense not to use the flashing lights on the light bar atop the car. All I needed to further enhance my image as a disruptive influence was for my neighbors to see me leaving with a sheriff's deputy in the back of a patrol car, lights flashing in the night. Rumors would be running rampant at Lefty's Bar-B-Q, the Shapely Woman Spa, and LaDonna's Cut Yer Guff Hair Salon.

"Augie, you have to understand one thing for sure before we get to the Sheriff's Office," I said, adjusting my seat belt for a little less discomfort. The patrol car had mysterious, unpleasant odors that I did not care to identify.

"What is that?" Augie asked as he reached the stop on Heavenly Oak Drive at Wanderwood Boulevard. He looked carefully both ways. Then he made the right turn and headed through the center of town on The Boulevard.

"I did not kill Anson Kerringer. However, I believe that someone who came into that office after the staff left did kill him very deliberately," I stated with emphasis on very deliberately. "Has the autopsy been completed? Have you learned the cause of death?"

"I'm pretty sure that I'm not supposed to discuss the case with you since you're our primary suspect," said Augie. A mile and a half past the traffic light, he turned left on County Road 118 to go toward Handlen, the county seat of Evritt County and location of the Evritt County Sheriff's Department offices.

"Stop and think," I cautioned. My scrambling brain was trying fervently to pull up reasons from my muddled cortex that would get Augie Dawge to consider another suspect---any other suspect than me. "There is a murderer loose in Wanderwood. If you waste a lot of your time trying to prove that I am guilty, that person will get away with murder since I did not kill Anson Kerringer."

"The Sheriff says that you're the one," Augie stubbornly stated once more.

"Augie, the Sheriff is hundreds of miles away in Corpus Christie. He is totally mistaken about me being the primary suspect because---because I have an alibi for when Anson died," I said emphatically. My frazzled brain had produced a moment of clear thinking.

"You do?" questioned Augie with a tone of doubt in his voice.

"I believe that the autopsy report will show that Anson died about an hour before I arrived at Champions Ramble. He looked to be pretty stiff when I saw him."

"Maybe---"

"No maybe, Augie. He was stiff," I postulated. "I've been giving the whole scene some thought. It seemed kind of obvious that he was poisoned. He was poisoned, wasn't he?"

"Yes, but---"

"No buts, Augie," I proceeded firmly. "Did the autopsy report say what kind of poison was used? What killed him?"

"The coroner's office in Austin did the autopsy, Addie. They are still trying to determine what kind of poison it was," Augie said with a sigh. "Anson Kerringer ingested a lethal dose of some kind of poison. It was strong enough to kill him very quickly. It did something in his stomach and in his brain."

"That fits with what I observed that day," I agreed.

"The poison was in the coffee pot and in his cup. That's why we thought that Mavis Corcoran did it, but she had an alibi. Shopping in Dripping Springs. Two shop owners confirmed her alibi. That leaves you," he said positively, still sticking to his previously erroneous statement.

"Augie, you think that I don't have an alibi, but I do. You see, I had lunch with

Lacy Tindal at Lefty's Bar-B-Q. Then I went home to change because I wanted to look fresh and very professional for my meeting with Mr. Kerringer. You saw how I was dressed at Champions Ramble. Lacy can tell you how I was dressed for lunch at Lefty's."

"I suppose I could check that out, but I don't remember how you were dressed," Augie Dawge protested.

"The TV stations have it on film, Augie. Reporters did interviews. Don't worry about that right now. As I was saying, while I was at home, Lottie Frisham came by the house to pick up a change of clothes for my grandson, Trent, because he had dripped chocolate ice cream on himself at the Wildlife Safari. Marty Gastbend was at the house, too, working on my kitchen remodel. That makes two people who saw and talked with me at home."

"Two people," he echoed.

"Lottie and I talked with Marty about the progress on the kitchen I'm having remodeled. That's why I didn't get to Champion's Ramble until around two-thirty. You can check all of that out with Lottie Frisham, Marty Gastbend, Lacy Tindal, and Ramona Aduddell."

"Ramona Aduddell?" asked Deputy Dawge.

"Lefty Aduddell of Lefty's Bar-B-Q," I explained. "Lefty's proper name is Ramona."

"Who'd a thunk it? Ramona," said Augie.

"We can put the information about my alibi into my official statement, Augie, as if you asked me about it on Wednesday afternoon and then checked it out."

"Are you sure that would be all right?" asked Augie.

"Professional investigators do it," I invented glibly. "That's why they call it an *official* statement---because it contains all of the information that has been collected. I'm sure that you want my statement to be accurate and have all of the facts, don't you?"

"I know that it sounds logical, but I'm not completely confident that what you're saying is right," Augie protested. "Anyway, the Sheriff isn't going to be happy. He's going to ask why I didn't tell him about your alibi when I talked to him on the phone."

"Tell him that you didn't have all of your notes in front of you, and that you hadn't been able to verify my alibi by the time you talked to him," I suggested. "The explanation sounds logical and official at the same time. Good law enforcement procedure." I nodded my head for emphasis although Augie probably couldn't see it in the darkness of the squad car.

"Logical and official," he repeated. "Good law enforcement procedure. Got it. But, Addie, now we don't have any suspects left on our list."

"Cast a wider net, Augie," I offered.

"What net?" He waved his hand in the air, showing clearly that he was not in tune with my thoughts concerning other suspects or trawling nets.

"What I mean is that now you have to consider his wife, his close friends or enemies, and that important client that he might have been seeing." I truly did want Augie to solve Anson's murder quickly. I had too many issues currently in my life to give up the amount of time that this murder was costing me. "On the police dramas, the detectives always say that the spouse is the most obvious suspect."

"Kassondra Kerringer has an alibi. Mrs. Kerringer was hosting a pool party in Lakeway for her son and daughter and a dozen of their friends," Augie said glumly.

"Who has a pool party at the end of March?" I questioned.

"They have an indoor pool," he stated.

"That must be nice," was all I could think to say.

"It was," Augie sighed once more. "Except that I had to drive all the way to Lakeway to verify her alibi. There was one curious thing, though. Mrs. Kerringer didn't seem very broken up when I told her that her husband recently died."

"Perhaps Anson and Kissie were having marital problems?" I questioned.

"Where would I get that kind of information? What good would the information do me anyway?" asked Augie glumly.

"Don't you see?" I proposed as Augie Dawge pulled into the county criminal justice complex in the center of Handlen across from the Evritt County Courthouse. "If the Kerringers were having problems, there possibly was another woman in Anson's life or other women." I couldn't believe that I had to explain this possibility to the deputy.

"For instance, a couple of weeks ago Lottie Frisham and I were at the Hays County Area-Wide Yard Sale. We saw Anson Kerringer with Viveca Laurin. Lottie thought that it was an odd place for the two of them to be together. We didn't see Kissie Kerringer with them. Viv seems like a nice person, but she is another person that you could check out."

"I don't know, Addie," said Augie Dawge hesitantly. "Mrs. Laurin is a really influential person around Evritt County. That could get me into trouble with Sheriff Post."

"You can't base your possible suspects list on who is influential and who isn't," I scolded. "A suspect is a suspect whether they have a lot of money and influential friends or not. You should be bold in your investigation. Ask Kissie Kerringer whether Anson was seeing other women and who those women might be. If she mentions Viveca Laurin as a possibility, then you are on solid ground to question Viv." I could hardly keep up with the possible suspects trotting through my tired brain.

"Also, you might talk with Mavis Corcoran again to ask her about any women whom Anson might have seen more often than one would expect to be usual contact. Mavis would know what went on around that office. Jack Cartoff and Benny Olesford could have information, too. Guys notice things like that about other guys." I was hoping that these suggestions would put Augie Dawge onto a more productive track.

"I suppose that I could talk to Mrs. Kerringer and Mrs. Corcoran again," he said with a profound sigh. "I hope that this doesn't get me fired. I don't have too long to go before retirement. My wife is very unhappy about all of this time that I'm spending running all over three counties investigating this murder. She's used to me going to work and coming home at regular times. No, Siree. Twila is not happy."

"Let's get my statement done then, so that you can get home to Twila," I said, exiting the patrol car. "Is this official statement thing a complicated process, Augie? Does this take long?"

"Not usually," the deputy sighed again.

The statement took longer than I expected that it would. Joyce Banyard, the Sheriff's Department stenographer, had finished work and gone home. She had to be called back. While I was waiting for Joyce's return, I made a call to my home to reassure Travis that I would be home shortly. Lottie answered my home phone.

"Lottie, why are you at my house? Is something wrong?" Suddenly my grandmother's worry machine was pumping at warp speed.

"Well, Travis asked me to come over," she stated.

"Is something wrong with Travis?"

"No, Addie, he just said that he needed to go out. Travis said something about a call from Amanda Ladd. Since Walter has the men's prayer group tonight at Melvin Hanby's house, I was able to come over right away. What is going on? Do you think that you'll be much longer?"

"I'm giving Augie Dawge my official statement about what happened that day at Champions Ramble. Augie had to send for the department stenographer. She'd already left for the day."

"The Evritt Sheriff's Department has a department stenographer? Is this someone new that I haven't met?" queried Lottie with her Wanderwood Info Radar on high alert.

"It's a woman named Joyce Banyard," I explained.

"Well, Joyce Banyard is the receptionist there. When did she get to be a Department Stenographer?" Lottie asked.

"I don't know, Lottie. If I hear the answer to that question while I'm here, I'll let you be the first to know," I answered a little shortly. "I'm sorry, Lottie. I'm unhappy with Travis for running off again."

"Travis said that he wouldn't be long," Lottie soothed. "You know that I don't mind staying with Tricia and Trent. They're already in bed sleeping. I'm watching television. No problem."

There were no problems in Lottie's World. I wished that I could say the same for Addie's World.

CHAPTER 15

Exhaustion was getting to be a way of life for me as I struggled to keep up with everything that was happening. My life was absolutely out of kilter. Events were piling up and tugging me in too many directions with too little time for rest in between. That's why I was relieved to see Lottie pulling into the parking lot of the Sheriff's Department facility. I hated to call her to drive over and get me in Handlen at night, but Augie Dawge insisted that it would be two more hours before a deputy would maybe be available to take me home.

Waiting around to dictate my official statement was so much more than depressing. 'No doubt the Sheriff's Department tries to keep the facility in Handlen clean,' I thought, 'but it shows the results of a long day of activity with a lot of foot traffic.' The depressingly dark beige walls did not encourage me to feel upbeat and energetic. The benches in the reception area could benefit from cushions---and cleaning.

After waiting over an hour for the dispatcher to locate Joyce Banyard and call her back to the Sheriff's Department, I spent another hour trying to dictate my statement. Augie wanted to make sure that what I was going to say in my statement jibed with his reports. We went over details of the day Anson Kerringer died again and again. It would have compressed the time somewhat if Augie had started this process while we were waiting for the stenographer to arrive, but he insisted on waiting until she was present.

Then, while Joyce was taking my statement, she repeatedly made errors which she blamed on her stenotype machine. She said that she couldn't understand why that was happening. The machine was working fine when she took the test on her correspondence course three months ago. Another hour later, after other errors were found and corrected and retyped, I was convinced that I should have taken Travis's advice and done the statement tomorrow.

"Well, what is going on, Addie?" were Lottie's first words as I pulled myself wearily into her gray van. Lottie had apparently pulled a red warm-up suit on over whatever she'd been wearing. Part of a lace-edged lavender collar stuck out from the crew neck of her pullover top.

"Lottie, I barely managed to avoid having Augie Dawge arrest me for Anson Kerringer's murder. That man follows logic to totally wrong conclusions."

"Was that why Mata Shatley called me from the Sheriff's office?" Lottie asked as she eased the van out of the parking lot and headed for Wanderwood. "You know that

Mata is Sandra Grotham's daughter by her first husband. Mata asked me whether I saw you last Wednesday. Well, I told Mata how I saw you twice on Wednesday... once in the morning when I picked up Tricia and Trent for the Wildlife Safari. I also told her that I saw you again at your house for a while after you had lunch with Lacy Tindal."

"I'm glad that you could confirm my alibi, Lottie. Thank you for coming to my rescue, and thank you for rescuing me from the clutches of the Sheriff's Office. Augie is desperate for someone to arrest for this murder. He told me that Sheriff Post is threatening him by phone from Corpus. Why the Sheriff doesn't come back from Corpus Christi and take charge of the investigation himself is beyond my comprehension."

"Well, Addie, now you see why you need to solve this murder. For Mavis, for Augie, and even for that ridiculous library!"

This statement had me totally confused. "I know that it is very late in the evening, and we are both tired, but I have to ask. Why would Anson Kerringer's death have anything to do with the new library?"

"Didn't you tell me that you went to Champions Ramble to get a donation of paint for the library?"

"Yes, Lottie," I said wearily, my brain cells failing still to follow her logic.

"Well, how will you get anyone to donate paint for the library while this case is unsolved? All anyone talks about or will consider is *who killed Anson Kerringer?*"

"I hadn't realized that the murder could be a problem for the library. I suppose that the case might put a damper on people and businesses being willing to donate for a new library in a community where the murder occurred." My befuddled brain was having difficulty trying to fathom what I, one tired, 58-year-old woman, would be able to do to solve the murder. The *wider net* that I had described for Augie might indeed cover two or three counties.

"Well, I think that we need to have a talk with Kissie Kerringer," Lottie announced and nodded her head emphatically.

"We?" I posed, wondering how Lottie thought that *We* would be able to reach Kassondra Kerringer. Getting Kissie to talk with us was an additional quandary.

But Lottie had an answer. "We'll get Lacy Tindal to help us. You and Lacy are pretty chummy, aren't you?"

"Lacy and I are friends," I allowed, "but what do you expect Lacy to do?"

"Well, I could be wrong, but I think that Mavis Corcoran will have Kissie's phone number in Lakeway." Lottie explained her convoluted thinking which often defied understanding by the best of minds. "I can get the number from Mavis and give it to Lacy. Then Lacy can call to invite Kissie to have lunch...in sympathy for her recent loss, of course."

"And why would Kissie accept that invitation?" I asked.

Lottie continued with her explanation. "Lacy can say that she and Burt were talking to Anson about the possibility of building a bigger house in Champions Ramble. Now she needs to discuss the probability of that house being completed."

"Doesn't that seem rather rude so soon after her husband's death? Kissie Kerringer is not likely to be thinking of Champions Ramble before she even has a funeral or memorial service." Lottie's proposal seemed rather preposterous to me. I couldn't fathom how Kissie Kerringer would receive this out-of-the-blue invitation.

"The business at Champions Ramble must be handled soon, Addie. Mavis told me that contracts have been signed, houses are already under construction, materials are on order, and subcontractors like Kilgore Pettigrew need to be paid." Lottie paused only a moment for breath after such a long statement. "Kissie must start dealing with all of that soon."

"I know that Mavis, Jack Cartoff, and Benny Olesford are hoping to be reinstated in the near future, but I don't see how our having lunch with Kissie is going to accomplish that. I can't imagine that Kissie would accept such an invitation while she's still dealing with the trauma of Anson's sudden death."

"Well, I suspect that she isn't that broken up over Anson's death," Lottie said in defense of her suggestion.

"Augie told me that she didn't seem that upset when he talked to her at her home in Lakeway," I agreed. "However, the full impact of his death may not have penetrated at that time. She may be in the throes of a terrible distress by now. When George passed, it took a while for me to deal with his loss."

"Well, while Kissie is dealing with his loss, she needs to deal with his business affairs, too. That's where you and Lacy come in."

"Lottie, how do you expect Lacy and me to bring up the matter of his business affairs at this speculative luncheon with Kissie? Even if she agrees to meet with us, what can we say to her?" I was beginning to appreciate having this conversation in a dark car traveling along a country road in the middle of the night. At least no one else could overhear our conversation. It certainly seemed ghoulish to be plotting against a woman who so recently lost her husband.

"Well, I'm pretty sure that Lacy must know Kissie. Addie, as the interim president of the new library, you would naturally have concerns for all people in the community of Wanderwood." Lottie was obviously creating this scenario as she talked. "It's only natural that you both should reach out to an unfortunate neighbor in her hour of need. As a civic leader it is your duty to do so."

"Now I'm a civic leader?" I could scarcely believe what I was hearing from Lottie. "That's really thin reasoning."

"Well, Addie, since you took on the mantle of interim president of the new library Friends, your status rose in our community. Everyone is talking about you... favorably for a change."

"For a change?" I questioned wondering what less favorable things were said about me in the past. Then I realized that I didn't want to know.

"You and Lacy are possibly the only persons who could convince Kissie to reopen the office at Champions Ramble," Lottie forged on. "Only you two could get Mavis and those salesmen, and even Kilgore Pettigrew, back to work there. Kissie doesn't know you, but she'll be impressed by your title and position in the community. I do believe that she will accept the invitation if only to find out whether all of the terrible things that Janet Makeshire and Clariss Padget say about you are true."

"We are talking about a woman whose husband died a few days ago," I protested. "We can't begin to know what is going on in Kissie Kerringer's life at this point. She could be totally distraught or overcome by the event of Anson's violent death. Being questioned by the sheriff's deputy surely upset her terribly. I know that it didn't do much for my peace of mind."

"Everyone deals with death in different ways, but I heard from LaDonna Del Valle that Kissie was hosting a dinner party the next day."

"Perhaps Kissie already scheduled the party and had no good reason or way to cancel it," I postulated.

"Since when is the death of your husband not a good enough reason to cancel a party?" Lottie demanded.

"Good point," I apologized. "I think that my brain cells are fried from too much activity. This has been a very long day in a very long week. I'll feel better tomorrow."

"Addie," said Lottie, "it is tomorrow now. I picked you up at ten past midnight."

Tomorrow didn't proceed any better for me than yesterday had. Travis was waiting for me when I got home. He had his own take on what to do about investigating Anson Kerringer's death. His ideas did not coincide with Lottie's plan. He had no difficulty telling me his thoughts on the matter.

"Mom, you have to find some way to distance yourself from this murder nonsense," he demanded. "I talked things over with Laddie, and she agrees with me. She has decided to accept my invitation to attend your party tomorrow no matter how inappropriate the party might seem under the circumstances."

"Under what circumstances, Travis?" My exhausted brain was inclined to be a little testy.

"You are a suspect in Anson Kerringer's murder. You're the Sheriff's prime suspect according to Laddie. Her friend Clariss has a connection in the Sheriff's Department. Laddie says that you have no alibi for the time of that man's death, and that the Sheriff's Department is very close to arresting you."

"Yesterday's news, Travis. You can tell Amanda and her friends that they are quoting a source whose information is out of date. I have a solid alibi for the time of Anson Kerringer's death, and I am no longer a suspect." The testiness was starting to get the better of my good judgment.

"You can tell Laddie yourself, Mom, when she comes for the barbecue tomorrow." Travis put forth a little testiness of his own.

"The barbecue is today!" I exclaimed. "And now I have another guest! I'll have to get up early to run to the Handy Sack for some more steaks. I can't cut them any smaller than I had planned. Travis, we need to get to bed. Now," I added more vehemently than intended.

"Mom, I think that we should be discussing what you are going to say to Laddie tomorrow." Travis's voice took on a slight whine.

"There is no tomorrow, Travis. It's always today. Trent and Tricia will be awake in a little over four hours. Then I have to get more food for this small barbecue that has now become a mammoth event. You may stay up all night if you wish, but I will be waking you up to help Trent and Tricia by six-thirty. I am going to bed." I turned on my heel and left him standing in the living room, still protesting.

Marty Gastbend was singing as he stained cabinets in my disaster of a kitchen later that morning. I acquired more steaks along with more soft drinks. Saturday was starting to look like a possibly doable day. What I was now calling *The Backyard Brouhaha* might actually shape up to be bearable. I was hustling to pull the food preparation together. Travis was pretending that he had been around all week like a good father taking care of his children.

Chuck Frengill arrived to deliver the flooring five minutes after I started cutting the added steaks to match the original set. The urge was strong to hide in my closet with a teddy bear and a six-pack of Dr Pepper. This barbecue was shaping up to be even more of a trial than the earlier part of the week had been, but I was lying to myself. I was telling myself that I could handle this *Backyard Brouhaha* and that it would be a success.

Travis started the charcoal burning in the grill and agreed to watch Tricia and Trent play in the yard while he waited for the charcoal to heat. Lottie wandered in with Walter in tow. Both of them were bearing bins of salad and bags of chips. Then they walked back to their house for more fixings for our gala extravaganza.

At least the weather was favorable with the sun beaming down but not too hot for an outdoor affair. With a reminding nudge, Travis proceeded to set up some extra seating in the form of sport chairs from the garage. My card table and folding chairs soon followed from the front hall closet. I started to believe that the affair wouldn't be too bad until the doorbell rang.

On the front porch stood Mavis Corcoran and her two daughters, Shelley and Salley. Shelley looked a little sullen while Salley was scoping out the front yard sleepily. They were an hour too early. I hoped to have the patio set and be assembling the food by the time the guests arrived. 'Best laid plans,' I thought. I'm afraid a small sigh escaped before I could catch it.

"I hope we're not early," Mavis said with an embarrassed laugh that proved she knew how early she was. "I was hoping to talk with you before the rest of the guests arrive." Mavis was wearing a long wrap skirt in a red, purple, and gold print with a pink blouse and white sandals. 'Does she have no sense of color?' my brain asked. I mentally gave it a slap for being judgmental.

I led them through the house which, unbelievably, I had managed to straighten after the emergency trip to Handy Sack. "Tricia and Trent are in the back yard. Why don't you go out to see what they are playing now, girls?" was all that I could manage to say. The two youngsters brightened up. I pointed the way for them across the kitchen, and they scooted through the plastic covered doorway and out the back door. Marty Gastbend paid them no mind as he spread stain on the cabinets. Travis was due for a surprise and a half with those two girls increasing his chores.

Then I addressed the mother of those two *active* girls. "I'm sorry, Mavis, but I don't know how much time I'll have to talk. I'm still putting things together for the barbecue."

"Lottie said that you're going to have lunch with Kissie Kerringer on Monday," Mavis blurted out. "You just have to get my job back, Addie. I don't know what my daughters and I will do if I don't get back to work right away. I don't have much money in the bank. That job at Champions Ramble didn't pay enough for me to save much."

"Mavis, Lottie surely didn't tell you that I'm definitely having lunch with Mrs. Kerringer on Monday," I stated in dismay. 'What was Lottie thinking?' I wondered. 'Why did she tell Mavis about that plan for lunch before the invitation was extended?'

"I guess that I have been a little emotional lately," Mavis said. "That's why it is such a help to have you and Lottie be there for me. It's so great to know that I have good friends like you and Lottie."

Uncharitably, I thought that Mavis was overstating things when she referred to us as *good friends*. I hardly knew the woman. Maybe at some time in the future we could become friends, but right now was not one of those bonding moments. 'I have a barbecue menu to assemble and the patio to organize,' I thought as panic mode knocked on my mental door. 'I do not need a whining, dependent woman in my kitchen distracting me with a repeated rendition of her troubles. Does that make me a terrible person?'

"Possibly you could help Travis watch the children while Lottie and I put the food together," was what I suggested since I glanced out the window and saw Lottie and Walter coming. They strode across the yard laden with another bowl, a plate of what looked like cookies, a box with packages of buns protruding from the top, and an angel food cake.

"Addie, I did think that we could talk for a bit," Mavis seemed insistent.

"I'm sorry, Mavis, but this isn't the time. Perhaps later," I said as we reached the patio in time for me to rescue the cake which was looking a little tottery, balanced on the bowl the way it was. I really needed to talk with Lottie in the kitchen without Mavis. "If you want to be helpful, Mavis, maybe you could ask Travis what you might do to help him straighten out the tables and seating on the patio," I suggested, thinking quickly. "Everything seems a bit bunched up, and there will be *numerous* guests."

"I-I suppose that I could do that," Mavis said, not too eagerly.

"That would be such a help," I said, hoping I wasn't going too overboard on the praise. "Lottie says that you're a really good organizer," I added. 'If Lottie can stretch the truth about me lunching with Kissie Kerringer,' I thought, 'I can attribute imaginary compliments to Lottie.' Before Mavis could change her mind, I dashed back into the kitchen with Lottie and Walter following me.

"Well, I think that we'll have enough food after all," Lottie said as she transferred the angel food cake to the green glass cake plate that I inherited from my grandmother. "And when did I say that Mavis *was a really good organizer?*"

I shot right to the topic that was more important to me at the moment. "Probably about the same time that you told her all about the Kissie luncheon. Lottie, did you really tell Mavis that I definitely was lunching with Kissie Kerringer on Monday?"

"Well, of course I did because you are." Her reply smacked me like an ice-cold glove to the face. "It's all arranged."

"How could you possibly arrange that so fast?" I asked as my harried brain hardly processed what she said so easily. My salad bowl was not large enough for the bin of prepared green salad that Lottie had on the dining table. I dug in the large plastic containers that held my dishes for the bigger gold glass salad bowl and quickly wiped it with a towel.

"I didn't arrange it. Lacy Tindal did. She is a woman of quick action." Lottie had the lid off a can of very pink cherry frosting and was deftly smearing it on top of the cake. "Since you are such good friends, Lacy was quite pleased to be able to help you out. She was not only happy to have Mrs. Kerringer's phone number, but she also insisted on calling Kissie immediately. Lacy invited Kissie to a small luncheon in Wanderwood for a few close friends. She said the friends would be you and me." With that amazing statement, Lottie slid the frosted cake into the microwave for fifteen seconds.

The cake emerged, melted pink icing drizzling down its sides, and Lottie quickly scattered multi-colored candy sprinkles on the top. The cake looked fresh from the bakery. Meanwhile, I emptied Lottie's bin of fresh fruit salad into the other salad bowl.

"Lottie, this whole *investigate the murder* thing is getting to be much too time consuming. I want to spend that time with Travis and my grandchildren. Beyond that, I have more responsibilities thrust on me with the library project. I also need to stay on top of this disaster occurring in my kitchen."

"I thought that Kilgore had the kitchen covered with his tight schedule." Lottie added a tsk or two and a shake of her gray curls.

"The new countertop is supposed to be set on Monday," I added a head shake and a sigh of my own.

"So?"

"Lottie, I think that the project is two days behind schedule. If Marty varnishes all afternoon, he might finish the cabinets by early Monday morning. But that won't happen." I deftly placed the wieners and burger patties on a tray alongside the halved steaks and moved on to seasoning the beef.

"Why ever not?" she questioned.

"Because the Longhorns are playing OU in baseball this afternoon. I overheard Marty talking on the phone to Bubba Kreske about watching the game with him. Marty said that he will find some excuse to leave before three."

"Well, maybe you could find some excuse to keep him here on the job," Lottie offered.

"How likely is that? Bubba said that he got a keg of beer and several other guys will be joining them."

"You're right. Responsibility of the job can't compete with a free keg of beer where Marty is concerned," she acquiesced.

"Kilgore is going to have a conniption fit and a half."

"Well, you're right about that, too, Addie," Lottie agreed. She was adding the last of the buns to a large, flat basket lined with a colorful cotton kitchen towel. Most of the non-refrigerated ingredients for *The Backyard Brouhaha* were now covering the plastic tablecloth on my dining table. "What will you say to Kilgore?"

"I plead temporary insanity," I stated as I double-checked all of the dishes and added a large dish towel over the top.

"For the kitchen or the investigation?" asked Lottie.

"For thinking that this barbecue was a good idea," I replied. A chiming doorbell interrupted this dismal statement. "That is probably Amanda Ladd…also early."

We raced to the front door, but Lottie won. We were eager to meet the often-mentioned Laddie, but it turned out that we had a little longer to wait. On the doorstep stood what I took to be Officer and Mrs. Augie Dawge. They were dressed in a style that would have been called *dressy casual* on the cruise ships.

"Addie, this is Twila Dawge, and you know Augie," Lottie stated as she stepped back to allow them to enter the foyer.

I half stumbled back to get out of the way in the narrow space, and I gave Lottie a look that said, *did you know that they were coming?*

"What a surprise," Lottie said and seemed genuinely nonplussed. "Is this a social call or something more official?"

"Actually, Twila suggested---" Augie started but his wife cut him off.

"I wanted to meet you, Addie, so I suggested to Augie that we stop by on our way to lunch."

"Well, we were just preparing for a barbecue with some friends," Lottie stated when Twila forged right along.

"A barbecue? Why, Lottie, how nice of you to include us. That will give us a chance to get well acquainted."

"Everyone is gathering in the back yard," Lottie recovered her usual aplomb. "Why don't you go on through the kitchen while we finish our preparations?" She smoothly pointed the way through the plastic to the back door. "Ignore the mess. Addie's remodeling."

Marty Gastbend stopped singing as they passed through. I still stood in the entry to the living room, probably with my mouth hanging open.

CHAPTER 16

Actually, Amanda Ladd did not ring the doorbell. When her car arrived, Travis trotted off down the driveway to greet her and escort her to the back yard. She, of course, was punctual, arriving only three minutes before the appointed time. When Travis introduced Laddie to me, she sized me up and down before extending her hand.

"We meet at last," Amanda said. She seemed like an Amazon; she was fully as tall as Travis and appeared very fit. Her sleeveless blouse was freshly-ironed crisp, and her Indian red shorts bore the Keena Torviale label.

"Yes," I agreed. "We should have met sooner, but I've been much busier than I planned to be this week."

"I can see how taking over the Library Friends organization could keep you busy," said Laddie. "That was quite a coup."

"There is no accounting for the choices that people dedicated to a cause might make," I parried. "The members' choice of me to be Interim President was a total surprise, but I'm glad that the remaining Friends members have confidence in me."

"Making charges of embezzlement against Clariss and Janet pretty much insured that, didn't it?" Amanda stated, a little more aggressively than I thought was appropriate.

"Obviously your friendships with both Clariss and Janet must color your interpretation of the events," I answered smoothly. "You no doubt were not present at the luncheon they hosted in Austin using Library Friends money. You must have been busy that day and missed the event. I hear that it was quite lavish. I'm only glad that they returned the money. It was a sizeable sum that we will need if we cannot get businesses or individuals to donate the paint for the inside of the school building."

"Oh, yes, that was your excuse for being at Champions Ramble when Anson Kerringer was killed," Amanda Ladd verbally thrust forward.

"Actually, according to the time of death on the autopsy report, I was not at Champions Ramble when Anson Kerringer was killed," I once more deflected her verbal assault and added a small parry of my own. "Apparently, Anson died somewhat earlier in the day."

"Really," was all that she offered.

"It seems that Anson's death occurred while I was at home after lunching with Lacy Tindal. Fortunately for me, Lottie Frisham was here to get a change of clothes for Trent, Paula and Travis's older child. You'll probably spend some time with Trent and Tricia this next week. I have a number of appointments with businesses to track down that paint, and Lottie will be helping me." I admittedly made up that last part. 'Won't that be a surprise for Lottie,' I thought.

Travis interrupted with filled plates for himself and Amanda, and they joined Trent and Tricia at the card table which seated only the four of them. Lottie filled Trent's and Tricia's plates, and I joined her and Walter at the picnic table with Augie, Twila, Mavis, Shelley, and Salley. Marty Gastbend ate early and, as predicted, quickly departed. Marty offered no excuse at all.

Twila Dawge was a large, heavyset woman with wide shoulders and an amazingly flat backside. Her gray-blond hair was cut short in a no-nonsense clip. As we exchanged casual chit chat, Twila appeared to be a woman in total charge of her life and Augie's as well. "Thank you, Addie, for being of so much assistance to Augie," said Twila. "With most of the department staff in Corpus Christi, this case was a real challenge to solve."

"Oh, have you solved the case now, Augie?" asked Walter.

"Not yet," Augie replied, "but I'm following a lot of leads, investigating suspects, and checking their alibis. In fact, I'm glad that you're here today, Mrs. Corcoran. I need to have another talk with you about people Anson Kerringer was working with over recent weeks. You see, we're casting a wider net now that all of the immediate persons of interest have alibis for the time of his death."

"I'll be happy to go over that with you, Deputy Dawge. It's not like I have a job to take up my time," Mavis whined, looking directly at me. Shelley picked this moment to punch her sister Salley on the arm, and everyone stopped talking while Mavis sorted out the conflict.

I took the break in conversation as a chance to offer more drinks around the table to everyone. Amazingly, Twila Dawge insisted on helping me fill the drink orders. As we bustled between the dining room table and the refrigerator in the living room, Twila got to the point of their visit.

"Addie, I heard around the area that you are a very honest and take-charge kind of person," Twila said while she filled glasses with ice and sweetened tea.

"My take-charge abilities are somewhat exaggerated," I protested.

"I've been following this case through Augie's reports about his days' work," she stated positively. "Your name keeps coming up. The things that you have done and said have helped greatly. That's why you must keep helping Augie solve this case. He is not an investigator. He's a clerk. But failing to solve this case could totally mess up his career with the Sheriff's Department. You obviously have more sense about investigating a murder than Augie has. Who do you think did it?"

"Twila, I truly do not know," I tried to explain. "Anson Kerringer may have been killed by a business associate. Or by a jilted lover. Or by some enemy that we don't know at all."

"Not that! Anything but that. Augie definitely has to arrest a known suspect before Bishop Post returns from Corpus." Twila's distress caused her to spill a little tea. I grabbed for the nearby roll of paper towels which I was now keeping on the sideboard with seemingly almost everything else from my kitchen. "You must have some thoughts about who could have done it," Twila said as she helped me sop up the spilled tea from the dining room table.

"I have been mulling over the situation. My only idea is that the murder had to be done by someone really close to him because they knew his habits," I offered.

"What do you mean, Addie?"

"The murder weapon was poison placed in the coffee pot at noon or later. How many people would know Anson well enough to expect him to drink from that pot of coffee in the afternoon? Not everyone drinks coffee in the afternoon. And who made that coffee for him? Mavis says that the coffee pot was empty and clean when she left." My brain was lost in those possibilities as we headed for the back yard once more with the drinks.

"Twila, have you considered joining the Library Friends?" Lottie asked when we were settled again at the picnic table. "Addie is the Interim President, and I know that she's looking for more volunteers to help with the project."

"I hadn't thought about it, but it does sound like a great idea under the circumstances," Twila said.

"Under what circumstances?" I asked though I thought I knew what circumstances Twila meant.

"You know, the library needing volunteers," Twila answered lamely.

"Well, the library group meets on Thursday night at the community center," interposed Lottie. "You should come. I know that I'm going to be there."

I was certainly surprised to hear that Lottie was coming to the Library Friends meeting. This day was just full of surprises. My brain could scarcely handle them all. Stray thoughts were pinging around in my skull like ricocheting bullets.

"Lottie, I hope that Travis introduced you to Amanda Ladd," I said to keep the conversation going.

"I made sure that he didn't overlook his social responsibilities," Lottie assured me. "It's not often that you have visitors from Willem Club. They do tend to stand on ceremony, don't they?"

"At the office, most of them walked past me like I wasn't even there," Mavis commented.

"Have some of the Willem Club folks been into the office at Champions Ramble lately?" asked Augie, perking up.

"Viveca Laurin was in a lot lately because she was working on a deal with Anson to make her house the model home for Champions Ramble. Anson told her that he would pay for some of the upgrades in her remodel if she let him use the house as a demo for future home builds. He thought it was cheaper than building a specific house to show the upgrades. They were negotiating how much he would pay," explained Mavis.

"Clariss Padget and Janet Makeshire" continued Mavis, "came in at least once a week to complain about one thing or another that they claimed was wrong with their houses. I think that they were just bored and wanted attention. Life in Willem Club can be pretty boring."

"Has anyone else been in a lot lately?" Augie prodded.

"Uh-huh. Cynthia Parkhal comes in a couple of times a week to go over landscaping plans for the new houses," Mavis added. "You know, she and her husband, Eldred, own Grow 'Em Tall Nursery. And there's Shelby Draper from the bank coming in when she has questions about financing on the houses. Oh, and Shaynie Millred was in twice last week because her septic system had drainage problems. Then, of course, Kilgore Pettigrew comes in almost every day because his company does a lot of the finish work on cabinets and trim in the houses."

"Have you interviewed all of those people, Augie?" asked Lottie. "My, you have been busy investigating."

"Not as busy as I'm going to be," Augie stated. "I still have a lot of work to do on this case. It won't solve itself. Thank you for this excellent lunch, Addie. I think that maybe we need to be getting along now, Twila."

"Yes, thank you for inviting us, Addie," said Twila. "The lunch was very scrumptious. I'll probably see you Thursday evening at the library meeting."

I managed to refrain from mentioning that they had invited themselves and headed them down the driveway. Mavis and her girls followed shortly behind them, thankfully, because it was obvious from their fussiness that Salley and Shelley needed a nap. Lottie quickly sent Walter on his way home, stating that she would be along after she helped me clear up things from the barbecue.

Amanda Ladd walked off down the driveway with Travis and did not even bother to say *goodbye* or *thank you* to either Lottie or me. "Good riddance," Lottie said. "That woman has an altitude problem. She has her nose so high in the air that she can't see beyond the end of it."

"Thank you for helping me clear away this mess, Lottie," I sighed. "I'm glad that we used paper plates and cups. This was an event that could be a lot harder to clear if we needed to wash dishes with no sink. Now I wonder whether the countertop company will be able to set the new countertop on Monday. Ernie Plott said that he can't put in the new sink and install the dishwasher until the countertop is set. You see that Marty Gastbend didn't finish coating the new stain with acrylic."

"Addie, I know one thing for sure," Lottie said as she tucked the plastic containers of leftovers into the refrigerator.

"What's that?" I asked.

"On Monday, Kilgore is going to skin someone's hide."

CHAPTER 17

"Madison, I am not in trouble and I'm not in danger. Your brother should not have called you and worried you." With the phone to my ear, I poked my head through the kitchen doorway but retreated quickly when I saw the chaos. "I have so much going on this week with Travis and the situations in the kitchen and at the Library Friends group."

"What will you be doing?" Madison, my second oldest child, asked.

"Somehow, I have to convince some merchants to donate the paint for the inside of the school building. At the Friends, we now find that we have to use some of the money that we collected for paint to instead repair the roof. Lottie is setting up some appointments with merchants that she knows who might donate paint, but the appointments will cut into my time with Travis, Tricia, and Trent."

"Mom, I know that you will be successful in whatever you set out to do. Now my coffee break is over, and I have to get back to comparing sizes of meeting rooms. I have to find a facility that will fit the number of people enrolled for the summer seminar sessions. This conference that I'm scheduling is majorly large. I may have to use more than one hotel. Stay strong. I'll call again soon."

Ending the phone call with my daughter, Madison, was an especially good idea. Monday had dawned. Kilgore was in the kitchen in a rage and letting Marty Gastbend know it. Life in Kilgore World on this busy Monday had taken a sharp right turn from its normal, controlled orbit. The countertop not only could not be set today, but it would not be set on Tuesday either.

On arrival, one section of the countertop was found to be damaged. In the larger section where the sink would go, the hole for the sink was cut in the wrong place. Both pieces of countertop had to be completely remade. Even if the countertop company could rush the order, the remade countertop could not be ready this week or possibly the next. That made the issue of the unfinished cabinet staining somewhat less of an issue...but only somewhat.

"Mom, I told Laddie that I could drive to San Marcos to shop at the outlet mall today," Travis announced as we took refuge in the living room, away from the disaster being discussed in the kitchen.

"You'll need to take Trent and Tricia with you, I'm afraid. Lottie just called to say that she has set three appointments with merchants in Dripping Springs. Lottie and I hope that they will donate some of the paint for the inside of the school building." I circled the living room while picking up toys and filling the makeshift toy box.

"Maybe Lottie has something that she wants to do with Tricia and Trent," Travis suggested hopefully.

I sat down on the loveseat and observed that my Siamese cat, Vanilla, was watching Travis and me from the safety of the top of the refrigerator. How my cat got onto the refrigerator I could only guess. "Lottie is accompanying me to introduce me to the merchants. And no, Travis, we can't take Trent and Tricia with us to these business appointments," I stated firmly. "This will be a good time for your friend Amanda to get to know your children and some bonding time for you and them."

"If you'll be through by lunch, Laddie and I could wait until then to go," the whine was starting to seep into his voice again.

"We're having lunch with Lacy Tindal and another friend of hers. Then Lottie and I have another appointment after lunch. I don't think that we'll finish before three o'clock, if then," I warned him.

Travis paced the now-crowded living room impatiently. "Mom, maybe you shouldn't have agreed to be in charge of the library group. It seems to be causing you nothing but trouble," Travis said. "And why would a little place like Wanderwood need a library anyway?"

"Wanderwood is growing, Travis," I scolded. "The population increases by two or three families each month. That may not seem like a lot, but it amounts to almost a hundred additional children in the school district in a year's time. Within five years, that could be over six hundred additional people in the area. Wanderwood does need a library, and this is our chance to create one with a minimum of expense."

"But why do you have to be the one in charge, Mom?"

"Things just worked out that way, Honey. Being Interim President is only temporary until new officers can be duly elected," I explained. "A lot of people stepped up to volunteer for this project, and they are donating a lot of time and money. I'm not the only one working on it."

"If you weren't doing library stuff, you wouldn't be finding dead bodies or annoying Laddie's friends at Willem Club." He paced around the room impatiently.

"Travis, you know that Laddie's friends at Willem Club misappropriated a large sum of money from library funds to squander on a fancy luncheon in another town. That was an illegal act that I couldn't ignore."

"According to Laddie, you didn't have any proof that they took the money. She says that you made the whole thing up."

"Janet Makeshire and Clariss Padget admitted to me that they took the money, and that they did use it for their personal party," I said. "The fact that they replaced the money they took is further proof of their wrong-doing. Being friends of Amanda Ladd is not a guarantee that they are honest or trustworthy, Travis. I question why you want to be such good friends with a person who believes that kind of dishonest behavior is acceptable."

"Laddie doesn't believe that her friends did any such thing."

"Laddie is mistaken. Her trust is misplaced," I insisted, trying to put a nicer spin on Laddie's attitude. "Possibly she should find some new friends who don't lie to her the way Janet and Clariss do."

Travis stopped sharply in front of me. "Mom, none of this is solving the problem of who will take care of Trent and Tricia today."

"Travis, there is no problem of who will take care of Trent and Tricia. They are your children. They are your responsibility. I have appointments. You have all day free to spend with them. End of discussion." In spite of the hubbub in the kitchen, I headed for that door before Travis could raise any more protest.

"Addie, I cannot apologize enough for the problem with the countertop," said Kilgore Pettigrew as I stepped inside the plastic curtained doorway. He emphasized his point with a wave of his ever-present clipboard. "However, we will not allow this minor setback to stop our progress. When the staining on the cabinets is finished, which Mr. Gastbend assures me will be tomorrow morning, we will proceed to laying the new flooring."

"I thought that the flooring needed to rest and acclimate. At least that's what Chuck Frengill told me when he delivered the flooring on Saturday morning," I said.

"Chuck must have been thinking that he had wood laminate," Kilgore disagreed. "That's one of the advantages of vinyl plank. It doesn't need those days to acclimate. By no later than Wednesday afternoon, we'll be able to proceed with installation. My crew will be doing all of the flooring installation so there should be no problems or delays." Kilgore glared directly at Marty Gastbend when he made this statement.

"Kilgore, I certainly hope that we can be finished within the three-week schedule that you originally set," I said doubtfully. "I have a lot going on right now that is making demands on my time, and I know that you have that big project for Viveca Laurin due to start in two weeks."

"The Laurin Redo was scheduled originally to start after your kitchen is finished. However, because of Ms. Laurin's schedule and the lack of work at Champions Ramble, I expect to be able to begin her remodel before the end of this week."

"That won't interfere with finishing my kitchen, I hope." I raised a small protest as a vestige of panic made its presence known in a few brain cells.

"Not at all," Kilgore assured me. "I'm sure that laying your flooring won't take more than a day, if that long."

"Addie, are you ready to go?" Lottie called out as she breezed through the open kitchen doorway. She was the picture of no-nonsense attire in brown twill slacks and a matching bolero jacket over a pale blue, long-sleeved blouse.

"I'll be with you as soon as I tell Travis that we're leaving and get my bag," I answered. I headed back to the living room hoping to find a more reasonable son.

Lottie and I managed to escape the house before Travis could slip away. Even though it was his vacation time, I didn't feel bad about leaving him with Tricia and Trent. *He should be spending more of his vacation with his children* was my rationalization. I concluded that they weren't tied to the house because Travis could always take Tricia and Trent with him wherever he wanted to go. Even to the outlet mall. The drive to Dripping Springs didn't take us long since there was seldom much traffic on RM150A.

Bolstered by Lottie's help and influence, the Library Friends soon had ten gallons of paint from the Ace Hardware and another ten from Kriender's Feed Store where Walter Frisham worked. The store managers at both places were much nicer to us than I expected. I was beginning to think that maybe this begging for donations wasn't as bad as I originally dreaded when I was cowering outside the office at Champions Ramble. Of course, I wasn't begging by myself today, and I did not find any dead bodies along the way.

Approaching the time of the luncheon, Lottie turned her gray van into the long driveway at the home of Lacy and Bart Tindal. We were surprised to see a black limousine with a neatly uniformed driver leaning over the large auto. He appeared to be polishing the hood. Possibly he was removing our rural dust from its well-maintained surface.

The Tindal home sat on twenty-five sprawling acres of natural Texas Hill Country. Numerous live oaks and elm trees dotted the landscape which was surrounded by a white, three-bar plank fence. 'The fencing alone must have cost Bart a bundle,' I thought as I looked at the white line trailing off over the hillside. The patches of bluebonnets were thick in the yard and field beyond. I suspected Bart had a very extensive sprinkler system on the grounds.

The house itself seemed huge to me, spreading out across the backdrop of trees, grass, and wildflowers with gray-white rock outcroppings here and there. Fieldstone covered the exterior, and a number of large gables protruded from the sage green, metal roof. Sage green shutters in a slightly darker shade than the roof completed the picture of a carefully designed house.

"Well, Kissy is here," Lottie stated unnecessarily as she started up the drive. "She must have a car service on call. I heard that she has a housekeeper who takes care of the house at Lakeway. The housekeeper sometimes works at the condo in Wanderwood as well."

"Lottie, maybe we should have made a plan before we got this far," I protested. "We don't even know anything about Kassondra Kerringer. She may be totally distraught by now over her husband's death. What do we think we can accomplish by basically giving her the third degree and causing her further distress? Possibly this wasn't our best idea."

"Well, Addie, do you want to be responsible for Mavis Corcoran and her two children for the rest of their lives?"

"Of course not!" I said a little too vehemently.

"Mavis needs to get back to work, doesn't she?"

"Yes, certainly," I agreed with the obvious recommendation.

"Well, we need to find out how much Kissy may know about Anson's business affairs to make that happen, don't we?"

"I suppose so, Lottie, but---"

"Well, what else do we need to find out?"

"We need to find out what went on during the time between Mavis leaving and when I arrived," I suggested. "Maybe Kissie talked to him on the phone. And I've been thinking that it might help if we could get into Anson's office to look around a little more," I said.

"Do you think that there's a chance she would let us meet her at the sales office? Maybe if we proposed to help her straighten out the mess?"

"I suppose we could ask," I replied.

"We'll try for whatever we can get from Kissie Kerringer, Addie. A minimum must be getting her to reopen the office and rehire Mavis."

"I agree with that last statement," I said.

Lottie parked her gray van opposite the limo. Getting out, I thought that the van looked a little shabby next to the gleaming, upscale black vehicle. I felt a bit disloyal to Lottie in having these thoughts. "Lottie, I truly appreciate you driving and helping me today," I said to assuage my guilty feelings. "I don't think that I would have been very successful on my own."

"You would have been fine," she insisted. "You did most of the talking and convincing. The library presentation was in good hands. How many times did you practice it?"

"Quite a few," I admitted while Lottie rang the bell. "I was so nervous. The fact that you knew the managers helped a lot." Then I had to ask her, "Do you really think that Kissy Kerringer believed the line about Lacy and Bart building a bigger house at Champions Ramble? She must be wondering after seeing this house." Lacy's house had to be at least three to four thousand square feet.

The door was opened by our good friend, Rita Carter. She was a local caterer who operated her catering business from her home. Rita was wearing a dark blue, uniform dress covered by a light blue apron. "Lottie, Addie, welcome. Lacy is in the Sun Room with Mrs. Kerringer. Please go on back."

Rita followed Lottie and me as far as the entry to the kitchen. We then proceeded to the Sun Room at the back of the house. As we neared the doorway, we were surprised to hear a hearty laugh from Kissy Kerringer. Sitting with Lacy was a woman in her mid-thirties. Her carefully styled, frosted blond hair and Nina Krasenski slacks and cotton knit sweater bespoke wealth.

Several bottles of chilled wine and a few crystal wine glasses occupied a tray in front of the yellow wicker sofa and chairs where Lacy was already entertaining what seemed to be a very merry widow. Whatever was said before we entered put a smile on Kissy Kerringer's well-made-up face.

Lacy quickly made introductions and offered us wine or some other drink possibilities. She settled us in a pair of yellow wicker tub chairs opposite Kissy so that we could *catch up*. While I was pouring the wine (rose for me, red for Lottie), my fellow inquisitor forged ahead with the Meet *Kissie Kerringer* mission. Handing a glass to Lottie, I dialed into the conversation.

"Yes, but please call me Kissie," Mrs. Kerringer insisted.

"All right, Kissie," Lottie said solicitously. "We sympathize with you greatly over this terrible loss. Addie is a recent widow, and we know that having to deal with Anson's affairs must be stressful for you."

"Oh, I don't have to worry about his *Affairs* now," Kissy laughed. "Anson won't be having any more *Affairs*, but he had plenty in the past. Believe me. He hit on every woman who bought a house at Champions Chase, Willem Club, and Champions Ramble. He didn't care whether they were single or not. Are you shocked that I'm so frank about his dalliances?"

Lottie didn't seem surprised by Kissie's statement. I clearly did not know how to process Kissie's attitude toward her dead husband. "Well, I know that isn't usual under these circumstances," allowed Lottie taking a sip of her wine. Then she proceeded even more boldly. "Did you know whether Anson was seeing any particular woman or women lately? We saw him recently with Viveca Laurin."

"If you're asking whether Anson was sleeping around with that realtor, absolutely not. I have been monitoring their relationship very closely. They didn't have an affair, and I was pretty sure that it never would become one. That woman is all about the money and business deals. His most current romance was with the wife of one of his salesmen. For Anson, the clandestine challenges were part of the thrill."

"Hannah Cartoff?" I asked incredulously and then sipped my wine to cover my embarrassment in having that thought. Hannah seemed like a nice person and a loving mother.

"No, the other one," said Kissie. "Joy Olesford."

"Well, how can you be so sure that it was Joy Olesford?" Lottie brazenly asked the question that was in my mind.

"Detective reports complete with graphic photos don't lie. I've seen the pictures," Kissie stated positively. "Can you believe that name---Joy?"

"Do you think that Joy's husband, Benny, knew about the affair?" I couldn't believe that we were discussing the topic of Anson Kerringer's sexual affairs so blatantly but asked the question anyway. This kinds of conversation made me uncomfortable.

"I'm sure that Anson saw to it that Benny Olesford hadn't a clue," Kissie said as she refilled her glass from the bottle of red wine. "Anson was all about pulling the strings and jerking those guys strings like puppets. He lived for power trips and sleazy relationships. If I knew what Anson was really like before I married him…well…I probably still would have married him."

"Why?" asked Lacy, jumping into the conversation and clearly curious.

"The kids," Kissie said cryptically.

"What did your children have to do with your decision?" Lottie queried.

"Not my children," Kissie protested. "Anson's children. They deserved better than the rotten father they had. Also, their mother lives in Barbados and rarely sees them. I can't have children of my own, so I got Anson's kids and a cushy life in Lakeway. He got to keep having affairs. That's why he put his developments out here in this Podunkville, no offense. He thought that I wouldn't find out about his affairs. Joy Olesford wasn't even close to the first."

"What do you plan to do about the Wanderwood housing developments now?" Lacy asked the question of the hour. "That is an awfully active, on-going project with loads of houses under contract, most partially built."

"I suppose I'll have to reopen the office at least for a while," Kissy stated. "The lawyer says that I have to find some way to complete the outstanding contracts so that I won't be sued. Maybe that pushy receptionist would take it on. She almost ran the office anyway."

"Mavis Corcoran?" questioned Lottie.

"Yeah, Mavis. Maybe I'll promote Mavis to Office Manager," Kissy speculated. "That should tempt her to come back to work. If she comes back into the office then I could step back to oversee things from a distance."

"Can you afford to do that?" I knew that I shouldn't ask but the words spewed out before I considered the consequences. "I mean, will you be able to run the company by yourself?"

"Most people don't know that I have a degree in business," said Kissy, "or that I was Anson's Sales Manager before we married. Yeah, without Anson draining off all of the profits for his speculative projects, I can afford an office manager. I can run the business myself at least short term. There's already a construction supervisor, Harley Grotham. I could even hire back one of those useless salesmen."

"Useless?" Lottie queried.

"Sure," Kissie laughed. "You'd have to be brain-dead not to know that your wife was stepping out with your boss."

The luncheon, fortunately, covered many more pleasant topics, including Kissie's views on the new RM150A roadway (too expensive). The new commercial area at Champions Ramble (not enough population to support it). The new library (that could help her sell the development to some other developer).

Over a dessert of Rita's scrumptious Chess Tarts, I broached a new topic with Kissy. "Do you know much about a new project Anson was planning called Sendero Gardens?"

"The deputy asked me that question. If Anson insisted that cash money was missing, it had to be some money that Anson was hiding. I may never find all of his secret stashes of money. He regularly siphoned money from the company that seemed to be for speculative projects. Maybe he spent all those sums of money. Maybe he hid the money in foreign banks. I don't know. All except this mysterious money for Sendero Gardens. Maybe Joy Olesford took it or her husband. Wouldn't that be the height of irony."

"Did the deputy tell you that it was a large sum of money?" I blurted out.

"Though the deputy didn't tell me the amount, I'm not surprised that Anson would salt away a stash of cash," said Kissy Kerringer shaking her head.

"Well, Kissie," asked Lottie after swallowing her last bite of tart, "when do you think that you'll be able to reopen the office? I know that workers in the area will be relieved that you are reopening."

Kissie Kerringer thought a moment before replying. "Deputy Dawge says he can release the *crime scene* tomorrow. That's what he called the office...a *crime scene*," she scoffed.

"Kissie, didn't Augie Dawge tell you that Anson was poisoned?" I asked quietly.

"Some kind of food poisoning, I suppose," answered Kissie. "Anson would eat in some odd little cafes."

"No, Kissie," Lottie said. "Not food poisoning. He was deliberately murdered with poison in his coffee."

"I told Anson that he drank too much coffee," stated Kissie. "Isn't that ironic. I know that sounds callous. Look, I really care about the kids, but lately, not so much for Anson. He was spending a lot less time in Lakeway and, probably, a lot more time with Joy Olesford. Unless he had moved on to some other bimbo in the past week."

A thought hit me. "Was your detective still watching Anson on the day he was killed?"

"I guess maybe he could have been," said Kissie uncertainly. "You see, I was collecting evidence of his affair with this Olesford tramp because their relationship was going on longer than usual. If Anson decided to divorce me, I wanted to be prepared to protect myself and the kids. I haven't looked closely at the detective's report since divorce was no longer an issue."

"Well, Kissie," said Lottie, "did you happen to tell Augie about the detective's report?"

"Who?" asked Kissie.

"Deputy Augie Dawge," I replied. "Did you tell him about the detective when he interviewed you?"

"Oh, you mean that deputy," laughed Kissie. "He didn't say that there was anything unusual about Anson's death, so I didn't mention the detective. I could tell the deputy was embarrassed to be questioning me."

"Do you think that perhaps you could lend us a copy of the detective's report?" I suggested tentatively. "I have been helping the Sheriff's Department with the investigation. If there is pertinent information in the report, I could leak it to Deputy Dawge without mentioning you."

"That's a good idea, Addie," concurred Lottie.

"I don't know," Kissie said. "The deputy will want to know where you got the information, won't he?"

"Kissie," Lottie pressed, "lots of rumors circulate in a small town like Wanderwood. Augie knows that. And he isn't the brightest kind of officer. He's merely a file clerk who was forced to investigate because all of the regular investigators were out of town for a law enforcement conference."

"I think that Lottie is right," Lacy agreed. "Augie Dawge is so desperate for a lead that he won't question where it originated. Addie can be very devious sometimes. In a truthful way. But she's absolutely trustworthy."

"Oh, I suppose I could make you a copy of the most recent report and pictures," Kissie acquiesced. "I need to track down that office person, Mavis, and meet with her concerning reopening. I already planned to check out the office tomorrow. I'm staying at the condo for a couple of days. A friend of mine at Lakeway was kind enough to watch the kids for me."

"Well, we do want to help you through this difficult time. I know Mavis Corcoran, and I would not mind contacting Mavis for you," offered Lottie. "We could tell her to meet you at the office at, say, two o'clock."

"Make it one," said Kissie, "and possibly you could contact that Cartoff salesman, too, if you can find him. Have him meet me at the same time. I don't want to be in that creepy office by myself any longer than necessary."

"We'll be happy to help you with that," I said. "We wouldn't mind meeting you at the office if it would help you to feel safer."

"Safer?" queried Kissie.

"The office is a *crime scene*," Lacy explained. "Not that we think being there would be dangerous for you. We know that dealing with the business under these circumstances would be difficult for most people."

"I think that I'll be okay," Kissie reassured us, "But I do thank you for offering. I need to get that office sorted and arranged as quickly as possible."

"Well, you also might want to get whoever cleans the office to come in and scrub down and air out," Lottie suggested. "There's bound to be fingerprint powder all over everything, and Addie says that Anson did throw up on the floor in the break room. Also, those county officials searched the place, and they don't clean up after themselves at all." She followed this with a couple of tsks.

"Thank you for the information, Lottie, but I think that Mavis did the cleaning in that place. I expect that she'll know what to do." Kissie seemed pretty determined to take charge of matters.

No other idea for getting into the office seemed to present itself to my feeble, over-sugared brain. Therefore, we reluctantly bid goodbye and safe traveling to Kassondra Kerringer.

Lacy, Lottie, and I stood at the rail on Lacy's front porch and watched Mrs. Kerringer's limousine depart. For all of our efforts, we did not glean a lot of new information except about Joy Olesford and the detective. However, being able to get Mavis reemployed was a major accomplishment. Now, perhaps, Mavis's personal life would settle down, and we could concentrate on the traumas in our own personal lives.

"Kissie Kerringer is amazingly level headed for a woman her age," Lottie commented. "She seems to have a good head for business."

"Yes," I said. "She understood the true value of the new library to Champions Ramble and the community."

CHAPTER 18

"Travis, you need to look beyond the beat up, bare walls that you see here. Try to visualize what the library could look like once it is repainted. There will be bookshelves and books, colorful tables and chairs, and artwork on the walls. This building might become another hub for activities in Wanderwood like the community center…only busier."

My son and grandchildren were touring the old school building with me while we waited for the volunteers to arrive and start painting. "Marolly Hamilton is bringing ten more gallons of paint that was donated by the Ace Hardware in San Marcos," I said to a very sulky Travis.

Amanda Ladd cancelled their plans for the day. Now Travis T finally had time to spend with me and his children. However, Tom Hamilton already scheduled the Friends to start painting the walls of the classrooms on this Tuesday morning because a number of volunteers were available. Surprisingly, Lottie Frisham even offered to help us paint, although she stopped short of joining the Friends organization.

More surprisingly, on the list of volunteers for today I found the names of Benny Olesford and Jack Cartoff. The two men were currently helping Tom Hamilton distribute five-gallon drums of paint to the various rooms where we would be painting. We were starting with the office and one of the classrooms at the front and two of the classrooms at the back of the building. The rooms at the back were scheduled for office space and storage. The rooms at the front would become the beginnings of the library proper.

Tom Hamilton approached our little group with a satisfied look on his face. "Addie, would you and Lottie care to start in the back classrooms? We have two extra volunteers here and ready to paint."

"Jack Cartoff and Benny Olesford?" I asked.

"Yes," said Tom. "Isn't it wonderful how so many members of our small community are stepping up to help with the Library? Benny and Jack said that they could help only this morning because they are currently unemployed and looking for new jobs."

"That is generous of them to give up their downtime when they could be relaxing at home," I stated.

"We'll be happy to work with them," Lottie offered. "Travis, why don't you take Trent and Tricia out to the playground?"

"I brought the soccer ball and your old wagon in the back of my car," I reminded him.

Benny and Jack were laying out drop cloths adjacent to the walls in one of the back classrooms when we entered. Used drop cloths, leftover painting trays and rollers, and paint brushes were collected and donated by the Wanderwood Garden Club and by many other residents. "This room is going to be a book storage, so we are painting it first," I explained to my trio of helpers. "Once this room is painted and the floors are refinished, we can move all of the books that we've collected in members' garages from those garages into storage here."

"Hello, Jack, and you must be Benny Olesford," Lottie said to the man standing next to Jack Cartoff. "I'm Lottie Frisham, a friend of Addie Girard."

Benny Olesford was shorter than his fellow salesman by at least six inches, and his thinning hair on top was covered, almost, by a comb over. He had close-set gray eyes behind horn-rimmed glasses. I could see why his wife might be attracted to someone with more handsome features like Anson Kerringer. Benny might have been good looking when he was younger, but he hadn't aged as well as his fellow salesman, Jack Cartoff.

"Please excuse the subterfuge," Jack Cartoff said. "Benny was hoping to talk with you. When we heard about the need for volunteers to paint today, we thought that you would be here for the project. This was the quickest way we could think to possibly reach you."

"So long as you are painting a wall or two, I suppose we'll call it even," I laughed. "We're not proud. We take the work of volunteers however we can get it. I am curious about why you wanted to talk with me?"

"Have you found out who killed Anson?" blurted Benny.

"Well, it isn't our job to find out who killed Anson Kerringer," were the words that came from Lottie's mouth. "That's the job of the Evritt County Sheriff's Department." I couldn't see her face because Lottie had her back to me and was bent over to dip from a five-gallon bucket of paint into the liner of a paint tray she found on the floor.

"Everyone says that you both are asking questions in town about the murder," said Jack. "They say you talk to that sheriff's deputy a lot. You must get some information from him about his investigation."

"I expect that most of the town is asking questions about the murder, now that the Sheriff's Department has designated the death as a murder." I brushed off Jack's comment and dipped paint into an empty bucket. Lottie was applying paint to one of the walls with a roller. I grabbed a somewhat-used brush from supplies by the paint can and started working on a corner near Lottie.

"But are you making any progress with your investigation?" pressed Benny as he and Jack took their turns at the paint bucket. "Or is the deputy making progress?"

"We don't think that we'll be able to get back to work until this whole Kerringer matter is put behind us," added Jack.

"Well, with all of the activities in town lately, we haven't had a chance to talk with many people," said Lottie. "Addie is having her kitchen remodeled, and things are not going well on that."

"You should have hired Kilgore Pettigrew," said Jack.

"I did hire Kilgore Pettigrew," I sighed, "but the project seems to have gotten beyond his control. He keeps insisting that he can bring the project back onto schedule, but I don't see that happening."

"Don't worry," Jack assured us. "If Kilgore can't straighten out those issues on your kitchen, no one can."

"That's what concerns me," I said. "The *no one can* part." Another sigh escaped me as I moved a little farther from the corner with my painting.

"Well, that was certainly odd, Addie. What do you think they really wanted?" Lottie commented two hours later as we were helping to clean up after the painting session.

Benny and Jack left ten minutes before to go home and clean up. Benny Olesford claimed to have an appointment in Dripping Springs for a possible job interview. He groaned that it would probably not pay enough for him to accept the position if they offered it.

"Jack didn't mention the appointment we set up this afternoon with Kassondra Kerringer about returning to work," I stated. "Actually Jack didn't say an awful lot."

"Maybe he hadn't told Benny about the appointment," speculated Lottie.

"Poor Benny," I said as we took the brushes and rollers out to the school yard to be cleaned. "His wife was carrying on with Anson, and he and their children are the ones suffering for it."

"It's sad that he has children. Joy Olesford should have thought about them before she became involved with Anson Kerringer," Lottie fumed. "Joy Olesford didn't consider the consequences to her family when she got involved in an affair with, of all people, her husband's boss. I wonder where she was when Anson was killed."

"Augie told me that she was at work in Austin. He checked on her even though he didn't think that she could be involved." I put the brushes into plastic bags to help keep them ready to paint again which I hoped would be soon. We still had too many rooms to paint. "Are you coming with us to Lefty's for lunch? I hear that Lefty put the emu teriyaki plate back on the menu for a limited time."

"Well, that sounds like a really fun time after this workout. Why don't you let me treat all of you?" offered Lottie. "I haven't had a chance to take you all out to eat since Travis arrived. And, yes, I know that's not your fault."

"Lottie, I should be the one taking you out to eat after all of the help you've given us with Tricia and Trent." We were headed for the parking area where Travis and the kids were waiting impatiently.

"Well, we're still going to the Salt Lick on Friday, aren't we? Walter and I are looking forward to that. You know that they are supposed to have the best barbecue for five counties. It's served family style."

"Don't let Lefty hear you say that," joked Travis. "We might all find ourselves barred from her restaurant for life. She insists that she makes the best barbecue around."

I was glad to see that his mood had improved. Maybe Amanda Ladd's spell over him was broken. I could only hope.

People didn't drive from five counties for Lefty's Bar-B-Q like they did for the Salt Lick, but the restaurant was still bustling with its share of patrons. Patsy was on the jukebox letting us know how out of her mind she was for feeling so blue. All of the booths along the walls were filled, so Brenda helped Travis put two of the square tables together in the center of the dining area.

Lacy Tindal dashed through the door and over to where Brenda was sitting on the barstool behind the cash register talking with Lefty. After a brief consultation with Lefty, Lacy joined us at our table.

"Had to get some takeout to improve Bart's mood," Lacy explained. "Bart was in the middle of negotiating with Eldred Parkhal over a *fleet of two vehicles* for Grow 'Em Tall Nursery. I left while I could to get some lunch for Bart and me. I hope the negotiations are concluded before I get back."

"Do two vehicles really constitute a fleet?" asked Travis as his phone dinged. He checked the message on the display and slipped away from the table.

"Eldred thought that they should qualify for *fleet pricing* if he called the pickup and van a fleet," Lacy explained. "Cynthia wants to expand their delivery service. Grow 'Em Tall has a contract with Champions Ramble for landscaping the new homes. They heard from Mavis that work might speed up when the development office reopens."

"Oh, dear," I worried. "Mavis shouldn't say anything about the office reopening until she talks to Kissy Kerringer this afternoon. I would hate to think that something Mavis did or said could mess up that prospect."

"Well, Addie, at our luncheon with Kissy, the reopening did seem like a done deal," Lottie insisted. "No doubt spreading the word will help speed the process." I took this to mean that Lottie told Mavis about the purpose of the meeting and Mavis ran with the information.

Our food arrived, and getting Trent and Tricia set to eat took a little time. Shelby Draper arrived to pick up a to-go order for several bank employees and stopped at our table to chat. Shelby commented on Champions Ramble reopening. She said that she got the information from another teller, Anita Hanbie, who heard it at LaDonna's Cut Yer Guff Salon this morning.

Lacy's order came out of the kitchen, and she departed in a rush. When the dust settled, I noticed that Travis was no longer at the table. "Lottie, do you know where Travis is?" I interrupted my cutting of Tricia's barbecue chicken sticks (a popular item on Lefty's menu).

"He went outside to take a phone call," replied Lottie as she turned her attention to Trent's chicken sticks.

"I'm facing the front door," I puzzled. "How did I not see him leave?"

She supplied the answer. "I think that he went out the other door on that side hall by the restrooms. It must be a long call. He's been gone a while."

"I'm so sorry, Lottie," I apologized. "You are treating us to lunch. As old as Travis is, he should know that is rude. He certainly could postpone taking that call."

"Maybe it was Paula," Lottie suggested.

We dropped the subject while we tended to our own food which was delicious. Even the children were almost finished eating when Travis returned to the table. I fully intended to take him to task over running out on lunch. In his current mood, I was fairly sure that the call was not from Paula. He ate a few bites and then asked Brenda for a takeout box.

Our disappointment over not getting into the Champions Ramble office ended when Mavis called us at three o'clock. She said that she was feeling uncomfortable with being in the office by herself. Tricia and Trent were barely up from their nap. Of course, Travis took off in his car as soon as we got home from lunch. We had no choice but to take the children with us. To secure the children's cooperation, I promised (I'm embarrassed to say) to buy them ice cream cups at the Handy Sack afterward if they behaved well.

I understood Mavis's reticence toward being alone in the remote office as we approached the structure in my green Jeep. Mavis hadn't seen Anson's body; I had. I looked around the area as I parked in front of the metal building. Where had Kissie's detective stationed himself to watch Anson near the office last Wednesday? The trees at the end of the building away from the road promised a good screen.

But where did the detective leave his car? Was there a country lane winding through the trees with a place for him to park and watch the building and lot? Where was this detective when I came running out of the office? The biggest question was *could he see into the break room window when Anson died?* I was still looking and wondering as we stepped through the office front door.

"Oh, good, it's you," said Mavis with obvious relief. "You'll never guess how things turned out in my meeting with Mrs. Kerringer."

I thought that we could guess after hearing Kissie's plans at the luncheon, but we let Mavis tell us about the interview and her new promotion to Office Manager. Mavis produced a bin of plastic animals for Trent and Tricia to keep them amused. The new Office Manager was thrilled, and her excitement bubbled through everything she was telling us.

Reticently, Mavis took us back to the break room. "I couldn't believe that Mrs. Kerringer expected me to clean in here today. This room was gross! I was glad I bought some disinfectant a few months ago. While I cleaned, she had an interview with Jack Cartoff. Jack is back on the payroll. Kissy...Mrs. Kerringer, didn't say anything about Benny, and I didn't dare ask."

As she rattled along, I scanned the room. Then I glanced out the window at the trees. The closest cluster was at least thirty feet away or more. "The detective probably could not see inside even if he used binoculars," I thought with disappointment.

"The coffeemaker is missing," I noted when Mavis paused for a breath.

"Yeah. Can you believe that?' scoffed Mavis. "The Sheriff's Department took the whole thing, coffeemaker and carafe, and did not return it or replace it."

"Well, that's okay, Mavis. I doubt that anyone would want to drink coffee from that pot again," Lottie stated.

"Um. Yeah. I guess not," Mavis agreed. "But now I'll have to replace it." Then another thought hit her. "I guess there's no hurry to replace it. I don't think that anyone will want coffee from this break room for a while. They'll probably want to bring their own drinks...in sealed bottles."

"Mavis, have you been able to determine whether anything other than the coffeemaker is missing?" I queried. "Were any files gone or even so much as a coffee mug?"

"Don't you mean besides the coffeemaker and the one hundred and eighty thousand dollars for Sendero Gardens? I haven't had a chance to look things over yet," Mavis whined. "I've been cleaning every minute since Kissy...Mrs. Kerringer...left."

"One hundred and eighty thousand dollars? I didn't realize so much money went missing. No wonder Anson was upset." I led the way back to Mavis's front office to check on Tricia and Trent. The active twosome seemed fascinated with the plastic animals, and Tricia was even singing quietly.

"I'll have a few days to finish straightening up before Jack comes back to work on Saturday," said Mavis. "Anson's office is a mess. The deputy in charge apologized but said that they had to do it to be sure that the money was actually gone and not just misplaced. If it ever was there."

I showed Anson's office to Lottie, and we started picking things up as Mavis answered a call on Anson's phone. She put the caller on hold and excused herself to research something in her files in the front office.

I was retrieving some books that had fallen behind Anson's desk when I accidentally bumped the golf course painting. I turned to catch the painting if it fell, but it hadn't moved. A nudge with my hand on the frame caused the picture to swing away from the wall. The frame was on a piano hinge and in the wall behind it was a safe. Now we knew where Anson kept his one hundred and eighty thousand dollars. Until it was apparently stolen from a safe five feet behind his very own desk.

"Where did that come from?" asked Mavis as she returned to help us with the clearing of the mess made by the sheriff's deputies.

"You didn't know that there was a safe behind that picture?" asked Lottie incredulously. "How could Anson have a safe hidden from you? Didn't you tell me that you've worked here since the Champions Ramble office first opened?"

"The safe must have been there before he brought the building over from Champions Chase! I had no idea," Mavis exclaimed. "Anson had a different receptionist at Champion's Chase. Stephanie Jedison. But Stephanie moved back to Ohio to live with her folks when the Champions Chase development was almost completed." Mavis straightened the books that I had placed on the front of the desk.

"Anson moved the trailer to this location, and then he hired me for Champions Ramble. I've worked here since the site preparation first started about two and a half years ago," Mavis chronicled. "I thought it was a miracle to get a job in Wanderwood even if Anson was a bear as a boss. I am so grateful to Mrs. Kerringer for rehiring me."

A shriek from the front office sent us running. Tricia and Trent were flipping the plastic animals into the bin. "We probably should be going, Mavis," I said regretfully. "I'll call Augie Dawge and make sure that he knows about the wall safe. If he didn't know about the safe, Augie will probably contact you."

"I will be happy to hear from him," was Mavis's odd reply. Her next words made her attitude clearer. "Maybe Deputy Dawge will come to the office to check it out. I wouldn't mind having a sheriff's car sitting outside. I forgot how isolated this place is."

My call to Deputy Augie Dawge went unanswered for almost two hours. When Travis returned home bearing dinner from Pizza Pantry in Dripping Springs, my taking him to task was postponed while we sat at my dining room table and enjoyed either cheese and pepperoni or ham and pineapple. The latter choice was for me, I knew, because Travis wasn't fond of that combination.

"Were you out with Amanda Ladd?" I posed the sensitive subject while we were putting away the remaining pizza in the living room refrigerator.

Travis looked pained.

"Amanda did call you when we were at Lefty's for lunch, didn't she?"

"Mom, Laddie is concerned for you," said Travis. "She says people are talking about you investigating the murder. She told me some of the things that they are saying. Those things could hurt your reputation."

"I don't believe that anyone who cares about me would say bad things about me, Travis. I also don't believe that anyone who cares about me would repeat ugly gossip that might be circulated by hurtful people. Maybe I'm naïve that way, but I think that my reputation in Wanderwood is fairly safe. You might worry more about your own reputation."

"What do you mean?" he challenged.

"A married man with children, who spends most of his time with a single woman whom he claims is only a friend, is bound to cause some gossip. You may think that, while you are away from home, your actions won't get back to Lubbock. However, I know people in Wanderwood who talk regularly with people in Lubbock. The favorite pastime in this small town is what residents call *sharing news*."

We were interrupted by a knock on the door. 'What is wrong with people in this town?' I thought. 'Why can't they let me have a very important conversation with my son?' Impatiently, I opened the door to find Augie Dawge on my front porch.

Augie was dressed in a sports shirt and some rather wrinkled denim shorts and very grubby tennis shoes. "I was ready to relax and watch some TV, but Twila insisted that I answer your call," he stated glumly.

"You have my number, Augie," I said. "You could have used the phone."

"Twila was in one of her moods. *She insisted*." Evidently, when Twila insisted, Augie obeyed.

"I'm sorry, Augie. I wasn't calling concerning anything major," I said in apology. "When Lottie and I visited with Mavis Corcoran this afternoon at the Champions Ramble office, we happened to uncover a wall safe in Anson's office that Mavis says she didn't know was there."

"What were you doing at that office?" Travis demanded.

"Lottie and I were helping Mavis clean the mess that the officers left after their investigation. Mavis asked us to come over to help her. You have heard that Kissie Kerringer rehired Mavis Corcoran to manage the office at Champions Ramble?" I knew that I was fudging a little on the sequence of events, but the beleaguered deputy didn't need to know that. "Travis, weren't you going to get Trent into his bath?"

"Remember what we were talking about earlier, Mom," Travis said in a warning tone.

"Oh, yes," I replied, "the topic was the time that you are spending with Amanda Ladd instead of me and your children."

Travis gave a disgusted sigh and headed for the stairs followed by Tricia and, reluctantly, Trent. "Thank you, Travis," I called after him. "Where are my manners?" I added, turning back to Augie Dawge. "Come in, Augie, and sit down." The deputy obliged, and, after fetching each of us cold glasses of lemonade in paper cups, I joined him. "We weren't sure whether you knew the safe was there, so I told Mavis that I would contact you."

"Where was this safe?" asked the deputy as he made a note in his inveterate little flip notebook.

"It's behind the golf course picture over Anson's desk."

"And just how did you find it?" he asked suspiciously.

"I accidentally bumped into the picture frame when I was picking up some books from the floor behind his desk."

He paused in his note taking. "Addie, I went through that office myself. I didn't leave any books on the floor behind the desk or anywhere else," he said in an accusing tone.

"Really, Augie?" his answer surprised me. 'How did the books come to be behind the desk?' my brain puzzled. "That suggests someone must have searched the office after you were there," was the answer that my brain shoved out of my mouth.

"The office was locked, Addie." He was quite definite.

"Then someone who had a key must have done the search. They might have been looking for the missing money," I suggested. "Mavis told me that Anson claimed it was one hundred and eighty thousand dollars that was missing."

"One hundred and eighty thousand dollars?" Augie stopped writing. "Mavis Corcoran never said anything to me about one hundred and eighty thousand dollars."

"Anson's death and dealing with an authority figure like you probably caused her to forget." I hustled to protect the struggling single mom. "Mavis has been a little scattered in her thinking lately. I think that losing her job caused her a lot of panic. She has two children to support, you know."

"Is there anything else you have found that you think I should know?" Augie seemed a bit testy when he asked this.

"Only that it might be possible for Jack Cartoff or Benny Olesford to slip out of Lefty's Barbecue without being missed," I offered. "Lottie and I were at Lefty's for lunch today, and my son, Travis, slipped out a side door supposedly to take a phone call. We didn't notice that he was gone until he returned quite a while later. Wasn't their alibi that they were at Lefty's the whole afternoon?"

"That's just great!" Augie huffed. "Now I'm going to look like a total lummox. I cleared those two salesmen as having alibis, and now you tell me that maybe they don't? What am I supposed to do about that now? Sheriff Bishop Post will nail my hide to the Sheriff's Department door and hang a sign that says *Ignertz of the Year* on it. How will I live this down?"

"You could look like a hero for double-checking their alibis," I suggested to calm him down. "Also, you might check with Mavis about who had keys to that office building. I would think that both Jack Cartoff and Benny Olesford would have keys."

"Possibly that might work," he mumbled. "More probably, I'll get chewed up one side and down the other by Sheriff Post. I do not think that he likes me, and he especially doesn't like me being in charge of this murder case."

"However, Augie, you have one thing in your favor."

"What's that?" he asked.

"He doesn't dislike you being in charge enough to come back from Corpus Christie to take charge himself."

"You think?" asked Augie with a sigh. "I believe Sheriff Post thinks of me like I'm a doorstop."

CHAPTER 19

"Lacy, I am so pleased that you devised this idea." We were checking the progress on the repainting of the school building on Wednesday morning. The old building seemed to look worse instead of better. Maxie Chalpers had convinced Kilgore Pettigrew to check out the internal walls, and large Xes now adorned sections of the hallway. At the front, Tom Hamilton had wisely concentrated the painting effort on walls adjacent to the outside of the building.

Lacy and I were discussing her future fund raiser. "These non-repainted sections of wall containing the Xes will be partially removed to open up the front three classrooms and the front office area," I interrupted our conversation to explain. "The school board had no problem with that idea because these are not load-bearing walls and because we are not removing any entire wall. The built-in counter of the school office is a big plus that we can utilize later for the library's circulation desk." The counter very carefully was covered with a heavy tarpaulin to protect the surface.

"You can thank Bart for the fundraising idea," Lacy replied. "His new hobby has him fired up to clear out the house. His plan is for the Friends to have this Wanderwood Community Yard Sale so that he won't have to haul all of that stuff very far. This way he can make two trips to bring twice as much stuff in one day. Oh, let me correct that. Bart says that it's not stuff. Our *old stuff* is now *vintage items and collectibles*."

"Do you really have that many things left to sell?" I know that I sounded skeptical. "You cleared a lot of *vintage items and collectibles* at the Hays County Yard Sale, didn't you?

"Our garage is getting pretty full," she insisted. "Bart is on a *clear the house out* kick right now. Some things do find their way back into our house, but mostly it's excess that we've accumulated over thirty years of marriage. Things are tucked away. Guest room closets are crowded. We're unloading a storage room off the garage that was supposed to be maid's quarters if we ever wanted to hire live-in help."

"Possessions do accumulate," I agreed. "You don't even have to be a collector. Objects collect on their own---pictures, books, gifts from friends, souvenirs from trips, items inherited from relatives. I have boxes of Christmas decorations that I don't use although I've given decorations to my children."

Lacy deftly picked her way around a collection of painting gear and rolled drop cloths. "Bart is right, Addie. We have to deal with our excess stuff now or it will crowd us out of our own house. Bart says that the equation is *stuff x space x us* and that another yard sale is the solution to this equation."

"That is a rather extreme philosophy, isn't it?" I questioned.

"The space in our house for us to use lessens as stuff collects. At least that's what Bart says now," Lacy explained further. "We'll see whether he changes his *philosophy* when we get to his camping equipment and fishing gear. When our boys were teenagers, Bart couldn't resist adding to his camping equipment and his fishing gear regularly. That camping and fishing stuff takes up one-third of the storage room. Why would he need four tents, three camp stoves, or seventeen fishing rods?"

"I do truly understand what you're saying," I admitted. "When I prepared to sell the house in Lubbock, the kids helped me stage three garage sales. They didn't like that I was moving away from Lubbock, but they helped me clear some of the excess."

"You're lucky to have such good kids, Addie," said Lacy. "We both are."

"Yes, we are. My children were a great help in clearing things out. There was so much accumulation that I brought too much of it with me to Wanderwood. My attic and garage are still pretty full," I sighed. "This Wanderwood Community Yard Sale could help me eliminate more of my leftovers, too."

"You want to have a booth space?" she asked with amazement.

"I do," I stated emphatically. "I'll be our first vendor rental and be brutal about clearing my attic and garage."

"You can't be the first vendor rental, Addie," she protested. "I've already made up the vendor rental form and filled out one for Bart and me."

"Girl, you are too fast for me," I laughed.

"I used the form we got for the Hays County Area-Wide Yard Sale as an example. I think that it covers all of the legalities and liabilities. Now you merely have to get permission from the school district to have the sale here at the new library grounds."

"Is that all? You make it sound so easy," I protested. "Are you sure that we don't need some kind of permits, like permission to hold a public event?"

"Not so far as I know, Addie. Wanderwood doesn't have a lot of town ordinances. We probably should check into that. I was hoping that the permission from the school district would be all that we would need. I've heard that the consolidated school district is solidly behind the Library."

"Really?" I couldn't help questioning.

"The Library gives our kids something educational and constructive to do with their time in the Summer," said Lacy. "This place will add so many more books for kids and the community to read and space for activities. Why shouldn't everyone be pro-library?"

"Some people in Wanderwood aren't pro-library," I stated the obvious flaw in her concept.

"Forget that gaggle of snoot-faces at Willem Club," she laughed.

"Gaggle of snoot-faces?" I couldn't help laughing with her.

"Yes," she giggled. "they're just a bunch of stuck-up gooses."

"A gaggle of stuck-up geese?"

"Addie, I really think of those people as silly gooses. The word sounds more appropriate." Our laughter echoed through the empty classrooms. When we managed to bring ourselves back to the moment, Lacy asked, "where are the three T's today?"

"Who?" I couldn't fathom who she meant.

Travis, Trent, and Tricia," she explained. "The three T's."

"Travis is wherever he is and hopefully enjoying his vacation time. Trent and Tricia are at Lottie's house helping her make treats for the Friends meeting tomorrow night. Lottie volunteered to supply all of the food for the refreshment time after the meeting. Shelby Draper is decorating the tables."

"For a non-member, Lottie is awfully active in the Friends these days," Lacy observed.

"Isn't she? I think that perhaps she is starting to accept the idea of the Library. Maybe the chance to participate was too strong for her and overcame her reticence."

"Why is she so resistant?" asked Lacy. "You'd think that as a long-time resident, she'd be the first one to support a project like this."

"I've been thinking about that, and my thought is that it's the school building itself being changed."

"What do you mean, Addie?"

"You know, Lottie's parents had a ranch in this area of the county before Lottie and Walter were married. She was in elementary school in this very building. Later, Lottie and Walter bought a house and moved to Wanderwood. And you do know how resistant Lottie is to change."

"I should have realized," Lacy moaned. "But, hey! We could use that to get more county-wide financial support for the Library!"

"What are you thinking?" I asked, my curious brain deciding to show up and salute.

"We could dedicate one of these rooms," she twirled around to indicate the classroom doors down the hallway, "to recognize families who settled the area. We could have local history exhibits on the walls of that room."

"That's a great plan, Lacy!" My curious brain was already into thinking how we could research the original families.

"But back to the yard sale," she gave a yank to my curious brain as it was wandering away into research land. "We need to stay on task if we're going to get the organization and advertising scheduled."

"Oh, yes. We have to have advertising for sure," I agreed, "and quickly. The fastest way is distributing flyers, posts on social media, and, of course, the *Evritt Gazette*. We don't want to lose the local vibe."

"The local vibe? Who are you and what have you done with my best friend, Addie?"

It really felt good to be laughing again. I realized that the whirlwind of activities and responsibilities had been monopolizing most of my time and limiting my chances to have fun. Adding to that was Travis and Amanda Ladd, my disastrous kitchen remodel, and the murder of Anson Kerringer.

I resolved to work on correcting that situation. I had only a few days left with Travis and my grandchildren. Maybe a phone call and some reprioritizing would help with that resolution. God willing, I could get my errant life back on track with a little directed effort.

"Speaking of the local vibe," Lacy said, "we shouldn't forget word of mouth advertising. A few of the right words at the Cut Yer Guff Hair Salon or Shapely Woman Spa would have the news all over town in no time. I can take care of those."

"Lacy, I will try to see the school superintendent tomorrow to get his or the school board's permission to have the event on the old school grounds. With fees from the booth rentals, we'd be well on our way to having the library funded. You are such a good friend for planning and overseeing this fund raiser."

"The most difficult part right now could be dealing with the county, but I believe Andrea Dorting can help me with that. She works in the County Clerk's Office at Handlen," Lacy explained. "We need to know whether the county has any permit requirements, and we need to know how the county feels about providing officers for traffic control."

"You don't have much time to pull this together if it's going to happen before the end of the month."

"Don't worry, Addie. Bart will help me, too, and you have all of those wonderful volunteers. I don't see a problem."

'My cup runs over with happiness today,' I thought. I was driving in a euphoric cloud all the way home. 'What could possibly make this day any better?' my mind trilled.

Travis actually was at the house with an entire afternoon available to spend with me and his children. "Amanda said something that kind of put me off," he explained his unexpected presence.

"What did she say, Honey?"

"She said that you were too provincial to be the head of an organization like the Library Friends. Can you believe that? You? Too provincial to head an organization? I told her that in Lubbock you were a co-founder of the Arts Promotion League, three times president of the area gardening club, and vice-president of the local Buddy Holly fan club."

"That last one you probably could have left out," I laughed.

"It's good to hear you laugh, Mom. I did some thinking on the way back from Willem Club, and I know that I was a part of the cause. I'm sorry."

"Travis, I appreciate you having that epiphany," I said with my best Proud Mom smile. "While that is truly important, this afternoon is dedicated to fun.

We're putting up the badminton net in the back yard if we can find it in my overcrowded garage. Then you will have a chance to defend your title as champion of the Sometimes-Occasional Girard Family Badminton Tournament."

"I can't believe you remember that, Mom. No, wait. I can certainly believe that you remember all of the fun times in your kids' lives because you created most of them." Then he gave me a big, Texas-sized hug!

The afternoon was great fun, following badminton with a rousing round of Tallywack and a well-deserved nap. Lottie and Walter came by to drop off a pasta casserole, a bowl of fruit salad, and peanut butter cookies (left over from Lottie's earlier treat-making with Trent and Tricia). Tricia was especially proud of her assistance to Lottie in making the cookies. I mouthed a grateful *thank you* to Lottie across the table since I insisted that they join us for supper.

I managed to ignore the chaos in my kitchen all day as Kilgore Pettigrew's minions were frantically laying new flooring over the old, now-stained, vinyl tile. *Back On Schedule* was the goal for the next week in Kilgore World. Getting my life back on track was the goal in Addie World.

I thanked Kilgore for his assistance with the library project and promised to recognize him on our major donor list. He protested that action, stating that he could not afford any additional business requests added to his extensive schedule. His flooring crew finished, cleaned the area, and left before Lottie and Walter's arrival with the food.

After supper, I showed the new flooring to Walter and Lottie. We were walking the room and tapping our toes on the imitation, oak-print flooring to check out it's resiliency when the doorbell rang. Travis called that he would get the door. Shrieks from the living room brought us hurriedly to the entryway. We were blown away with the scene of Travis, Trent, and Tricia in a group hug with Paula Girard. I insinuated myself into the midst of that wonderful group. I thought the day couldn't get any happier.

CHAPTER 20

Thursday started early with the arrival of Kilgore and his painting crew to move the kitchen redo along. While he got the workers started, I put in a call to the school superintendent. Amazingly, the superintendent tentatively approved the yard sale over the phone, pending further discussion with school board members. He thought that they would agree with him. The day was off to a good beginning.

I barely clicked off that call when the phone rang in my hand. "Lindsey! It's so good to hear from you." I was surprised to get a call from my younger daughter.

"Mom, Trav called early yesterday and babbled something about you putting yourself in danger. I couldn't quite follow all that he was saying. What is going on there?"

"A lot is going on, but I'm not in danger. I'll e-mail you all about it next week when things slow down. The new library and the kitchen renovation are keeping me very busy."

"What new library? Mom, I also called to see whether you received my e-mail about the dates for the cruise next month. I found a great deal at the travel agency the other day. I hope you like it. I'm mailing you a brochure with a picture of the ship and more details."

"I'm looking forward to our time away together, Linn. Do you think that you could get a few more days off so that we could see more of Florida after the cruise?"

"Not happening, Mom. I'm so up to my eyeballs in work. I just wanted to make sure that you're okay. Why would Travis say that you're in danger?"

"Possibly he misunderstood the situation here. He's used to Lubbock, but I don't think he understands about life in a small town. Your big brother tends to take things too seriously. Sometimes it seems as if Travis T was born to worry."

"That's Trav to the nth degree. Tell him from me to lighten up," she laughed.

"I'll try to remember to pass that important message along," I said, laughing with her. Being around Lindsey always made me feel younger and more light hearted.

"Mom, you can't know how much I'm looking forward to this cruise. I miss you lots. We really need this time together to reconnect...and rest. Boss is coming. Got to go. See you in May!" Then with a click, the phone call ended.

Yet it appeared that I couldn't escape the phone yet. I was wanting to straighten the downstairs rooms and vacuum some of the construction dust from the furniture, although that seemed to be a fruitless task. The next call turned out to be Deputy

Augie Dawge. "What's going on, Augie?" I asked cautiously, fearing that he might be bearing bad news.

"Addie, I'm afraid you were right about one of the salesmen. His alibi at Lefty's didn't hold up. Brenda and Ramona weren't sure that he was there the whole time. I would ask the other salesman again whether he could guarantee that they were both there all the time, but they seem to be such close friends. Twila said that I should ask you the best way to handle the situation since you know both of these guys."

"Actually, Augie, I've met them both, but I don't know either of them well. Which one might have been missing from Lefty's?"

"Olesford. Brenda was pretty sure that Cartoff was there the whole time because he made a real nuisance of himself bothering the customers. Brenda's not so sure about the shorter guy. She says that maybe he was there the whole time and maybe not."

"On the TV shows, the detectives would take their suspects to the police station and question them separately about the time involved to see whether they contradict each other."

"The detectives on TV have lots of resources and backup, Addie, not to mention producers, script writers and a director. I just have me. The other two deputies that didn't go to Corpus are taking turns patrolling the county. Other than that, we have one full time dispatcher, one part-time dispatcher, and a receptionist. Everyone else is in Corpus, but they'll be back tomorrow."

"I didn't realize that Evritt County had such a small staff," I said.

"Sheriff Post is going to tack my picture to his office wall and cover it with darts over this. Twila is sure that not solving this case is going to mess up my retirement. That woman can surely get riled if her day doesn't go right, let alone an entire week, let me tell you. I purely do not know what to do. I'm sunk any way I try to swim and surrounded by sharks besides."

"Don't give up, Augie. I think that Benny Olesford is still out of work. Maybe he'll be at home," I suggested. "You and whichever of your deputies is on patrol today could bring him to the station for questioning."

"I suppose that's possible," Augie accepted.

"Once Benny is at the station, you could work on getting Jack Cartoff. Jack might be at the Champions Ramble office or at home. I heard that Jack is starting back to work on Saturday. You could call around to locate him and then let the junior deputy pick him up for you while you question Benny. That's my best suggestion."

"I hope it works, or I'm in a real pickle," fussed Augie. "What if I can't prove that Olesford is the guy? I doubt that he's going to confess to me, and I can't charge him with a crime without evidence. Do your TV detectives have a Plan B?"

"Those detectives would probably put him in a cell and try to hold him as a material witness until Sheriff Post shows up tomorrow. I think that you might be able to hold him for up to forty-eight hours without charging him." I knew that things didn't always work in real life like they did on TV detective shows but that was my best guess.

"Yeah. Maybe that sounds right. Twila might know. But do you think he's the guy?"

"Augie, if his alibi doesn't hold up, he had opportunity and motive. I don't know what type of poison was used, so I don't know whether he had means."

"Addie, almost anyone in the county had means, including me. The final autopsy report said that the poison was distilled oleander."

"Wow! You're right. There is oleander growing in hundreds of gardens around the county," I said. "How does a person distill oleander?"

"I asked the coroner in Austin that exact question. Distill just means that you boil a big bunch of leaves in some water," Augie explained. "She said that it wouldn't take much distilled oleander to kill a person, and that it would be easy to hide the bitter taste in coffee."

"So, Benny Olesford could have means as well, Augie."

"What was his motive?"

"I heard somewhere that his wife, Joy, was having an affair with Anson Kerringer." I slid this nugget of information in neatly, not mentioning that my source was Anson's wife. "I think the story came from a reliable source---originally."

"You're sure about that?"

"I believe that you can find proof, Augie. If the story is going around town, someone is bound to have seen them together when they shouldn't be." I didn't want to tell him that I was expecting pictures and a copy of a private detectives report in the mail. I felt that I needed to have those materials in hand and read the report before I told Augie that they existed for sure.

"Do you absolutely think that I should pull in both of those salesmen for questioning again?"

"Augie, at least it would show Sheriff Post that you were working on the case. Actively trying to solve the murder."

"Twila definitely won't be a happy woman if this murder case messes up my retirement," said Augie Dawge with a deep sigh. "I may call you later today, Addie, in case I need a Plan C."

"Bye, Augie. Good luck."

"Um. Yeah. Bye."

"That officious deputy wasn't bothering you again, was he, Mom?" Travis was munching some Doritos from a disposable paper bowl.

"Augie called to reassure me that he is looking at other suspects and that I am no longer on his list." I couldn't help stretching the truth a tad. I didn't want to spoil the type of family day that I had planned. "I hope it's okay with you and Paula, Travis, but Lottie and I thought we would take Trent and Tricia to BoompaLand one more time before they go home. That way you and Paula could spend at least a day of your vacation time together."

"Mom, there's not a lot of activities for me to do with Paula in the area of

Wanderwood. I had other plans today, but I cancelled them." Travis seemed uncomfortable and not too happy about that statement.

"Why don't you and Paula drive to south Austin or San Marcos and see a movie unless you spend a lot of time going to the movies at home."

"No, we rarely get time for movies at home. The kids take up a lot of time, you know, and we'd have to get a sitter."

"Travis, that shouldn't be so difficult...getting a sitter, I mean. You did not have problems arranging for a sitter when you wanted to spend time with one of your friends here."

"Mom!"

"Well, I know that you said money wasn't a problem, so why couldn't you afford a sitter once in a while?" I nudged. "However, today you don't have to arrange for a sitter because I want to spend some time with my grandchildren, and you know how Lottie feels about them. Take some time for yourself with Paula while you have the chance."

"I don't know---" Travis started to protest but I forged right ahead with my meddling.

"That new James Frobish thriller is currently playing at the theaters in Austin. I saw it advertised on TV, and it's supposed to be really good. You know that it won't get to Lubbock for weeks. Movies never play as soon in Lubbock as they do in Austin."

"Maybe we'll do that. We'd enjoy a movie," Travis allowed. "I should check that out with Paula to see if she's up for a trip to Austin."

"You could probably have lunch in Austin if you start early enough. Trying to fix meals in this dusty house has surely gotten old, and I think the paint smell is not too conducive to eating here. I could beg something from Lottie for lunch again, I suppose."

"That's okay, Mom. I'll take the hint. Lunch and a movie with Paula in Austin sounds like fun. I'll check with Paula to see whether she's okay with that." He headed up the stairs where Paula was catching up on lost time with Tricia and Trent.

Now all I had to do was call Lottie to make sure that she was on board for another morning at BoompaLand. "Lottie, what are you doing this morning?" I got right to the point when I had her on the phone.

"Well, I'm trying to finish the teddy bear project that our church is doing. You know, making teddy bears for the Victims Assistance Unit. Each member of our Women's Service Group is supposed to make ten teddy bears to donate."

"Didn't you finish your ten bears two weeks ago?" I questioned. I was fairly sure that she announced completion of her part of the project right after our trip to the Area-Wide Yard Sale at Woodcreek.

"Yes, Addie, I did finish my bears, but then Delia Struthers fell and broke her hip last week. What could I do but offer to finish her bears? I thought it would amount to four or five more bears, and that wouldn't be a problem for me because I work fast."

"Yes, you certainly do work fast," I agreed with my clever and capable friend.

"Well, would you believe that she hadn't even started her bears?"

"Oh, Lottie, no!"

"Oh, yes. Then Margaret Jewitt's brother got sick, and she had to go to Amarillo to take care of him. She asked me to finish her bears."

"Oh, my."

"At least Margaret said that she completed two bears before she left. But then I got Laura Lendson's bears as well."

"What's wrong with Laura?" I was amazed at the problems Lottie was having with her church group project.

"Well, Addie, nothing is wrong with Laura. She's young and has a new boyfriend. Laura didn't think that she had time to do the bears because it interfered with her active social life. And it was her idea to donate the bears in the first place!"

"How many more bears are you making?"

"Well, I have seven of the additional bears finished plus the two that Margaret started. That leaves twenty-one more bears to sew and stuff. The bears are printed on fabric, but they are not all the same. It's a family of bears like for the Goldilocks story."

"Can't you merely donate fewer bears? I mean, does the project have a quota or something?" I didn't understand this bear project at all.

"The problem is Eula Banks. She's the minister's wife. And, while we do like having Brother Banks as our new minister since his sermons are interesting, and he's so conscientious, we find Eula to be a bit demanding. She finished her ten bears as she keeps reminding us, but she didn't offer to do any more."

"You know, Lottie, I would be happy to help you with the bears maybe next week. You could sew and I could stuff. Travis, Paula, and the children will be heading home after lunch on Sunday. The new, larger windows for over the sink and for the end wall by the cabinets are scheduled to be installed on Monday. They arrived in good shape according to Kilgore. His crew will have to cut holes in the walls and reframe. I don't think that I want to be in this house while they're doing that."

"Well, I totally understand. Totally."

"I'm sorry you're so busy, Lottie. I thought that we could take Tricia and Trent to BoompaLand one more time this morning."

"Well, how soon would you like to leave? I could be ready in about ten minutes if you can wait," Lottie said. "Since you are helping me with the bears, it's the least I can do to help you."

I had to laugh. "I think that I could give you fifteen minutes. I'll work on getting Tricia and Trent ready to go. They still may be in their pajamas. See you when you get here."

CHAPTER 21

Paula protested about being separated again from her children after she was separated from Trent and Tricia for more than a week, but the protest wasn't too strong. "You'll have them after Saturday," I told her. "These are my last few days to spend with them. I don't know whether that's enough time for all of the hugs I want to give them."

"You're right, Mom. I'm being selfish," she apologized.

"Who wouldn't want to be with them," I soothed. "Tricia and Trent are such sweethearts. You and Travis are doing a very good job of raising them. The past two weeks, I've had a great time with them. I wish there weren't so many distractions this past week."

"Mom," spoke up Travis. "I hope you'll be careful. BoompaLand is pretty isolated."

"There's no reason to worry, Travis. Lottie Frisham is going with us. In fact, Lottie will probably drive her van. We know how out of the way BoompaLand is, but there are always some other visitors there. The Bumpers are on site, too. We'll be fine. Why do you insist that I am in danger?"

"I've heard the talk at Willem Club," Travis countered. "Your name is mentioned a lot, and they sound like they are plotting against you. They say things like *bring her down* and *chase her out of the county.*"

"That's only talk by some disgruntled people who find that they have lost a little control of town activities." I brushed off his effort to put too much emphasis on what I considered idle threats. "Trent. Tricia. Grab your backpacks. Aunt Lottie is here, and we're going to BoompaLand. Won't that be fun?" My question was drowned out by two shrieking kids who were now bouncing up and down like they were attached to bungee cords.

"Lottie, I am very glad to be escaping the over-the-top frenetic activity that we're experiencing in Wanderwood lately," I said as we bumped along the curvy RM150A toward Austin and the turnoff for BoompaLand. "Travis is convinced that the Willem Club group is plotting against me. Augie Dawge keeps calling me wanting help with his investigation."

"Well, why is he calling you?"

"He says that Sheriff Post and the rest of the deputies will be back from Corpus Christi tomorrow. The case has to be solved by then, and he is in a major panic He's afraid that, if the case is still unsolved, he could lose his job and his retirement. Plus, Twila's pushing him toward me."

"Augie actually has done much better than I thought he would," admitted Lottie. "You know, Addie, that he never had to handle anything more difficult than a tangle in his pile of paper clips before this case. You really have helped him pull things together."

"Lottie, I think you may be crediting the wrong female," I contradicted her statement.

"Well, then, who do you think is behind his turnaround?"

"Twila Dawge."

"I stand corrected, Addie. You are probably right. Twila Dawge can turn into a tornado if someone leaves mud on her rug."

"Do you speak from personal experience?"

"A major rain storm on canasta day when Twila was hosting." The extremely winding section of road caused Lottie to slow down. "Augie might be more afraid of Twila than he is of Sheriff Post."

We reached the turnoff for BoompaLand and slowed even more for the turn into the parking lot. I counted fourteen vehicles before we found an open space to park. "You'd think that it was June," I commented. "This is quite a crowd."

"I think that Della is using social media to get the word out," said Lottie. "Their children and grandchildren are doing the posts for them."

We could barely hold onto Trent and Tricia as they danced, bounced, and tugged their way to the entrance. Of course, the children wanted to start on the carousel, but Trent was not happy when he found that the lion and tiger already were taken. I managed somehow to convince them that they should try driving the side-by-side red car and blue car. Then they could pretend that they were in a car race on a round track.

All of the benches were occupied, so Lottie and I perched on a huge, flat boulder under a nearby elm tree. "I certainly was pleased that you could come along today, Lottie. What I meant to tell you on the phone and forgot was that I wanted to give Paula and Travis some alone time. She and Travis are spending the morning together in Austin. Lunch and a movie."

"Hallelujah! That couldn't have worked out better if you had arranged it," exclaimed Lottie.

I gave her a look and then continued, "I don't know what I will do about Augie Dawge. I've proposed every lead that I can think he could investigate. Today, he's picking up Benny Olesford and Jack Cartoff to recheck their alibis."

"Why is he doing that?" asked Lottie as we gave Trent and Tricia a wave when they slowly raced by in their cars.

"When you took my family to lunch the other day at Lefty's," I said, "do you remember Travis slipping out the door by the restrooms? He was missing quite a while and I didn't notice."

"Well, don't worry about that, Addie. I didn't miss him at first either."

"Lottie, he was gone long enough to have gone somewhere nearby and returned. You do realize that with Wanderwood being so small, it takes no time to get anywhere in town."

"Yes, I suppose that is true."

"Don't you see?" I explained. "If he could do that, and we didn't miss him, one of the salesmen possibly could have slipped out and gone to Champions Ramble."

"Well, I wouldn't have thought about them doing such a thing," Lottie said. "That would take a very devious mind."

"Augie has been rechecking Benny and Jack's alibis, and one of them could have slipped out the way Travis did," I told her. "Today, Augie is trying to interview both salesmen again. He wants to see whether they contradict each other some way. He's hoping to get proof that Benny Olesford did slip out for enough time to go to the Champions Ramble office and back."

"Well, that proof really could crack the case," Lottie enthused.

"What might give Augie proof would be that detective's report. I wonder why Kissie hasn't sent it," I moaned. "From what she said, I thought that she would possibly overnight it. I truly don't want to call her about it."

"Didn't the postal van deliver something to your house yesterday?" asked Lottie. "I was sure that I saw a delivery being made at your house when I was taking my walk."

"I was in and out yesterday," I said. "We played in the back yard because Travis actually was there for a change. Travis didn't say anything about any envelope or package being delivered. He hasn't been good about relaying messages the past two weeks. Now I'm anxious to get home to see about that delivery."

"Well, that won't happen until Tricia and Trent have petted a bunch of animals, played some carnival games, hit the ball through five holes of mini golf, and ridden the carousel at least once more." laughed Lottie. "Then, of course, they'll want to ride the carousel at least two more times."

"I guess we might as well enjoy ourselves," I laughed along with her. We were not headed home until more than an hour later, but there were a couple of tired, singing grandchildren in the back of the van.

My kitchen was in chaos when we got home. Marty Gastbend and Ernie Plott apparently were in conflict over the sequence of work that was to happen. Somehow, Ernie had not been notified that the countertop was not set. I called for a truce, and they quieted down.

"Ernie, I'm sorry that no one notified you that the countertop pieces came in damaged and made wrong," I said apologetically. "Also, someone should have notified you that the dishwasher has not arrived."

"Addie," interrupted Marty, "the dishwasher did show up."

"Really?" I questioned.

"Sure," he said. "We put it in the garage by the stove yesterday when Alf Moody and I were staining the baseboards there. Alf insisted on helping me make up for what Jasper did to your floor."

"That was nice of Alfred," said Ernie.

"Yes, it was," I agreed. "Now may I see the dishwasher to be sure it's the correct one?"

"Okay," said Marty, "but I checked the delivery slip carefully myself. The number on the box matched the number on the paperwork."

We adjourned our meeting to the garage where there was indeed a boxed dishwasher. On top of the box was the delivery paperwork and a large, cardboard, USPS envelope. "How did this envelope get here?" I asked, picking it up to examine it. The return address was Lakeway.

"Oh. Cindy Macklund delivered that envelope after the appliance truck left. I was double checking the paperwork on the dishwasher when she came," Marty explained.

"I've been waiting for this envelope," was all I dared to say.

"Addie, you won't believe this," said Ernie.

"What won't I believe?" I asked with trepidation.

"Somehow the top-loading model of dishwasher must have been ordered by mistake," replied Ernie. "Who do you think should tell Kilgore?"

Luckily, I managed to retain my sanity and my equanimity until Marty and Ernie left for lunch. Trent and Tricia were lunching at Lottie's house and baking cookies until nap time to let me have a rest break, so Lottie said. I microwaved a leftover wiener in the bowl of leftover chili while I excitedly opened the envelope.

Inside were the detective's pictures in a clear plastic bag. Also included was the detective's report in which he stated that he ended his surveillance after the removal of the body bag and the arrival of the TV vans. I had to call Lottie. But first, I had to call Deputy Augie Dawge.

"No wonder Kissie Kerringer wasn't shocked when you notified her of Anson's death. The detective already had told her the bad news," I reported. "I promised not to reveal my source. I can't tell you how I got this copy of the report, but I'm sure that the detective agency can verify its authenticity. Were you able to pick up Benny Olesford?"

'We did find him at home working in his garage," said Augie.

"Is he in custody now?" I asked as I pulled the hot bowl of chili from the microwave while trying to balance the skinny cell phone on my shoulder. 'You should have put the phone on speaker, ninny,' Lottie's voice in my brain fussed.

"We didn't arrest him, Addie, so I don't think that *in custody* would be the correct term," Augie stated with a sniff.

'Was Augie crying?' I wondered. 'Did he let Benny go?' "This is no time to quibble over terminology, Augie. Is Benny Olesford at the Sheriff's Department?"

"Sure he is and Jack Cartoff, too," said Augie with another sniff. "And get this,

Addie. Cartoff says that he never noticed whether Olesford was with him all the time. He was busy trying to hustle some customers to get him back into Anson Kerringer's good graces. *Now* he says that." I took my ear away from the phone briefly as Augie noisily blew his nose.

"According to this report," I told Augie when he had stopped snuffling, "three people went into the office between the time that Mavis and the salesmen left and the time that I arrived. Shaynie Millred arrived shortly after the salesmen left together, and she left nine minutes later. Then Viveca Laurin arrived and was there for eighteen minutes. Last was Benny Olesford and he was only there for four minutes."

"Probably just long enough to make the coffee and put the poison in the coffee pot," said Augie.

"That's an assumption, Augie. You cannot base a murder arrest on an assumption," I insisted patiently. "No, Augie, you make an arrest on the basis of motive, means, and opportunity. Benny Olesford has all three of those elements. You were ready to arrest me on a lot less evidence."

"But does the detective's report prove that his wife was having an affair with Anson Kerringer?" Augie stubbornly resisted.

"There are explicit pictures with the report. I don't think that there could be any doubt of the affair," I said.

"I'll hold Olesford and send a deputy to pick up the copy of that report," said Augie. "But if he's not the one, I'll be in a peck of trouble with Sheriff Post tomorrow and in an even worse predicament with Twila tomorrow night."

"You should be okay with Sheriff Post because you are holding a viable suspect with evidence to back up your conclusions," I reassured him. "I make no guarantees about Twila."

The call took so long that I had to reheat the chili while I spread mustard on a leftover bun. I didn't even care that it was a hamburger bun. I was so relieved that Benny Olesford was in custody and that I would soon be distanced from the whole investigation process. 'Life is good,' I thought as I sliced the wiener in half lengthwise and crosswise to fit on the round bun. "Travis and Paula are where they should be and hopefully mending fences. Anson Kerringer's death is no longer my problem. Dealing with the Library should be a walk in the proverbial park.'

I managed to finish my round hot dog lunch. Then I called Lottie before the deputy arrived to retrieve the detective's report and pictures from wherever that deputy was in the county. "The detective managed to station himself within a cluster of trees near the end of the trailer. He was able to watch both the front and back parking lots, according to his report," I explained to Lottie, now on speakerphone.

"Did he see anyone enter the office from the time Mavis left at 11:37 and when you arrived at 2:30?" questioned Lottie.

I explained to her about the document pages that I had thought to scan into my computer. I described what the detective recorded after the two salesmen left.

"At 12:14, Shaynie Millred entered. At 12:23, Shaynie Millred exited. At 12:40, Viveca Laurin entered. At 12:58, Viv exited. At 1:22, Benny Olesford entered. At 1:26, Benny exited," I read.

"At 2:32, unknown female arrived and sat in her car watching office. My license tag number was listed with a note to check later. At 2:38, same unknown female entered. At 2:41, unknown female exited and ran to the car and remained there watching office. At 3:56, sheriff's deputy arrived. Arrival of additional sheriff's staff, removal of body bag, and arrival of TV crews was also noted. At 5:00, surveillance discontinued."

"That office was a busy place after Mavis left. Which one do you think killed Anson Kerringer?" asked Lottie.

"It doesn't look good for Benny Olesford. He was the last one entering the office before I arrived."

After scanning the report and pictures into my computer, I carefully placed them in a manila envelope and sealed it with some blue painter's tape from the project in the kitchen. The deputy could not believe that Augie had called him away from his patrolling to drive all the way to Wanderwood to pick up an envelope.

Unfortunately, Travis and Paula drove onto Serenity Lane as the deputy was backing out of the driveway. "Mom, are you okay?" Paula called when they came through the kitchen door.

"I'm in the living room, and I'm fine," I called back.

"Mom, why was there a deputy here?" asked Travis as they brushed past the plastic sheet in the doorway.

"The deputy needed to pick up some paperwork that I had," I replied. "Did you have a nice time? Was the movie as exciting as the reviewers said?"

"Oh, yes," said Paula. "By the end of the movie, we were on the edges of our seats and holding our breath. I will certainly recommend it to my friends when I get back to Lubbock."

"Maybe we'll see it again when it opens in the theaters at home," agreed Travis.

"Are Trent and Tricia napping?" asked Paula. "Maybe we should have been quieter when we came in."

"The children are at Lottie's house for lunch and then they are baking cookies," I said. "They promised to bring some cookies home for us when it's nap time. We all had a very fun time at BoompaLand, and I'm sure that they'll need a nice, long nap."

"I thought that Paula and I might drive around Wanderwood and check out some of the changes since the last time that we were here," Travis proposed.

"That sounds like something interesting to do," I approved. "You might want to put the children down for their nap before you go, Paula. Lottie should be bringing them back soon. I have to make a call to Kilgore Pettigrew about things in the kitchen."

"Are things progressing better on your kitchen redo?" Paula asked.

"I'm afraid not," I replied, laughing and shaking my head. "I hope Kilgore doesn't develop blood pressure issues over it. He is not going to be pleased with this latest snag to his tight schedule."

Before I could tell Paula the latest problems with the kitchen redo, Trent and Tricia noisily arrived with Lottie. Each child was carrying a basket of freshly-baked cookies. "We made sugar cookies, Gammy. We made them for Mommy," said Tricia.

"I made cookies, too, Mommy, because we missed you!" crowed Trent.

Lottie asked Paula and Travis about the movie and then excused herself to go home and clean her kitchen.

Paula gave each little baker a hug while I took the baskets to the dining room. Then I had to give each of my grandchildren a hug before Paula happily trundled them to bed.

"What did the deputy really want, Mom?" demanded Travis.

"Lighten up, Travis T. The deputy came to collect some papers that Augie needed," I said, giving him a spare hug that I happened to have left over from the hug-fest. "I don't think that the Sheriff or his deputies will be bothering us much in the future. It's possible that Augie has solved his first murder case."

"Are you sure about that?" Travis questioned. For some reason he seemed not to believe me.

"As sure as I can be at the moment," I told him. I couldn't help giving him a big smile. I was really pleased and relieved that the investigation was over. I wanted to ask Travis what he planned to do about Amanda Ladd, but I didn't dare. I didn't want to disrupt the positive mood between him and Paula.

"Maybe you should take a nap while we're gone, Mom. You look a little tired today," Travis said as he put his arm around my shoulder.

"I promise you that I will rest a little after I make that call to Kilgore. I'll need the rest to prepare for the Library Friends meeting tonight."

"Do you have to go to that meeting tonight? Couldn't someone else sub for you?" he asked. "Paula even mentioned that you looked tired. She thought that taking care of Trent and Tricia might have been too difficult for you. I told her a little of what's been going on here---about Anson Kerringer and Deputy Dawge and the library. I realize now that I should have been here more to help you handle all of these problems."

"Honey, I don't know that your being here would have made things too much easier. I know that this is your vacation time, and I wanted you to have some fun while you were here." I soothed his conscience that was obviously trying to deal with his issues.

"Travis, I do need to attend this meeting. Lacy has offered to ramrod a big fund-raising yard sale for us. I have to introduce the plan and report on what progress we've made toward setting it up. Why don't you watch something on TV while you wait for Paula? Right now, I must make that call to Kilgore before I lose my nerve. I'm afraid Kilgore World might implode over this latest problem."

"What is it, Mom?"

"Travis, I'll tell you about it tomorrow," I said laughing. "I do not want to think about it anymore today, once I pass the problem on to Kilgore, poor man." I slowly picked up the phone, shaking my head. Kilgore took a few rings to answer his end of the call.

"Addie, it's good to hear from you. I meant to call earlier today to set up another appointment with you. We need to go over that tile for the backsplash. Have you chosen another selection?"

"I am so sorry, Kilgore, but I haven't made it to Moore Décor yet," I apologized. Truthfully, I completely forgot that little detail.

"Do not give it another thought, Addie, because I found another solution. Well actually, my wife, Sara, was the one who located the tile. You see, we sometimes deal with suppliers in Houston as well as Dallas. A supplier in Houston had enough of the tile that you originally chose to be able to do your backsplash. It isn't a large amount of tile, after all. Since the pattern is discontinued, we were able to buy at a substantial discount."

"That's wonderful news, Kilgore," I said, realizing that this might make the ordering error on the dishwasher less distressful. "Did Marty Gastbend call you concerning the dishwasher?"

"He did, Addie, but thank you for also wanting to confirm the delivery. That should move things along more smoothly when the new countertop arrives."

"I'm sorry to be the one to tell you this, Kilgore, but there's nothing to do except say it right out." I took a breath and plunged ahead before Kilgore could voice any more assurances. "The dishwasher is the wrong model. Ernie Plott checked it, and what came is the top-loading model."

I could almost hear Kilgore's teeth grinding over the phone. "You are not to worry, Addie. We still have time to get this corrected before the countertop arrives. I currently have some leeway in my schedule because Mrs. Laurin is rethinking the details of her project."

"Viveca is changing her plans?" I queried.

"She thinks that the death of Anson Kerringer might change the scope of her remodel. Ms. Laurin thinks that she may change some of her material choices, and she wants to make definite plans before we start. She may need to consult with Mrs. Kerringer before finalizing anything, you understand."

"I certainly do, Kilgore. I certainly do understand."

CHAPTER 22

By the time I reached the Community Center for the Friends meeting, I felt fairly rested and ready to host the event. The news about the Yard Sale was going to be exciting for the members, I was sure. We needed all of the money that we could raise. I debated with myself and decided that the less said about Anson Kerringer the better. The Friends should concentrate on library matters.

Although I thought that I would be the first person early at the meeting, Lottie and the Hamiltons were there before me setting up. They all rode in Lottie's van since she was bringing all of the refreshments. I was doubly pleased that Lottie was not only participating but also volunteering. I took this as a positive sign that she might overcome her difficulty with joining the Friends.

"You certainly have outdone yourself, Lottie." I couldn't help praising her efforts effusively. "How did you have time to bake brownies, cupcakes, cookies, and make finger sandwiches?"

"Walter helped me ice the cupcakes," Lottie preened. "Of course, he ate three of them, so I hope that the count doesn't fall short."

"Not to worry," chortled Marolly Hamilton. "Some of our members are dieting and may not opt for a frosted cupcake."

"Yes, Lottie. They'll probably pig out on the cookies instead," I laughed, trying to ease my friend's concerns.

When Tom and Marolly went to Lottie's van to fetch a couple of floral centerpieces, I quickly explained to Lottie that a deputy had gotten the detective's report (minus the envelope with Kissie's address) and that I would tell her what Augie was doing about it later. Lottie was impatient to know more, but Tom and Marolly returned too quickly.

Members filtered in and the meeting proceeded in an orderly fashion. The members didn't disappoint me in their reception of the plans for the Yard Sale. Lacy received a standing ovation. Seven members offered to rent booth spaces, and many more volunteered to work at the sale. Velma Plott offered to collect paperback books to resell in a booth for the Library, and Lottie proposed to host a bake sale in the same booth.

I was pleased to report that I obtained tentative approval from the Superintendent to use the school grounds and to remove parts of the proposed walls marked with Xs. No one mentioned Anson Kerringer, but several people did ask me how my kitchen remodel was going. I told each of them that the mess was difficult to handle and that seemed to satisfy them. 'Why go into the more unfortunate details?' I thought.

Getting into my car after helping clean and lock up, I saw that I had a phone call from Augie Dawge during the meeting. The unpredictable early-April weather was getting chilly again, so I decided to return the call while the car warmed up. I waved to Lottie as her van pulled out of the lot and onto the Boulevard. Then I punched electronic buttons to tell the phone to redial Augie's call. I hoped the car would warm up quickly because I forgot to bring a jacket or sweater.

"Deputy Augie Dawge," came Augie's voice in my ear.

"Augie, this is Addie," I replied as the passenger door on my car was flung open and Viv Laurin slid into the passenger seat---with a gun pointed directly at me!

"Put the phone down," Viv demanded.

I slowly lowered the phone and set it in one of the cup holders on the center console. "Viveca," I shrieked. "Why are you pointing a gun at me? What do you want?" I grabbed the steering wheel, shaking with fear and the chill in the car.

"Put the car in gear and drive," Viv demanded.

"What?" I asked, trying frantically to think. My brain cells seemed to be as frozen as my hands were on the steering wheel.

"I said, put the car in gear and drive," Viveca demanded once more with increased volume and emphasis.

My brain cells thawed enough to move to the gear shift. The car lurched a mite as my shaking hand popped the lever into reverse.

"Carefully," Viv ordered, waving the gun at me.

I eased my Jeep out of the parking space and crept over to the exit onto the Boulevard. "Turn right!" Viv commanded. I put on my blinker and turned onto the roadway heading right, opposite to the direction and the safety of my home. I drove slowly away from the miniscule business area, passing the shops across the street in Twin Oaks Plaza. Only the Handy Sack had lights showing and a few cars parked on the lot.

"Where are we going, Viv?" I asked.

"Just drive. I'll tell you where to turn."

"We missed you at the Friends meeting tonight," I said to calm my brain cells that were frantically yelling *Turn back! Turn back!* "Tom and Marolly Hamilton brought some beautiful flower arrangements from their garden to decorate the tables. The Community Center looked really lovely."

"What do I care for flower arrangements?" laughed Viv. "You are such a goody goody. Turn right at the next corner."

"Do you mean Crockett Drive?" I asked to be sure I didn't make a wrong turn and upset her more. The next turn to the right was Crockett Drive, and it was almost a mile further on 150A.

"Crockett Drive is the next corner, isn't it?" She seemed to sneer at me as if she was saying *how dense can you be.*

When I reached the next street, I slowed the Jeep, put on my blinker, and made the turn. My brain, at this point, seemed to lapse into nervous giggling. I gave it a mental slap to get my focus back. I needed to say something. Do something. "Why are you doing this, Viv? What have I done that has you basically kidnapping me and pointing a gun at me?" My voice seemed to want to yell at her while I was trying my best to calm down.

"You shredded all of my carefully laid plans. Don't try to deny it! You started your insipid little kitchen project and monopolized all of Kilgore's time. He should have been working on my house so that I could sell it quickly and move on to Grand Cayman. I could be on easy street with the money from the sale of my investments and my house and Anson's money from Sendero Gardens."

"You took the money that was missing---the one hundred and eighty thousand dollars?"

"I saw it in the safe. Anson shouldn't have made it so easy," Viv crowed. "Can you believe it? The combination was 2-4-6-8! Who puts a load of money in a safe with a combination so simplistic. Anson was never cautious. He made it so easy for me to see the numbers when he punched them into the keypad. Anson was begging to have that money stolen, and I was more than willing to oblige him." She seemed self-satisfied.

"Slow down! The road is too curvy to go so fast," Viv ordered and I complied. "Of course, it's all your fault that rotten road still is going to be straightened."

"What do you mean?"

"I made permanently sure that Anson Kerringer couldn't put that road through---a little oleander in his hot coffee to stop him cold. But you had to get the company reopened. At Shapely Woman Spa, Mavis Corcoran told everyone within earshot that you were responsible for Kissy reopening the office. Now *that cow* Anson was married to will put in the road---probably in his memory." Viv gave a macabre laugh that caused me to shiver more. "The Anson Kerringer Memorial Highway, monument to a total scumbag."

'Try to keep from exciting her,' my brain cells cried out. 'I just want to keep her sane,' I mentally replied.

"Slow down more. We're going to turn up here soon."

'Oh, no!' my brain panicked again. "We're going off the main road?"

"Slow down more," Viv fussed, and I actually was ready to go as slow as I could manage. Better yet, I wanted to stop altogether and leave this scene and this mentally deranged woman behind. She could have the Jeep.

"I don't remember a road along here," I said. "Maybe we missed it. We could go back---"

"No! Stop running off at the mouth and watch for some silver streamers of Christmas tinsel," Viv yelled harshly.

'Fat chance I'm going to watch for that tinsel,' I thought. 'I wouldn't tell you if I saw them. I'll just move on by and never mention them.'

"Stop the car! Now!" she shouted. I slammed on the brakes which didn't disturb much since I was creeping along. "On the left---there---turn to the right side of that post with the tinsel hanging on it," instructed Viv with a wave of the gun.

"I don't see a road there," I whined.

"You're driving a Jeep. We're going to do a little off-roading," she laughed her manic laugh again.

I put on my blinker although no one else seemed to be on Crockett Drive with us. Slowly I turned toward the side of the tinsel-adorned post that Viveca Laurin indicated. As my headlights swept over the tall grass, I could barely make out a dirt-covered culvert over the drainage ditch and a somewhat rutty, two-lane track heading into the live oak trees and scrub brush. I clicked the lights up to high beam as I crept slowly forward, straining to see this nearly invisible track while trying to avoid the rocks, bushes, and especially the trees.

"Stop!" Viv yelled and I gladly complied. "You almost hit a tree!"

"I can see that now," I grumped, staring at the trunk of a huge, sprawling live oak that had suddenly loomed in front of the Jeep. I waited for Her Royal Nuttiness to figure out where we were.

"I think that we turn right at this tree," she said a bit uncertainly.

"Are you sure?" I asked.

"Yes, I'm sure," she sneered. "Bear to the right."

My frightened brain cells conjured a rearing grizzly bear with sharp teeth and long claws, ready to maul that gun right out of her hand. I carefully eased the car around the tree to the right, searching with one eye for the track and with the other for more tree trunks.

There, I could see it to the right of a small boulder protruding from the ground... the track, not a tree. This section was ruttier and the Jeep waddled along at the pace of an inch worm. "Did you find this place when you were showing land to some client?" I asked. I gritted my teeth and mentally apologized to the Jeep as we hit a particularly deep rut.

"No, Addie dear. I found this place when I needed to get rid of my worthless sleaze of a husband two years ago. Watch that tree on the right!" I managed to veer enough to miss a tree that had multiple chipped places where it had been hit. "I've dinged my SUV on that tree four times already, including the night that I buried the remains of that dirtbag and his luggage. Can you believe it? He was going to take off for Brazil and leave me. He and that lowlife Glorie Shovenhower."

I peered through the gloom and inched along as Viveca continued her rant. "People in town gossiped that he was seeing Carla Mott, but he only took her to dinner a couple of nights. Clark wanted to sell her a big life insurance policy. He thought widows were likely targets for that kind of policy. I knew that his real affair was with Glorie Shovenhower."

"Who?" My brain didn't recognize the name. It was too busy helping me concentrate on the path ahead and trying desperately not to think about the ominous gun pointed at me. That gun seemed as huge as a cannon!

"Glorie Shovenhower. She's Glorie Helvig now. What a name! Big improvement, huh?" Viv almost cackled. "You may not know her since she lives at Willem Club. You're not very popular at Willem Club these days, are you? I didn't mind helping that along Miss Nosybody."

Viv shifted in her seat, and I let my eye flick momentarily to the gun. She was holding it firmly and keeping it pointed at me! "You should have put your little kitchen project aside and let me get on with my remodel, but no matter. I've sold my house for a very good price to a buyer from California with plenty of cash to pay. We close on it in two weeks, and I will be off to Grand Cayman to relax for a while."

We exited the trees into an area that was flat, sandy dirt, and fairly flat limestone rock. The track almost disappeared because of the rocks and the Jeep snaked along now with only a small bump or two every few feet. "You'll be sad to know that we'll soon be there, Addie. We'll soon arrive at your point of total disappearance. Of course, you'll have my cheating, sleazebag husband's remains for company. Maybe the two of you could fly off and haunt Brazil together!" Her laugh sounded more bizarre than the last.

"Stop here!" yelled Viv.

I stopped. Looking around, I could scarcely make out that we were close to some large trees at the edge of the flat area. What I could see clearly by the headlights on my car was a shovel leaning against the large trunk of a live oak tree.

"Leave the lights on and get out!" Viv insisted. I might argue with *her*, but I wasn't going to argue with *her gun*. Carefully, I got out of the Jeep and closed the door. The night chill almost made my teeth chatter. "You see that shovel? You're going to do a little digging. In front of the car where I can see you."

I walked over to the shovel and for a nanosecond, I thought of making a dive behind the tree. But my eyes were adjusting to the dark and I could make out that there was open ground all around this small cluster of trees. No chance to run or hide.

"Quit stalling. Get over here and dig," Viv ordered.

I tried the ground much closer to the front of the car, but it was hard and the shovel thunked a rock. I moved a little further toward the trees once again, and the ground was a little softer. 'Maybe an underground spring is near these trees,' I thought. My quaking brain cells instantly produced the image of a huge torrent spraying from the ground and knocking the gun from Viveca Laurin's clutching hand.

In what seemed like half an hour but probably was only ten minutes, my digging hadn't turned much dirt, but the ground was getting softer as the hole became wider and a little deeper. "This ground is so hard, I could be digging half the night," I grumbled.

"Don't worry about that, Addie dear. You'll have all of eternity to rest," she laughed.

At least the laugh wasn't the Nutsy Woman laugh from our drive to this place. I said a fervent prayer to God for assistance from this terrible predicament which I somehow felt that I had created. "Please. Please," I kept whispering as the hole got deeper. "Please help me, Lord."

Suddenly headlights appeared across the expanse of dirt and rock which my Jeep had recently crossed. "Who is that?" Viv shrieked. The Queen of Nuttiness was back! The headlights seemed to prowl stealthily across the flatland, coming toward us slowly but surely. Then they stopped for a few minutes, poised like a stalking cat ready to strike! Viv and I were transfixed watching this incursion of a strange vehicle which was now moving forward again.

With a lurch, the headlights sped up and tore across the rocky turf like a demon possessed. Viveca moved over to the darker area by the driver's door and behind the glow of the headlights, watching as the speeding vehicle bore down on us. Boing! The flat blade of a dirty shovel slammed into the back of her head! She pitched forward, hitting her forehead on the back, passenger door. The gun flew away from the Jeep into the rocks and tall grass.

The charging vehicle slammed to a stop, both front doors flew open, and a female voice rang out, "Sheriff's Deputy! Drop your gun and get your hands up. We've got you covered!"

"I dropped the dirty shovel, raised my hands, and moved closer to the headlights. "Don't shoot. It's just me," my quivering voice called. "Addie Girard. I think that my captor is unconscious. Hopefully she's only stunned."

The owner of the voice came forward wearing a housedress and fuzzy house slippers and carrying a very large, double-barrel shotgun. From the passenger side of the vehicle came the hulking bulk of Deputy Augie Dawge, also well-armed. I put my hands to my face and started crying in relief and limitless joy!

CHAPTER 23

The *female deputy* voice belonged to a very outraged Twila Dawge. "Twila is a provisional deputy that the department can call when we need extra help," explained Augie as he got into the squad car. He said that someone had to go back to Crockett Drive to watch for the ambulance. Augie turned the car slowly toward the dirt track.

"We were cleaning up after supper," Twila explained, "when your call came up on the phone. Augie looked shocked and yelled *grab your gun, Twila. Addie's in trouble!* I grabbed my shotgun, and we ran for the squad car. He handed me the phone, and I listened to your directions while he drove."

"My directions?" I was totally puzzled. We were waiting by my Jeep for the ambulance to arrive for Viveca Laurin. "How could I give you any directions?"

"You didn't disconnect the call, and we could hear most of your conversation in the car. You were very clever to ask Viveca Laurin to explain where she told you to turn," complimented Twila. "We were able to follow you once we got to Crockett Drive. Letting us know that you were starting from the Friends meeting at the Community Center in Wanderwood helped us get our bearings."

"I didn't even know that I did or said those things," I sighed pulling my blanket closer around my shivering body. I was huddled in my emergency blanket that I had retrieved from the back of the Jeep. Viveca was still lying on the ground by the Jeep, covered with a blanket from the squad car. She had not regained consciousness yet, but Augie had handcuffed her anyway. *Just to be sure*, he told us.

I truly hoped that Viv would regain consciousness soon. I knew that I hit her pretty hard with that shovel. "When Viv wakes up, she may deny everything that you heard, and that I heard," I told Twila. "We don't have much evidence to prove that she kidnapped me or that she did any of the other things that she confessed to me."

"Augie hit *record* on the phone as we left the house, so we have the whole conversation recorded. Augie was afraid that we might have to play the call back if we missed one of your directions. Besides, deciding to kidnap you won't be Viveca's biggest issue," Twila scoffed. "She confessed to the murder of her husband, Clark Laurin."

"But do you think that you'll be able to find his body after two years?" I questioned looking around at the clump of trees and the open ground surrounding it. "This is a lot of open land around these trees."

"We'll find him," Twila said with assurance. "We'll be out here with metal detectors and borrow some cadaver dogs from Austin or San Antonio. You can bet we'll find him."

"You don't have a very large Sheriff's Department staff in Evritt County."

"We also can maybe borrow some students from the Criminal Justice Department at Texas State University in San Marcos. They are always looking for chances to get practical experience," Twila explained away my doubt. "Oh, yes. We'll find him. And when we do, Ms. Laurin is going to be up to her platinum earrings in trouble."

"I apologize for interrupting your evening, but I'm awfully glad that you came to rescue me."

"You didn't seem to need much rescuing, Addie. You appear to be a very resourceful woman," Twila disputed. I took that as her way of saying *you're welcome*.

After about five minutes of waiting around while the Provisional Deputy looked over the immediate area, Twila located Viv's weapon where it landed about ten feet away. I checked on Viveca Laurin once more. I was tired of standing by the car shivering and opened a car door to sit down.

"Addie, I want to thank you for helping Augie and me through the past couple of weeks. This was his first official case, and I hope it will be his last. Fighting crime is way too disruptive to our home life," concluded Twila.

"I do feel bad for the deputies who have to do this kind of work on a regular basis," I agreed.

"In Evritt County, the deputies mostly have to deal with speeders or drunk drivers or somebody's lost child or pet," said Twila. "If it only had been one of those, I think Augie could have managed---but murder?"

"Hopefully these problems soon will be over," I sighed. 'Thank you, Lord,' I thought.

"Thanks to your help, Augie has a suspect in custody for Anson Kerringer's murder and a solution for a cold case of a missing person, Clark Laurin. You made him look awfully good, Addie."

"Don't forget my kidnapping. You should be really proud of Augie. He worked very hard and tried his best to follow procedure and solve the crimes," I said, sighing again in relief. "Who knew that a huge crime spree would break out as soon as the Sheriff and the main part of the force left town." We both had to laugh at that thought.

At last we saw lights of the squad car returning followed by an ambulance. "Oh, no!" Twila moaned.

"What now?" I questioned.

"Addie, I just realized that someone will have to be on guard at the hospital tonight since we will have a prisoner there," Twila explained. If Augie stations a deputy in the hospital, we won't have anyone left to patrol the county."

"Well, it's not like Evritt County will have another *crime spree*. Maybe the county could do without being patrolled for one night," I joked. "And remember that Sheriff Post will be back tomorrow."

"Amen," said Twila.

I was amazed that my Jeep handled the rough terrain without suffering any damage, other than a slight dent in the back, passenger door where Viveca Laurin fell into it. With relief, I headed home after promising Twila that I would make an appointment to give another official statement about tonight's events. I promised myself that I would make that statement during daytime hours when the department steno would be working.

My Jeep was the last vehicle in the parade that crept across the wide stretch of dirt and rock to finally weave its way back through the trees, boulders, and brush. As I slowly made the turn off the blacktop of Crockett Drive and onto RM 150A turning toward the center of Wanderwood, I realized that my hands were gripping the steering wheel like extremely tightened clamps.

The turn onto the Boulevard should have helped me relax, but it didn't. I watched in my rearview mirror as the ambulance and the squad car sped away from me in the opposite direction on RM150A, lights flashing and sirens wailing. I guided the Jeep into Twin Oaks Plaza by the Trinity Street entrance. Then I stopped under the parking lot lights in front of the Handy Sack that was now definitely closed for the night. Next, I made sure that all of the car doors were locked tight.

I sat for a few minutes, shaking in spite of the warmth oozing from my vehicle's heater. Then the tears started to flow---again. While the ambulance crew checked Viveca Laurin when she was at last fully conscious, I found myself quietly crying for no apparent reason. The ambulance crew checked me as well for injuries or shock, but I bravely insisted that I was all right.

Now I was sitting in a parking lot, shaking and crying. I obviously was not all right. I had the fright of my life tonight. The realization of how desperate my situation had been swept over me. I pushed my mind to think of home and safety. I wanted to think of anything but that awful time with Viveca Laurin pointing a loaded gun at me.

'Home!!!' My feeble brain at last showed up from wherever it had been cowering and shook me back into the moment. "George, now what am I going to tell Travis? He's been warning me to be careful, and I didn't take his words seriously. Yes, I know that I'll have to tell him what happened. Yes, I know that I need to be careful when I explain it. And, George? Thank you for answering me. Yes, it is a difficult time."

I put the Jeep into gear and pointed it toward home. Sometimes it was a nuisance to have George's voice rattling around in my head. But other times, like now, it could be a great comfort.

Travis and Paula were pacing the floor when I entered the house. Lottie and Walter were there, too. "Mom, where were you?" my upset son demanded. "You should have called to let us know that you were running late." My words to Travis during his thoughtless teenage years came back to scold me. "We were really worried."

I couldn't help myself. I started laughing. It made no sense, but I was laughing. Lottie was eyeing me suspiciously. "I'm sorry," I finally managed to say. I knew that this was more reaction to the traumatic evening that I had, but that realization didn't help much.

"Addie, why don't you sit over here on the sofa," said Lottie. "I'll get you a Dr. Pepper, and we'll talk." My good friend opened the door of the hulking white refrigerator, pulled out a can, popped the top, and handed it to me. "Why don't we all sit down and calm down for a moment." She gave Travis a look that sent him scurrying to the loveseat with Paula taking the seat beside him. Lottie sat by me on the sofa. Walter gravitated to the recliner.

I sipped. Looked around at the expectant, concerned faces. And sipped again. The normalcy of the drink and sitting in my own living room did make me feel a little better...a little more secure. "I'm sorry that I caused you to be anxious, all of you, and thank you for helping us out again, Lottie. Walter. This was a very difficult evening, but I am going to try to tell you about it." The tears started to well up again, but I worked to hold them back.

Lottie patted my back softly. "What happened, Addie?" she asked more gently than I'd ever heard her speak to me.

"I---I was kidnapped," I said simply.

"What?" came four surprised voices.

I took another sip and proceeded with my explanation. "After the Friends meeting, Viveca Laurin got into my Jeep and pointed a gun at me. Viv kidnapped me, and forced me to drive to a place outside of town."

The faces around me looked, first, rather shocked and perplexed. Then their expressions shifted back to concern. "Well, why ever did she do that?" asked Lottie for all of them.

"Viveca stole the one hundred and eighty thousand dollars," I said.

"What one hundred and eighty thousand dollars?" asked Travis, seeming thoroughly confused.

"Anson Kerringer's missing money. The Sendero Gardens missing money," answered Lottie which didn't answer much for Travis or Paula.

"What is Sendero Gardens?" asked Paula.

"I think that Sendero Gardens is a project name that Anson set up so that he could siphon off money from his business and deduct the money as a business expense. His wife, Kissie, told us that Anson did this to hide money away in secret stashes. His cash for a rainy day, I suppose. We'll likely never know what his plans were for that money. Viv found out about the money and managed to steal it from his office safe. She told me tonight that she had taken it."

"Well, were we wrong about Benny Olesford? Did Viveca Laurin actually kill Anson Kerringer?" queried Lottie.

"Tonight, Viveca told me that she permanently kept Anson from putting in the new RM150A by adding a little oleander to his coffee." My nerves were calming down a fraction. "However, Viv also confessed to killing her husband, Clark Laurin, two years ago."

"She killed Clark Laurin?" Walter asked in disbelief. "I played golf with Clark. He was a regular guy, a member of Kiwanis. You mean that Clark never left town to go off to Brazil?"

"Clark told Viv that he was leaving her, and she killed him. Then she buried him on some ranch property that she thought would never be disturbed. It probably wouldn't have been disturbed if Anson Kerringer hadn't decided to put a road there," I explained.

"The new RM 150A," said Lottie.

"It seems that the proposed roadway is what set this horrendous series of events into motion," I agreed.

"Actually, Clark's death," said Walter with surprising insight. "If he hadn't been buried in that field---"

"Then none of the rest might have happened," Lottie finished the thought.

"Even before that. If Clark hadn't decided to close his insurance office and run off to Brazil with Glorie Shovenhower, he might be alive today," I added.

"A domino effect," Lottie summed up the narrative. "Because of the want of a horseshoe nail---"

"Two people are dead," I stated.

"That's why married couples should stay together," Travis said, "and be supportive of each other." He took Paula's hand and they both smiled.

I smiled, too. My little family world once more seemed to be in sync with the universe at large.

Lottie interrupted the moment with a question. "Well, if you were kidnapped by Viveca Laurin, how did you escape? We need details. You can't sit here and say that you were kidnapped without telling all."

"I was rescued by Deputies Augie Dawge and Twila Dawge. Did you know that Twila Dawge was some kind of provisional deputy, Lottie?"

"I never knew that, Addie. Are you sure?" I couldn't believe that I was telling Lottie something that she didn't know about Evritt County and the people in it.

"Maybe you could start from the Friends meeting and explain it all to us, Mom," suggested Paula. "I'm starting to feel that I need a program to know who all of the players are."

I sipped a little more Dr. Pepper and then started the narrative over more slowly. The story seemed short compared to the actual events. When I was driving Viv Laurin through that dark woods in my Jeep, the episode seemed much longer. As I was almost finished, Tricia wandered down the stairs and said, 'Gammy, are you home?"

CHAPTER 24

All of my family slept late on Friday morning, at least as late as two noisy children would allow. For once, none of Kilgore's crew showed up to work on the kitchen. The activity of preparing breakfast for Trent and Tricia helped to push back the terror of the previous evening. Thoughts of that ordeal were positively surreal in my memory. Oatmeal from the microwave topped with brown sugar, warm milk, and banana slices caused me to feel rather virtuous in the care-giving department and definitely more grandmotherly.

Paula was helping me clear up the disposable paper bowls, plastic spoons, and paper cups when the doorbell sounded. On my front porch stood Sheriff Bishop Post who, upon his return to duty, had wasted no time before taking charge of the murder investigation. I had never met Sheriff Post and was surprised by his appearance.

Sheriff Post was no taller than me and wiry, almost thin. 'He must have his uniforms custom made,' I thought. "How else could he find any to fit him. Did they sell law enforcement uniforms in the Juniors Department?' That uniform was crisply starched and ironed. His hair was medium brown and curly atop a very oriental, sunburned face, somewhat shaded by his uniform cap. Apparently, the indoor seminars did not take up all of his time in Corpus Christi.

"Adelaide Bonner Girard?" he said as soon as I opened the door.

"Yes, I am Addie Girard," I replied.

"I'm Sheriff Bishop Post, and I need for you to come with me at once," he stated.

"What is the rush, Sheriff?" asked Travis, standing behind me.

"I am investigating the death of Anson Kerringer, an investigation that has been thoroughly confused by Officer Dawge. I need to take your official statement covering what happened the day you found Anson Kerringer's body."

I noticed with consternation that his police car was parked across the end of my driveway with the lights flashing. "Sheriff Post, I have already given my official statement. I really have nothing to add to what I stated earlier when the matter was fresh in my mind." I was sure that some of my nearby neighbors were already on their phones calling friends to report on the Sheriff's visit to my house.

"This is an urgent matter, Ms. Girard," the Sheriff insisted.

"If you thought it was so urgent and important," I countered, "why didn't you return from Corpus Christi to handle the investigation personally? Or why didn't you, at least, send one of your trained detectives back early to do the job?"

"My officers and I were in Corpus Christi for an extremely important law enforcement conference. Evritt County provides support for our staff to improve their skills and interact with other law enforcement groups from around the country."

"No doubt the conference was a well-earned opportunity for your officers, but I fail to see how that translates into a need for me to rush off to Handlen. As I said, you already have my official statement which took up quite a few hours of my time and inconvenienced my neighbor, Lottie Frisham, as well. I might consider making an appointment for some time later to review my statement. Possibly I could drive to Handlen on Monday."

"I must insist that you accompany me now, Ms. Girard," said the Sheriff, sounding somewhat threatening.

"Sheriff Post, this investigation has already taken up a lot of my time over the past couple of weeks. Anson Kerringer was killed well over a week ago, so that *need-for-urgency* ship sailed many days back. My son, daughter-in-law, and grandchildren are visiting only through tomorrow. I plan to spend the next two days with my family." I knew that I was on slippery ground, but I was tired from stress and lack of sleep.

"Unless you are prepared to officially arrest me now and chance being sued for false arrest, I will not be accompanying you to Handlen or anywhere else. Set an appointment time for Monday, and I will drive myself to Handlen." I was determined to be firm and not to be bullied by the officer who was so obviously in the wrong, at least in my mind.

"I told you, Ms. Girard. The timing is urgent. We need you at Handlen now--today!" The man was not only stubborn but adamant in his demand. "We must wrap this case up while we still have our two suspects in custody."

"Two suspects?" I asked.

"Deputy Augie Dawge says that you were helping him with the case which never should have happened," Sheriff Post said. "You are not an employee of the Evritt County Sheriff's Department. However, after last night's incident, we need for you to help us sort out the evidence. We do not have your official statement for what happened last night."

Lottie chose this time to stroll up the street with what looked like some of her bear project in a clear plastic bag. I was relieved to have another witness to this exchange with the very officious sheriff. Bishop Post appeared to think that everyone should drop whatever they were doing and accede to his demands.

"Addie," called Lottie, ignoring Sheriff Post altogether. "Do you have a few minutes to go over these bears? I'm having a real problem with some of the ones that Margaret Jewitt started. Maybe you could look at them and explain to me what Margaret was thinking when she decided to sew them this way."

"I don't have too much time today, Lottie," I said, knowing full well that Lottie did not require instructions from me no matter what she was saying. "I maybe could take five to ten minutes to look at them, but I have plans to go to New Braunfels with Travis and Paula. Schlitterbahn is open for a three-day weekend, and I want to take Trent and Tricia for a family outing." I was totally making this last part up because I had yet to discuss the possible trek to Schlitterbahn with Travis or Paula.

"Yoo-hoo! Addie!" called Marolly Hamilton as she crossed from her front yard to my front yard. "Do you have time to talk with Tom about the scheduling for the painting project at the school? Also, he's wanting the phone numbers of those new volunteers that signed up for the project. He hopes that you have the list with you at home."

"Lottie. Marolly. Do you know Sheriff Bishop Post? He's finally back from Corpus Christi. Sheriff Post is taking over the investigation of Anson Kerringer's murder," I announced loudly to my two friends and whatever other neighbors might be listening inside the open windows of their houses.

"Well, it's about time!" Lottie said. "Poor Deputy Augie Dawge has been working his tail off trying to cover for you and your absent investigators, Sheriff. We all have been surprised by what a good job he's done under difficult circumstances. You must be really pleased that Deputy Dawge nearly has this case wrapped up for you."

"Oh, my, I must say," agreed Marolly. "Deputy Dawge certainly has been extremely industrious trying to question so many witnesses and separate suspects from innocent persons like Addie and Mavis Corcoran. Do you think that he'll get a commendation for his hard work with so little help?"

Sheriff Post seemed flustered by all of the neighborly input and interest that his visit generated.

"Ms. Girard," he managed to say, pulling himself together. "I will expect to see you at my office in Handlen by four o'clock today. Monday simply will not suffice." This statement made, the sheriff turned sharply and stomped over to his flashing vehicle. We could scarcely keep from laughing as we watched him turn the car and head back along Serenity Lane.

"Mom," suggested Travis. "Maybe Schlitterbahn is a bit too adult level for Trent and Tricia."

"I hope you don't mind," said Paula from behind Travis. "Possibly we could find an activity that would be a little easier on the children."

"I don't mind at all," I laughed. "It was merely a thought of something to do. I didn't have any definite trip scheduled. Take some time and think what we might like to do with the children today."

"Addie, I actually do need to have you look at these bears and tell me what Margaret has done. They may all be ruined and useless if we can't figure out a remedy," Lottie said holding up the bag.

"We'll take a little time and look them over," I assured her. "And I'll get that list for Tom as well. There's no rush---now."

My family and neighbors all segued back into my house which looked like two active children were playing there. Between the laughter of the adults and the squeals of two playing children in the living room, chaos reigned for the moment. I retrieved the volunteer list for Tom Hamilton and gave it to Marolly after marking some possible volunteers to call for painting.

"Mom, maybe painting could be a good family activity for today," Travis suggested. "Paula and I have some practice in painting the walls at our home. I haven't been much help to you on your library project. We were talking yesterday, and we wanted to do something to make that up to you."

"That's very sweet of you both." I said and gave them each a very sincere hug. "What do you think, Marolly? Is Tom planning to paint today?"

"Tom is planning to paint every day this week and the next, until we get all of the painting done," Marolly laughed. "That's why he's looking for more volunteers. Tom would like to have enough done so that we can give tours of the building during the yard sale. He believes that will encourage more county-wide participation." Marolly looked over the list.

"We got a text this morning that Kilgore's second construction crew took out the walls that needed demolition yesterday. Tom went to the building to check things out. He reported to me that Kilgore's crew were amazingly good at cleaning up the mess. They even framed the ends of the walls so that you can hardly tell that the missing sections of walls were ever there. I think that Kilgore is doing this to make up for the problems on your kitchen. The walls are all set to be painted."

"I can't wait to see how that came out," enthused Lottie. "I wasn't too sure about converting the building to a library at first, but now I can see your vision. That school building has a lot of history. It influenced a lot of children who are grown now. I'm glad to see that it can continue serving some of those former students."

"We are very glad to have you on board, Lottie, because you are such a great asset to any project. I'm not saying that simply because we've picked up a bunch more volunteers since you joined the effort." I knew that I was telling the truth and speaking for everyone in the Friends group.

"Well, speaking of projects, Addie, please take time to look at Margaret's bears and help me figure how to salvage them. She got one of those fancy new sewing machines, and I think that she was trying all of the different embroidery stitches around the edges."

I looked at the printed bear cutouts. The images were inside out facing each other as they should be, but Margaret Jewitt had sewn completely around each set using various machine embroidery stitches as Lottie described. She left no opening for turning and stuffing the bears. Apparently, she had done this with all of her bear cutouts.

"Lottie," Marolly mused, turning one of the bears in her hand, "If you pick out some of the stitching at the bottom of each bear and run a row of straight stitching around inside the machine embroidery stitching, I think that you would be able to turn and stuff them. That will no doubt be tedious extra work, but it could be done. In fact, I could help you do that on Monday afternoon. I have garden club on Monday morning, but I'm free after that."

"I could surely use your help," said Lottie. "Addie said earlier that she would be available on Monday, too. We could get together around one-thirty at my house if that fits your schedules."

"One-thirty. I'm in," I agreed.

"Then one-thirty it is," said Marolly. "I will see you later at the school building, Addie. Wear old clothes."

When Marolly was gone, I hit Lottie up to go to Handlen with me to find out what Sheriff Bishop Post really wanted. Travis and Paula were getting the children changed for our trip to the school to paint. "There is safety in numbers, Lottie, and I don't trust that man enough to go there alone."

"I don't blame you, Addie," she concurred. "That pushy Sheriff wanted something from you, and we should be on our guard. He likes to throw his weight around, doesn't he?"

"He may be covering up for staying in Corpus when he should have been here," I proposed. "Perhaps he's looking for someone else to blame if he botches the investigation."

After painting walls till our arms and backs ached, I sent Travis and Paula home to have lunch and put the children down for their naps. Lottie and I headed for Handlen to have lunch at Essie's Diner and afterward to see Sheriff Bishop Post.

"It was his idea to bring us here," said Lottie, a bit miffed after we had waited on the hard benches of the reception area for over fifteen minutes. "You'd think that the Sheriff would not keep us waiting so long."

"Since Evritt County doesn't have much crime, I have to agree that it's probably his little power trip," I soothed. "In a small pond like Evritt County, an official could get the idea that he is a very big fish. He might forget the fact that he's an inconsequential county official in a small, inconsequential county."

"Ms. Girard, here at last!" boomed Sheriff Post's voice.

"Sheriff Post, here at last," I called out in reply.

"Come back to my office," he ordered, turning and stomping down the hallway behind him. Joyce Banyard, manning the reception counter, buzzed the wooden gate open, allowing us to follow the Sheriff. She gave us an apologetic look as we passed her desk.

The Sheriff's office was much nicer than the room where I had worked with Augie Dawge. Large oak desk. Framed certificates and pictures on the walls. Potted Ficus tree in the corner by a window. Oak file cabinet in another corner. Three chairs faced the front of Bishop Post's desk, and we selected two of them side by side. 'Safety in numbers,' I thought.

"What can we do for you, Sheriff?" I asked to break the silence which he seemed to let hang in the air.

"You've caused us a lot of problems, Ms. Girard," he boomed.

'Didn't he have an indoor voice?' My ears and tired brain cringed at the noise level in the closed room.

"Your meddling has left us with two...count them...two murder suspects with no way to prove which one is guilty. What do you have to say for yourself?"

I found that I had plenty to say for myself but somehow settled on one solitary, misguided question. "Do you suppose that you could do better if you had torn yourself away from your fun week on the beach?"

Lottie jumped into the conversation to save me from myself. "You should be glad that Addie was able to help you find two possible suspects since you weren't here to do the job." That statement didn't seem to help our situation.

"I would be within my rights to lock you up for obstruction of justice," the sheriff countered loudly.

"If you did that, you could kiss the Wanderwood vote goodbye in the next election, as well as the votes of all of their relatives who live in the county," Lottie stated calmly in a matter-of-fact tone. "You are an elected county official, are you not? And Adelaide Bonner Girard is a well-respected leader of the community and president of the Library Friends organization in Wanderwood. Her influence is widespread in this county." Evidently, Lottie could run a bluff as well as the most skilled poker player.

Sheriff Post altered his tone and said quietly, "Ms. Girard's influence doesn't seem to extend to the residents at Willem Club."

"They are a small handful of malcontents whom you might find needing to be investigated by you in the future." Lottie scoffed. "You should keep your eye on them. They may be the ones that you'll need to arrest down the road since some of them, like Viveca Laurin, seem to think that they are above the law."

"About Ms. Laurin," said Sheriff Post.

"She confessed to killing her husband, Clark Laurin, when she kidnapped me at gunpoint last night," I stated. "She also confessed to putting the distilled oleander into the coffee that killed Anson Kerringer. Deputy Dawge has that conversation recorded."

"Kidnap is a strong word that may not be easy to prove," said the sheriff.

"Murder is a strong word," I stated, "and finding Clark Laurin's body along with her confession on that recording should help you prove it."

"Yes," said Bishop Post slowly, "but that is not the case of the moment. The big problem for today is proving *Who killed Anson Kerringer?* Benny Olesford or Ms. Laurin?"

"Have you read the private detectives' surveillance report?" asked Lottie.

"At least twice," said the sheriff. "According to the detective, Benny Olesford was the last person to see Anson Kerringer alive."

"Maybe not," I disagreed. "Benny Olesford was in the office only for four minutes. Viveca Laurin was there for eighteen minutes at which time she says that she made the coffee and put the deadly oleander into the coffee. I am thinking that maybe Anson was already dead when Benny Olesford got to the office. That might be why Benny was in and out quickly."

"Where is the proof?" Bishop Post demanded, roaring with his outside voice once more.

"In Viv's recorded confession," I replied, remembering one thing that the realtor said the night before. "Viv said that she thought she made permanently sure Anson couldn't put through his road plan. Benny Olesford may not be the best witness that you could have. However, if you questioned him, and he could describe finding Anson Kerringer's body, then you could compare his description to your crime scene photos. With Benny's testimony, you would know and have a witness and proof that Viveca Laurin killed Anson."

"After a night in jail, Benny Olesford brought in a lawyer. As you might guess, on his lawyer's advice, he's not answering questions," Sheriff Post said perfunctorily.

"Then talk to the lawyer," interposed Lottie. "Convince him that it's in his client's best interest to answer questions if he didn't kill Anson Kerringer and doesn't want to be charged with the murder."

"I don't think that would work," said the sheriff.

"Who is his lawyer?" Lottie asked.

"Gifford Bradenton," he answered.

"Gifford's my cousin," Lottie announced to my surprise. "I'll speak to Gifford and let him know that his client needs to tell his story. Lest you should be concerned, I know not to tell him any of the details of your case. I'm sure that Gifford will listen to me."

'Small town life,' I thought. 'It works in mysterious ways.'

CHAPTER 25

Friday night was a real celebration when I was able to use my BOGO coupon from the Hays County Area-Wide Yard Sale. I was pleased to take Lottie and Walter to The Salt Lick restaurant by Driftwood, although we did travel in Lottie and Walter's gray van. My excellent Jeep, capable as it might be, was not large enough to carry seven passengers.

The Salt Lick had an indoor/outdoor rustic feel while they still served a first-class barbecue menu. The smoke from barbecuing beef, pork, chicken, and sausage hung faintly in the air, making our mouths water in anticipation. We were seated on chairs pulled up to a long picnic table on what appeared to be a porch that had been enclosed. Windows lined the walls and gave a pleasant view of the trees and bushes beyond.

All of us were determined not to waste our time talking about Anson Kerringer or Viveca Laurin. The library project, however, was fair game as well as talk about Paula's school and job. I thought that it was good for Travis to hear people giving some positive and encouraging views toward Paula's efforts.

"Lottie, I went by the workshop where Maxie Chalpers has been working on the donated chairs on Wednesday. Early on, the Friends changed their minds about staining and opted for painting the tables and chairs in various colors. The furnishings committee settled on red, blue, green, and yellow. All of the tables are red, and the yellow, blue, and green chairs around them look very cheerful," I said, visualizing the effect.

"The mix and match colors on the tables and chairs are quite striking and fun at the same time. I think that they will look really charming, especially in the open areas at the front of the building. She has a number of bookshelves that were donated as well, and Maxie painted those in the blue and red to match the chairs and tables."

"I still can't picture what that will look like," said Lottie.

"Maxie Chalpers has a great eye for form and color," Walter stated. "You can tell by her wood sculptures. The feed store made her a deal on the paint."

"I've been thinking that possibly someday soon I can talk Derald Markey, the owner of the *Evritt County Gazette*, into donating a page or even a half page ad," I proposed. "We need to recognize and thank all of the organizations and businesses in the community who helped make the library possible."

"Well, you can tell Derald an ad like that would be good for the *Gazette*," commented Lottie.

"Why would you think that?" asked Travis.

"Because everyone likes to see their name in the paper, and the ad would mention most of the people in the county or their organizations," explained Lottie. "That kind of thing sells papers."

"I suppose I could use that as an incentive when I talk to Derald Markey at the *Gazette*."

"Mom, you are so creative that you should write articles for the *Gazette*," offered Paula.

"Oh, no," protested Travis. "I think that Mom is at her limit in projects. In fact, I wouldn't mind seeing some of those projects completed and off her schedule. The past couple of weeks have been very stressful for her."

"I cannot argue with your logic, Travis," I said. "I am looking forward to my life returning to the peace and quiet for which I moved to Wanderwood in the first place."

Peace and quiet did reign in my household on Saturday morning except for the usual happy noise from a couple of active grandchildren. Kilgore, for some reason, decided to allow me another day off from the chaos and racket of construction. I was hoping that he hadn't surrendered on ever getting the project back on track. I assured him that I knew his work usually proceeded better than my remodel had done so far.

Lunch on Saturday found my family group once more at Lefty's Bar-B-Q. Lefty's special of the day was a broccoli, carrot, and cheese soup accompanying her popular pork chop smothered in an onion and walnut sauce. Walter, Bart, Lacy, and Lottie were with us around some center tables squeezed together for the event. Tom and Marolly Hamilton brought me a lovely vase of early roses from the blooms in their garden. Everyone was celebrating my salvation from the clutches of an oh-so-obviously mentally-disturbed Viveca Laurin (at least that seemed to be her current line of defense for her actions in my alleged kidnapping).

This was also a farewell luncheon for Travis, Paula, Trent, and Tricia. They would be leaving for Lubbock after church services the next day. I felt sad and glad about their leaving. I would miss them in two ways. I would feel sad that they were not with me, but I would be glad to finally get some rest. Looking after Tricia and Trent on top of my other ongoing activities had worn me out in spite of all the help that Lottie and Walter gave me.

"Addie, what will you do this week without your company and without so many things going on in your life?" asked Bart Tindal.

"Actually, Mom's life is still very busy," Travis answered for me. "Her kitchen is a mess, and I don't think the job will be finished next week as planned."

"Kilgore tells me that won't be a problem time-wise now that Viveca Laurin's project is cancelled," I said. "He now estimates that it will take at least two more weeks to finish the redo. I can't wait to finally hang my painting by Rebecca Ratleif in my updated kitchen."

"Viv cancelled her entire remodel?" questioned Bart.

"Viveca told me that she sold the house without the remodel to a couple from California with plenty of cash," I explained. "She said that she's doing the closing on the house in two weeks."

"Where do you think she'll live during the trial?" asked Lottie. "Harvey Lackie is her lawyer. I expect that he'll try to post bail to get her out of jail."

"Viveca's bail could be set pretty high," Lacy speculated. "The district attorney is bound to charge Viv with both murders."

"I think that the DA's office is waiting to charge her with Clark Laurin's murder," I said, "until they find her husband's body."

"When Viv bought her car last year, we did a credit check, of course. I understand that she owns various properties that she could use as collateral," said Bart."

"I suspect that Viveca has been selling off those properties lately," I said. "After the remodel, she planned to sell her house and move to Grand Cayman."

Willie once more was warming the jukebox with a familiar tune as Brenda Aduddell interrupted us to refill our water glasses and take our dessert orders. Slices of Lefty's incomparable pies were popular choices along with scoops of butter pecan ice cream (flavor of the day).

"How are the plans developing for the Community Yard Sale fund raiser, Lacy?" I asked to move us into a happier topic.

"Shelby Draper is helping me with the planning. So far, we have devised a layout for the booths," said Lacy. "We're thinking that there is good space for about one hundred and fifty-six booths. We plan to have a double row with the rows facing each other along the perimeter. Possibly we can put eight or nine food and drink booths in the center of the open space. There's a light pole in the center of the yard with four covered electrical outlets in a locked box at the base which the town uses to power yard tools. Some of the booths may have their own gas grills."

"Will that raise enough money to make the yard sale worth doing?" Marolly questioned. "Yard sales can be a lot of work."

"Shelby told me she estimates that the booth rentals could raise upwards of nine thousand dollars if we charge fifty-five dollars for the regular booths and eighty-five for the food and drink booths," Lacy replied. The library Friends' booth could bring in another thousand. "The proceeds of the sale will be a good addition to our fund of donations."

"Lacy, I was talking to Twila Dawge, and she says that we need to get a permit from the county clerk's office," I reported. "I also asked her about getting a couple of deputies to help with traffic control. We probably should talk with Sheriff Post about parking and traffic issues. Maybe it would be wise for you to get another volunteer to talk to the sheriff since I don't seem to be his favorite person at the moment."

"The sheriff doesn't have his head screwed on right if he can't see that you and Lottie saved his bacon on this investigation," scoffed Walter.

"If the yard sale works out, you might make it a twice-yearly fund raiser," suggested Paula. "Lots of people like to go to yard sales in the Fall as well. And maybe you could get the TV stations to mention it on air since you're getting so much attention in Wanderwood."

"We could use some good publicity," agreed Bart, "instead of sensational stories about Anson Kerringer's death. Wanderwood businesses would like to see a more positive image on TV." He slapped the table for emphasis.

"You know," interposed Travis, "a lot of people will probably come to the yard sale just to see where the murder happened. People sometimes can be ghoulish that way."

Nine happy, well-fed friends and two nap-ready children wended their ways to their homes or business after a very special get together. We couldn't know then that Viveca Laurin would get out of jail on bond a week later when Harvey Lackie posted ten percent of a fifty-thousand-dollar bail amount. Or that after closing the sale on her house near Willem Club, Viv would disappear altogether.

Speculation in Wanderwood was that Viv had gone to Brazil to join her husband Clark---at least, until his body was found buried about twenty yards from the clump of trees where I had been digging.

Acknowledgements

Addie Girard lives in the real world of Central Texas, but Wanderwood TX is a totally fictional town bearing only vague common similarities to real small towns of Central Texas. Austin is the real capital of the state of Texas. San Antonio TX, Dripping Springs TX, Woodcreek TX, Wimberley TX, San Marcos TX, and Texas State University therein, and New Braunfels TX are real entities and interesting places to visit. All characters are fictional though you may envision the characteristics of some of your friends and neighbors in the folksy community of Wanderwood.

Special thanks must go to my stalwart proofreaders: Jan Fendley, Louise Beyer, Linda Sandoval, and Kate Ertel. Any remaining errors are mine alone.

While *A Fistful of Death* is a fictional narrative, the following are not fictional: Fritos, Cheetos, and Doritos are registered brands of Frito-Lay, Inc. of Plano TX; Dr Pepper is a registered trademark of Dr Pepper/Seven Up, Inc. of Plano TX; Kiwanis International is an international service club headquartered in Indianapolis IN; Shriners International, Inc. is an American Masonic society headquartered in Tampa FL; Civitan International is an association of community service clubs based in Birmingham AL; LaQuinta by Wyndham is the registered name of a hotel chain brand, one of the Wyndham Hotels and Resorts family of hotels; Jeep, Wagoneer, and Grand Cherokee are registered brands or trademarks of FCA US LLC; Volkswagen is a registered brand of Volkswagen Group; The movie *Overboard* (1987, MGM, Star Partners Ltd.) was produced by Nick Abdo, Roddy McDowall, Alexandra Rose, and Anthea Sylbert, directed by Garry Marshall, and written by Leslie Dixon; Norman Rockwell (1894-1978) was an American painter and illustrator; Whataburger is an American restaurant chain headquartered in San Antonio TX.

CROCHET PATTERNS – *For Red Dog Puppet, Whitey the Dog Puppet, and Hausbol patterns, send money order for $3.00 to Addie Girard Mysteries, P.O. Box 30281, Edmond OK 73003-0281.*

About the Author

Judy Spoon Ertel, world traveler and author extraordinaire, grew up in several towns (Chickasha, Duncan Altus) in Oklahoma. A former columnist and teacher in Central Texas, she is very familiar with life in small Texas towns like Wanderwood, Texas, the fictional setting for the *Addie Girard Mysteries*. Currently, she co-habs with her daughter Kate and their three cats in Central Oklahoma.